> Arnold —
> Depending on your view of me —
> as an author, this is either
> a valuable first edition or a
> handy doorstop. Keep in
> touch — and watch for
> "The Secret of Possum Hollow"

Saving Magnolia

bdharrell

Copyright © 2014 by bdharrell.

All rights reserved.

This book or any portion thereof may not be reproduced or used in any manner whatsoever without the express written permission of the publisher except for the use of brief quotations in a book review.

Printed in the United States of America

First Printing, 2015

ISBN: 13: 978-1503011243

For Norm

Table of Contents

Opening Shot 1
Refusing to Remember 10
On Replacing a Legend 14
Taking Stock 20
Premonition and Recollection 26
The Fraternity 30
Committing to the Trip 33
Dotting the "T's" and Crossing the "I's" 36
The Broken Date 43
Spit-Take 47
Magnolia Revisited 53
The Texan 57
Trying it on for Size 62
Back to the Stomping Grounds 66
Key to a Mystery? 72
Getting Grilled 77
Call To Glory 82
Dreaded yet Anticipated 84
New Plans for Old Business 94
Reality Check 97
Persistent Questions 104
Upsetting News 107
Tribute 110
The Unknown Ally 115
The Stoned Guest 122
Guests - Welcome and Otherwise 127
He's Poison 137

Pro-Bono Advice 140
Confession 147
The Missing Link 153
Knowing Without Saying 156
Trojan Horse 158
On the Warpath 166
Starting Over Again 170
Simmering Frustrations 175
Unrealized Consequences 176
Meeting a Deadline 182
Evolving Revenge 184
Alternate Plans 186
Covering Bets 194
Coming to a Decision 197
Running Away 200
Randy's Problem 203
Proposal 209
Evading and Abetting 212
The Prisoner 219
Dodging the Goons 223
Escape 227
Earl Strikes Out 231
Cutting It Close 234
On the Razor's Edge 241
Missing Puzzle Piece 246
Captive Audience 250
Racing to the Rescue 254
In the Best Interest of Magnolia 258
The Odds and Ends 265
You're Welcome to Come Back to Magnolia! 269

Opening Shot

"This is it," thought Glenn Michaels. "So this is how it ends, with a bullet to the brain. For what I've done, I deserve it." His next thought was that the scenario playing out in front of him was strangely inappropriate. A bullet to the brain was too easy; too convenient. He should suffer as part of his imminent death. That's what he <u>really</u> deserved.

There was nothing Glenn could do once Delbert Jones had stomped in anger to his car in the parking area of Beasley Brothers Appliances in this suburb of Dallas, Texas. The entire incident took less than a minute, yet for Glenn Michaels it represented a lifetime spent making other's lives miserable.

Delbert had made an ugly scene in the store, stormed out, went to his car, pulled out a gun then took two steps back toward the building as Glenn watched him.

Glenn certainly wouldn't be missed. His wife - rather his ex-wife - would point to his demise and tell their children that he got what he deserved for making her life a living hell and the ruin he had rained upon them all. Never mind the fact that it had been Alice's dalliance which led to the divorce in the first place.

His children seldom contacted him anymore because of her fabrications. They might miss him but he wasn't placing any bets on the prospect. His son, Christopher, had already blithely informed him that he and his sister were in discussion about who would get what when he died. He wasn't surprised. Alice had completely estranged their children from their father within five years of their divorce. Now, the estrangement would be permanent. His death would help to obfuscate the fact that Alice was, at the moment, in the process of divorcing the man who had put her marriage to Glenn on the rocks.

There appeared to be a momentary distraction. Delbert Jones paused on his second step toward the doorway where Glenn was standing.

Glenn's marriage to Alice was actually in peril from the moment he married her. For that matter, it was in peril from the first time they met because of Hannah Smith.

Glenn had never let go of Hannah Smith.

Even at this moment when he was facing his demise, Hannah Smith came to him. He would join her soon. They would finally be together. Maybe she would forgive him for not taking a stand… for stepping out of her life.

He had no choice. The difference in their ages prevented him from pulling her out of the situation she was in when it was still possible to interrupt her life path and divert it into one where they could grow, bond and prosper.

Her life ended twenty-five years earlier in a trailer home outside of Magnolia, Ohio as a result of Glenn's best intentions to reset both of their lives. Glenn felt that his imminent death was well deserved due his role in Hannah's death.

The madman rushing toward him turned. His face contorted into a look of surprise. In an instant which seemed to last a lifetime, Delbert Jones put the barrel of the gun he under his chin and pulled the trigger.

Glenn watched in horror as the final moments of Delbert Jones' life played out in slow motion in front of him. He realized in an instant that, for the second time in his life, his life had been saved from a bullet meant for him.

"YOU'VE RUINED MY LIFE YOU BASTARD!" Glenn could still hear Delbert Jones screaming at the top of his lungs just moments before he left Glenn's office. Delbert made a big deal about tearing up his severance check as he was making a scene for the benefit of the other people in the building.

Glenn wanted to fire Delbert Jones but up to this point he was reluctant to do it. He knew good and well that Delbert's life had spiraled out of control in the past year and it was affecting sales, and the morale of the other employees at Beasley Brothers Appliances.

"YOU'LL REGRET FIRING ME, MICHAELS!" Delbert had stopped after he opened the front door of the store, turned and still screamed. "I'LL SEE THAT YOU PAY FOR THIS!"

Glenn came out from behind his desk, hoping to catch up with the employee he had just fired. Maybe there was something he could do, something he could say to get Delbert calmed down. Delbert needed help, that's all. It had been hoped the firing would lead to an intervention, not the bloody mess which ensued less than a minute later.

On his way to the door, Glenn noticed that Delbert's co-workers had started heading toward the loading dock at the back of the building, herding several frightened customers before them.

What Glenn didn't notice was an act of serendipity which had saved him and the other people in the building from being a victim of Delbert's rage. A police officer catching a smoke in front of the police station half a block away heard the ruckus, threw down his cigarette, shouted inside for assistance, and then started running toward the Beasley Brothers Appliance Store while pulling his gun out of his holster.

What Glenn saw was Delbert yanking open the door to his car, diving in then pulling out a gun. The next thing Glenn knew, Delbert Jones pointed the barrel of the gun under his chin and pulled the trigger.

The gunshot and the lifeless body slumping down to the street propelled Glenn back twenty- five years to the incident which took the life of Hannah Smith. He had not been an eyewitness to the event, but the actions he witnessed were quite similar to those described to him about the previous incident. He had been told that Brother Murphy was enraged because of what Glenn had done and that Brother Murphy was armed and coming to get his revenge.

Back in the Beasley Brothers parking lot, chaos ensued. Glenn watched the first officer on the scene stop to vomit as Delbert's lifeless body slumped to the ground.

Brother Murphy had also pulled a gun on himself when he was confronted at a traffic stop. Rather than have to deal with the carnage he had already created by killing his wife and his children, Brother Murphy put a bullet through his head as he was approached by the highway patrolman who had pulled him over.

Bob Beasley, owner of Beasley Brothers Appliances, had raced downstairs at the commotion. "DAMMIT!!! MICHAELS!!! WHAT THE FUCK HAPPENED?" Glenn heard his boss yell while Claire in the office was screaming hysterically.

"Just like Brother Murphy," Glenn said again and again as events swirled around and in front of him. He felt a pair of arms come up from behind him to support him just before he blacked out.

"…hyperventilated, that's all… looks like he's coming to…"

Glenn found himself flat on his back, looking up at the ceiling of Beasley Brothers Appliances. An EMT was hovering over him as were the familiar faces of Bob Beasley, Steve Crabtree and Claire Williams.

"Are you okay, Mister Michaels?" the EMT asked.

"Glenn, buddy, it's okay," Bob told him. "It's over. You can relax."

"Does he need to go to the hospital?" Claire asked.

"Hey..." Glenn interrupted. "I'm... I'm fine, really. What happened?"

"You hyperventilated and passed out," the EMT told him.

Glenn looked at the EMT's name tag: "H. Smith". She appeared to be in her mid-twenties, although her face and her demeanor made her appear at least a decade older.

"Hannah," Glenn stated. "Hannah Smith. Is that really you?"

"Yes," answered the EMT. "Do I know you?"

"No," Glenn said, starting to get up. "No it can't be. Hannah died years ago... she was the cause..."

"You need to take it easy for a while, sir," the EMT told him. She shook her head then asked Bob Beasley if there was somewhere Glenn could rest for a while.

Minutes later, Glenn was in the recliner in Bob Beasley's office still shaken by recent events. The EMT had been shooed away as were Glenn's fellow employees. It was just Glenn and Bob.

"Care for a snort?" Bob asked. Bob offered to share the bottle of Jack Daniels he had produced from his desk.

"You had me fire Delbert for abusing drugs and you have a bottle of Jack in your desk?"

"Medicinal purposes. Besides, Jack is legal." Bob poured himself a shot before he put the bottle away. "I'm sorry that things turned out like they did, but you weren't going to fire Delbert unless I gave you a little push. He and that whore of his have been ruining my reputation."

"You should have done something yourself. It's your name on the building."

"And your name as store manager is on the window next to the front door," Bob pointed out. "I did do something. I pushed you to finally have the balls to fire the son of a bitch."

Glenn sighed, indicating that he had conceded the point.

Bob downed his shot.

"So, who's this Brother Murphy you kept babbling about before you went down?"

Glenn said nothing. He had kept the incident involving Harlan Murphy bottled up inside of him for a quarter of a century. He wasn't about to open that bottle, no matter how good a friend Bob Beasley had become.

"'Just like Brother Murphy' is what you were saying." Bob was trying to probe.

"Did I? I was probably having a hallucination."

"Have it your way, partner," Bob went on. "You have your mind set and knowing you, you aren't going to talk about what's going on inside your head without a fight, so have it your way."

Glenn glared at Bob for attempting to break through the wall he had so carefully built around him.

"Let me tell you something, buddy… if this is a secret, you need to cut it loose, or it'll drag you down. You're too damn good a manager and human being to let something drag you down. You've said yourself that confession is good for the soul."

Glenn continued to glare at Bob.

Bob shifted gears and changed the subject.

"You could have gone down the same road that Delbert did, you know. You didn't. I admire you for that."

"Thank you," Glenn told him. "Could I get a drink of water?"

"Sure, no problem," Bob answered. He reached over to the small refrigerator next to his desk and pulled out a bottle of water. He opened it and gave it to Glenn.

"Thanks," Glenn said after taking a drink.

"Why would one man come out of a divorce with his wits intact while another goes off the deep end inside of a year?" Bob mused when Glenn was finished.

"Delbert didn't stay focused. Besides, he was blindsided. I knew what was coming and I was prepared to handle it."

"Did Delbert have a list like the one you made when you and Alice separated?" Bob thought for a moment. "Of course not... he had his whore."

"I tried to get him to make a list like mine, but he didn't think it was important."

"It kept you focused when your wife ditched you, didn't it?"

"Yep..."

"Did you ever get everything done on your list?"

"I still have two items left to take care of."

"It's been ten years, Glenn. You have no excuse not to have finished."

"Yep..." Glenn nodded his head. "Maybe it's time to get it done, out of the way."

"Glenn..."

"Yes, Bob..."

"None of this was your fault, you know."

"I'd like to think so, too, but I know better. Alice, the kids, Delbert, Hannah..."

"Who's this Hannah? How's she figure into this?"

"It's not important. She's gone... she's been gone..."

"Is she the same gal you mentioned you knew when you were a kid in Ohio? Are you still clinging to an ancient memory? You can't do that and keep on living, you know."

Glenn took another long pull on his bottle of water then sat and stared into space for a long minute. Bob was right. He was still mourning the loss of Hannah Smith long after he went off to the job which was waiting for him in West Virginia. He felt the sadness of losing her long past the time he could have made a difference in her life.

"I've seen your list and I know that one of the items on it was a promise to yourself that you would cut yourself loose of that girl's memory and try to live for once in your life. It's time."

Glenn sat quietly while Bob got up and paced in the office.

"You need to take a vacation. Scratch that. You are going to take a vacation. You haven't taken any time for yourself for at least two and a half, maybe three years. You need to take a hike for your own sake."

"Bob's right," Glenn thought. "On the other hand, if I can just maintain the status quo for just a little longer…"

"You need to reconnect, Glenn. You need to find out just who you are so you can get focused. I can't afford to let you run my business when you can't keep your head on straight."

Glenn knew that he was in a rut. It wasn't a bad rut, really. His children had both made lives for themselves, leaving him alone; fallout from the poison Alice fed them after she and Glenn had separated. He learned to survive without his kids. He'd go to work, make lots of money then go to the house he owned and into the arms of 'Mrs. Michaels du jour' - usually some woman he met on the internet who was interested in nothing more than casual sex.

Glenn didn't commit to any one woman, discreetly referring to the "smorgasbroad" available to him. As far as he was concerned, commitment had become a four letter word.

He took another drink of water. "I can't afford a vacation, Bob. I have things to do, sales to plan…"

"All that's unimportant, Glenn. I need you to go for the sake of you. We'll manage. Trust me."

Bob leaned over, opened a drawer in his desk and produced a checkbook. "Tell you what," Bob said as he wrote a check, "I'm giving you three weeks time off and three weeks' pay. I want you back here on… the twenty-fourth… no, the twenty-sixth, of July. I want you to finish with the items on that list and then I want you back in here in one piece, in mind and in body, so we can start kicking some ass on the sales floor. Can I get at least that much of a commitment from you?"

Glenn reluctantly took the check which Bob had just written and put it in his front pocket. Slowly he got up from the recliner. It took a moment for him to steady himself while thanking his mentor for his generosity.

He left Bob Beasley's office knowing that if he hadn't taken up the offer, he would have walked out of that office without a job.

Glenn shuffled down to his office on the ground floor, picked up the simple vase with the yellow rose which sat as a sentinel on his desk, then went out the front door to find that he had become the center of attention of what seemed to be every news reporter in North Texas.

"No comment," he said repeatedly.

He walked past the crime scene tape, hopped across the street and walked home. It took him twenty minutes. He closed the door of his house, his refuge, to the world outside to sit in a fetal position with his back to the door.

"I need to finally make my peace with Magnolia and Hannah Smith," he said out loud. He contemplated the yellow rose before getting up from the floor and taking the rose in its vase to his bedroom so it could stand watch over him. He thought he felt her presence. "I'm so sorry," he said. For the next twenty minutes, he cried like a baby. "I should have saved you from that bastard Harlan Murphy."

Refusing to Remember

Glenn woke up on Saturday morning next to Tina Kay, the latest in the string of girlfriends he had met through the internet. She had come over late Friday night after hearing about Glenn's experience at the store.

"Good morning, lover," she purred in his ear. "Do you think you can get it up for me now?"

Glenn felt her hand moving up the inside of his thigh, trying to stimulate an erection with no result. The image of the chaos of the previous afternoon overrode any desire he may have had. "Let me, uh, use the bathroom first." Her hand withdrew to her side of the bed. He got out of bed, walked into the master bath and used the toilet. He came back to find her in a provocative pose, attempting to tease him into attention.

He glanced over to his dresser. The yellow rose was still standing guard over the bedroom. This was the first time he had ever brought the rose home and somehow, uninhibited sex with Tina Kay didn't seem to be the right activity to indulge in at the moment. He felt as if they were being watched.

Still nothing. He started to sulk.

"Bad timing?" she asked.

"Most likely," Glenn answered. "It's my fault, not yours."

She drew her legs back together and swung them over the side of the bed, sitting on the side. Glenn sat down next to her, nuzzling her out of habit, attempting to gain his attention. She tried again to elicit a reaction, again, coming up empty.

"I thought I'd come over for a good fuck last night and here you are, limp as a wet noodle… Jesus." She got up and went to the bathroom.

"I thought you came over last night to at least try to be a good companion," Glenn said as she went about her business.

"I would have liked it if you had at least tried to satisfy me," she scolded.

He looked over at the rose again.

"Sexual satisfaction. That's all I am to Tina Kay… for that matter, that's all that Tina Kay means to me," he thought.

Just after he heard the toilet flush, she came back into the bedroom heading over to the nightstand to pick up her bath robe.

"Sorry," she said, putting the robe on, "I feel naked and exposed." Her tone reeked of disappointment.

Tina Kay swept from the bedroom into the hallway leading to the kitchen. Glenn followed.

"What's it been… two weeks?" she asked. "You give good head, Michaels, but I was really looking forward to another night of passion like we had on Wednesday. I was hoping for more, that's all."

"All that I wanted last night was companionship."

"And that's all you got. Not even the decency to show some appreciation for a girl," she huffed.

Something seemed to have caught her eye on the refrigerator. She went over and pulled off a list being held by a magnet. "What's this?" she asked.

"It's my to-do list. It's usually not out. Could you put it back, please?"

"In just a minute," she said. She looked over the list while Glenn fumed. "What's this down here on the bottom? 'Cut my ties with Magnolia and clear my life of Hannah Smith?' What's this Magnolia and who's Hannah Smith?"

"It's a long story and it's rather private, thank you."

"An old girlfriend… how old?"

"Twenty-five, no, thirty-five years."

"Was she a good fuck?"

"I never got that far with her," he lied… or did he? The relationship he had with Hannah Smith went far beyond the animal act being demanded by Tina Kay. "She was too young for us to pursue a proper relationship."

"You had an improper relationship with her, I suppose."

"It cost her… it cost me… It was… different. I'd appreciate it if you would put the list back on the refrigerator, please." Glenn felt annoyed at the intrusion into his private life.

Tina Kay put the list back on the refrigerator as she was asked. "That deal with Delbert really fucked your mind good last night, didn't it?"

"To tell you the truth, I put off dealing with Delbert far too long," he told her. He sat down on a kitchen chair. The cold, hard surface provided him another excuse to keep from being intimate with the nearly naked woman in his kitchen.

"He and his girlfriend were dealing drugs. My boss told me to get rid of him at least six months ago."

He looked to see Tina Kay had taken the list back off of the refrigerator and was intently poring over it.

"I tried to get him to make up a list like the one you're reading. His wife left him and took everything – apparently she took his self-esteem, too."

"Did your wife take yours when she left?" she asked.

"I was lucky. I got to keep most of the stuff. Sure, she got my kids, but I was relatively unhurt. I suppose it was because I knew what was coming.

"Anyway, the business with Delbert got me to thinking if nothing else. I hadn't had the list out for a couple of years. All I have left to do are the last two items."

She peered down at the list again. "You used to be on the radio?"

"For twenty years," he told her. "It was a waste of time."

She looked over at him. He too, was starting to feel naked and exposed. More importantly, he felt as if he were cheating on a dream which had been ripped from him by the petty concerns of decorum in a small Ohio town.

"God, I want you!" Tina Kay sounded almost desperate. She put the list on the kitchen table before trying to stimulate him one more time. Failing, she went into the bedroom and put on her clothes.

Ten minutes later, she was gone, leaving Glenn naked and alone. He stared at the list while the echo of the door closing behind Tina Kay reverberated in his ears for the rest of the morning.

On Replacing a Legend

"Zeke Collins, you are impossible."

John 'Wild Jack Jay' Jankowski firmly placed a stack of folders on a desk in front of the older man with thinning white hair and runaway eyebrows.

"In the past four months I have been here on five separate occasions to have you come up with the same conclusion each and every time. I came up here again Wednesday; we spent Thursday and Friday hashing over all of your choices and here it is, Saturday morning and I'll be damned if you haven't come up with the same conclusion all over again."

"Jack," the old man came to life, "I just want to be sure. As I say, it's not like I'm giving a toy to a favorite grandchild or nephew, this is my life's work… and it's a community at stake. Here…"

Zeke opened the top folder.

> ***MICHAELS, GLENN***
>   *1/76 – 6/76: Saturday & Sunday*
>   *** Referred-Truman Howell.…*

There was further information regarding Glenn Michaels's work and social history, some typed, some hand-written.

For instance there was the notation: = **Alice Baker 6/78** followed by the penciled-in date: **7/00**. In the margin, again, penciled in was:

= **Hannah Smith** with a line crossed through her name and a further notation: ***d. 7/85***.

"Jack, you once told me that Michaels's the best talker you've ever heard… even went to bat for him behind the scenes when he was almost booted from that station in Parkersburg."

"I was in Florida. Truman sent me a tape. The kid was good… but that was over thirty years ago. He's been out of the business for nearly half that time. Hell, Zeke, he runs a goddamn appliance store!"

"A business is a business, Jack. It shouldn't be much different running a restaurant and a pair of radio stations than it is running an appliance store."

"But he hasn't been on the air…"

"He's not mute and he's not deaf, at least he wasn't when I talked with him last week."

"So did you even think of asking him to take over the operation?"

"The question hasn't come up yet. I will make the offer and I will be making the offer in person."

"Zeke Collins, you are impossible."

"I know, Jack… that's why you're here. I need your constant reminders."

Zeke closed the folder, set it aside and stood up.

"Walk with me, Jack…"

He slowly came around the desk, dodging some of the trophies and reminders of his importance in his younger days.

"I understand that there was an incident last night which may have stirred our Mr. Michaels up a bit."

"The shooting - yes. It made the morning paper."

"Knowing him, he'll be up here at latest a week from today. I expect the call to come sometime this afternoon. He has a demon he needs to get rid of. When he comes here, Jessie and I'll take him out to the Town Lake Club and present him with the opportunity."

"Jessica still approves, then…"

"I don't make a move without her knowing, Jack. Never had… well, maybe once, but I heard about it for a solid month."

"And if he refuses, what's 'Plan B'?"

"We'll give him some room… he'll take it. The lawyer Fischer will help persuade him. He'll show him my will and Glenn most likely will go along."

"You didn't put it in your will," Jack protested. "You had said that you would put Jessie in charge and I-"

He stopped short.

"And you were going to come up from Lexington and run the stations. Don't act surprised, Jack. Jessie told me about your proposal and I almost thought it would be a good idea, but I've built something here which needs to continue and needs a steady hand on the tiller. I love you to death, but I need Glenn Michaels to take over when I'm gone."

Jack got up and headed toward the door.

"And what happens if you kick off between now and whenever it is when you modify your will? Does Alvin know about your plan?"

"Jessie's already said something to Alvin. If I do shuffle off before the changes are made, I'm depending on you to come back here and see that everyone does the right thing. We've been through this before. If I go without someone strong to take over, the stations die, the restaurant dies and Magnolia will follow. I've built a town, Jack. Like it or not, the force of personality has kept this town prosperous in the face of numerous recessions. Magnolia's health as a community is my legacy."

Jack took a long, hard look at Zeke Collins. "I suppose you're right. It's just I'm disappointed that you don't trust me enough to let me have at least one last hurrah."

"I trust you to do what I want you to do. That's I keep you around Jack, and that's why I've paid you at least twice what I should have paid you for your advice. Now, you have a safe trip home."

They patted each other on the back after shaking hands. Jack took one last look at Zeke as he tottered his way back behind his desk.

"I wonder if Legal has a way around a will," Jack thought as he went downstairs to his car. He went across the street to sit for a moment or two on the bench facing Zeke's Café. "Maybe I should cover my bets and have a talk with Alvin."

Jack watched Zeke Collins make his Saturday morning rounds of the various groups of people in Zeke's Cafe through the front window. The old man didn't have much time. Jack saw the signs during their meeting. The question was if there was there enough time for Jack to turn Zeke Collins' decision around so that he could be entrusted to handle Zeke's business affairs after he died.

Jack got up from the bench to go see Alvin Bates before heading back to Zeke's for a quick lunch and some friendly conversation prior to returning to Lexington.

"I'm afraid we might have a problem on our hands."

A short, rotund man with red cheeks wearing suspenders which were almost as red pointed his fork to a larger man with a genial disposition. Zeke had just been by the round table in the center of the café, making his usual Saturday morning appearance.

"You afraid of the next election, Mayor?" the larger man laughed.

"You know exactly what I mean, Mulligan," the Mayor responded. "It's Zeke. He had his heart attack last fall and that fool Jack Jay thinks that he's going to move in and take over the whole shebang!"

"I doubt that will happen," a woman's voice chimed in. "Zeke is well aware of Jack's intentions."

"Well? You've been talking to him, Knox. Tell us what he intends to do." The Mayor pointed his fork at the middle-aged woman, demanding an explanation.

"Well, the only reason Zeke's had Wild Jack Jay over here in the past few months has been to help him along," Ms. Knox replied. "All Jack has left in life is a couple of rooms and a kitchenette down in Lexington. Zeke's known Jack for years and knows that Jack won't just take a hand-out, so, he's made Jack a consultant and is paying him for his opinions."

"When Zeke dies, what happens to the station? What happens to Zeke's Café?" the Mayor asked the others gathered around the table.

"Zeke told me not to worry," Mulligan answered. "He said he was working something out with a lawyer."

"You mean Bates? That fool has no idea."

"My understanding is that he's working with someone else."

A server came by with fresh coffee. The Mayor suspected that she was listening in to what amounted to an informal meeting of the Magnolia Town Council.

"If you ask me, I hope that this place will stay open," the server opined. "Heaven knows that all of us need our jobs. Without Zeke in the window on weekday mornings, we may as well shut 'er down."

"She's right, you know," the Mayor spoke up. "Without Zeke Collins sitting in that front window every morning, no one would bother coming to Magnolia, much less spend the money they spend when they show up."

An older man wearing thick glasses and a well-worn suit came to the table and sat down to join the party.

"The usual, Pastor Kellough?" the server asked, pouring him a cup of coffee.

"Just a half order today, thanks," the pastor replied.

The server noted the order and took it to the kitchen.

"We could be in a lot of trouble, that's for sure," Mulligan said, picking back up the string of the conversation. "Has anyone locally shown any interest in buying Zeke out, Hank?"

"No one's been by with any proposals," Hank told them. "I think anyone who might be interested is scared off by Big Thicket."

"Zeke's the only operator in this neck of the woods who's stood up to them, that's for sure," the Mayor interjected.

"That's because the stations' success is built on Zeke's personality," Ms. Knox pointed out. "Quite honestly, when Zeke goes, the only hope of saving Magnolia will be for someone to come in and take his place in the window every morning."

"We already know that Jack can't handle it. My business went down twenty percent when he was running the place after Zeke's heart attack," Mulligan stated.

"The Lord will provide."

Pastor Kellough's voice rang out loud and clear.

"There will be someone, you'll see. The Lord will provide. When a door closes, a window opens."

The party sitting around the table nodded their heads in agreement. The server came with Reverend Kellough's half order of Miss Annie's biscuits and gravy.

"If the Lord's going to provide, Ezra, he's cutting it mighty damn close," the Mayor observed.

Taking Stock

Not long after Tina Kay left, Glenn called the store and received the pre-recorded message announcing the closing of the store for the weekend. He called Bob Beasley at home to let Bob know that he was alright.

"That's good," Bob told him. "I hope you take this opportunity to get out of town for a while… maybe go down to Houston to see your kids."

"I have something else in mind. Besides, Alice is in the middle of a divorce. Her kids - our kids - tend to circle the wagons whenever she's in trouble."

"You've talked about cutting your ties with that place in Ohio… Magnolia, wasn't it?"

"It's crossed my mind…" Glenn paused for a few moments. "Actually, I just… oh, never mind."

"Never mind what, Glenn?"

"It's just that… well…"

Bob waited patiently.

"I have this feeling that maybe this time I need to go."

"Will you be taking the current so-called Mrs. Michaels with you?"

Glenn thought that he had been discreet regarding the parade of girlfriends who came in and out of his life since his divorce from Alice. Apparently he wasn't.

"No…" he stated firmly. "She walked out of the house with her belongings about an hour ago. It was probably good riddance."

"You need to do what you need to do then, buddy. The members of the group will be praying for you until you get back."

Somehow Bob's words gave him a small comfort. Something told him that he might never make it back.

Glenn came home from church on the fourth feeling refreshed. He fixed lunch then started making preparations for what he determined was going to be the last trip he would make to Ohio. He had not said a word outside of the hint he had given Bob the day before. For most of the rest of Saturday, a voice inside of him told him that he had to go.

"Shirts…" The closet yielded several shirts which might be suitable. The chest of drawers provided several more; golf shirts with the Beasley Brothers logo on them. He took pride in the fact that he was trusted to run a profitable store, despite the occasional turmoil in his personal life.

"Damn that Tina Kay."

He briefly considered calling her to try to make amends.

"No more Tina Kays," he said to himself. "No more Julies, no more… Alices."

Just the thought of Alice made him burn. She took away some of the best years of his life, but she had given him Corey. She had given him Christopher. Just as surely, she took them away, too. He sighed, wondering if his children would ever come back to him.

"Did she really?" he asked himself.

He checked socks and underwear. The washing machine needed to be busy over the next few hours.

"She was the manifestation of an imaginary lover. She was Mary, as I would have imagined she would have been."

"Does that make Corey any less your daughter?"

He pulled his clothes out of the hamper, separating items by color or whether or not the item was permanent press.

His internal dialogue continued.

"I should have latched on to Hannah when I had the chance. She would have made a great mother."

"How do you know that she wasn't?"

Socks and underwear went into the front of the washing machine along with detergent and a little bit of fabric softener.

"How about Christopher? He might have liked Hannah's boys."

The washing machine had finished filling. It was merrily thunking the clothes back and forth, getting them clean.

"I've already made up my mind about what I need to do to get my life back on track."

"When?"

"When I was almost the target again the other day, and when Alice left. When I made up the list - that was another time. I set some goals – some reasonable expectations. For example:

"1.) Expand my boundaries beyond where I've been. Head west, at least head over to New Mexico."

"You took care of that detail within a few months of your separation. The rented camper and the trip to Carlsbad Caverns, Roswell and as far west as a small roadside park where "they 'dumped' Smokey Bear". He paused to snicker for a moment. "Dumped Smokey Bear." The thought was amusing to him.

"2.) Get more involved with the church."

"Cursillo. You joined what some people would call a cult. Even inside the Episcopal Church, you joined a cult."

"It wasn't a bad thing, you know…"

"At least you and Bob became closer. Otherwise he most likely would have fired you for dragging your feet on firing Delbert."

"Delbert deserved a chance…"

"And you gave him that chance. He blew that chance and as a result, he nearly killed you."

"3.) Get off your ass, get out and exercise."

"No need to avoid what happened between you and Delbert…"

"Delbert brought his problems on himself. I could have saved him…"

"But you didn't try hard enough."

Glenn took a deep breath on that point. Maybe he didn't try hard enough to keep Delbert on the straight and narrow after Delbert's wife kicked him out of his house. Bob repeatedly told Glenn that there was a situation which needed his attention and Bob repeatedly asked Glenn to take care of it.

"Maybe I didn't," he finally sighed, "but maybe it was meant to happen that way. It's all in His hands, okay?"

"For the moment, yes."

"Now, for item number three…"

"Okay, you can tick that box. You <u>have</u> been walking to work and to the grocery store more often, and you've been riding the bicycle, too."

"4.) Sample a new cuisine at least once a month for a year."

"Now there was a damn good idea. You helped that girl make an item on her list, and she helped you by suggesting the list in the first place."

"I remember her… her name was Brenda. She was easy on the eyes and good company. I don't think she liked the idea of my moving into a different apartment complex."

"She was good company, and the list she suggested has come in handy."

"Yep… for one date only, if you could call lunch at the Thai place a proper date."

"Maybe you should have waited. Maybe you came on too strong."

"Maybe we were doomed to failure before we even started."

"5.) Ride Amtrak somewhere."

"Avoiding the subject? Perhaps you needed a few years to realize that you needed to be with someone you could relate to for a change instead of going after an easy fuck."

"I'm headed in that direction, now, thank you. Let's get back to number five."

"Very well. You had a choice of heading to San Antonio or Chicago. Since San Antonio was closer, you chose San Antonio where you spent three days getting sun burnt while living out of a too-expensive hotel and indulging yourself with a prostitute."

"I was lonely…"

"You were stupid."

"6.) Keep a journal."

"You changed that to keeping a blog. Six months, rather regular… I guess that qualifies…"

"7.) Take a college class."

"I'll admit that you did quite well with that assignment, taking those business courses and getting number eight crossed off the list in the bargain."

"8.) Manage the appliance store."

"You almost blew that on Friday. On the other hand, if you did blow it, you would not have been around to worry about it anymore, would you?"

Glenn came down to the last two items on his list. He stared at the refrigerator for ten minutes looking at number nine:

"9.) Prove that I still have what it takes to be on the radio."

Below that he had written: "Show the bitch that I really could have made a good living if she would have let me."

"Are you sure about that? Alice may have been right about that one, you know."

Alice had convinced him that he was a no-talent bum with no future in his chosen field, rather, the career which chose him. Over and over again, his customers at the appliance store remarked on his 'radio voice', and he found that his 'radio voice' helped him to attract women… mostly the wrong kind.

He had spent the better part of twenty years on the air before Alice convinced him that he needed to allow her to pursue a career of her own in the Dallas area. He took a job selling appliances; she took a job elsewhere, found someone else who suited her better and dumped him.

The only silver lining of the whole affair, at least as Glenn was concerned, was that husband number two proved to be a total schmuck. The schmuck was in the process of divorcing her.

There was one item left on the list:

"10.) Cut my ties with Magnolia and clear my life of Hannah Smith."

"You need to do it. You need to say goodbye to that girl and close out that chapter of your life."

"Yes, I know."

"If you're going to have a companion, you need to have someone you can trust, someone who is willing to live life with you… an equal partner."

"Yes, I know."

"You will find her if it is meant to be."

"Yes, I know."

The washing machine finished its final spin.

"I know," he told himself again.

Premonition and Recollection

Zeke Collins knew that his time was short. Doc Swisher over on Cherry Street told him that he needed to be getting his affairs in order before Easter.

Easter came and went, yet Zeke soldiered on. Magnolia, Ohio needed him to stay the course… to stay on the air and keep the town afloat. The town's economy depended on him. Nearly every morning for the past forty years, Zeke Collins drew people into Magnolia by sitting in the front window of his café (formerly Annie's Coffee Cup) and broadcasting platitudes on his radio stations. People from all over southern Ohio would listen, then come to Magnolia to sample Miss Annie's biscuits or visit the antique shops on Cherry Street, or purchase fresh, home-grown pork from Mulligan's IGA… or to visit with Zeke.

Everyone felt as if they knew Zeke Collins personally.

On the first day of summer, Doc Swisher told him that he would be lucky if he made it to Labor Day.

That was good enough for Zeke until Friday afternoon. He sat in his office after lunch and experienced… well, he wasn't sure what he experienced.

"You have less than two weeks, Zeke," a voice told him. "It's time to wrap it up."

He ignored the voice.

"You heard me… <u>NOW</u>!!!"

"If you say so. I'm ready."

That was on Friday morning. Sunday afternoon, Zeke was in his office attending to details he should have paid attention to after the minor heart attack he had the previous fall.

His desk, usually not the prettiest sight by a long shot, was littered with half a dozen manila folders, his office littered with the mementos of a lifetime of memories.

A light knock at the door was followed by the appearance of a woman he had known and loved for over sixty years.

"Hi, Jess,"

"Love you, Zeke."

Jessica Collins closed the door behind her and placed a folded newspaper in front of her husband.

"Have you and Jack already decided?"

"Pretty close."

"Glenn?"

She could read his mind. Sixty-three years of marriage can do that. He nodded his head.

"Did you read this?"

Jessica pointed to the article in the Columbus newspaper she had placed on Zeke's desk.

"He's an incredibly lucky young man, you know. It was an incredible circumstance."

Zeke re-read the article about the near tragedy which had occurred two days before in a suburb of Dallas, Texas.

"Saved by a cop sneaking a smoke," Zeke laughed. "I wonder if Harold has seen this?"

"Harold would appreciate it, I'm sure."

"There was no name in the article, how do you know that this was Glenn Michaels?"

"I tried to call him at the store yesterday afternoon. The store was closed '…due to yesterday's events…', at least that's what the answering machine said. Then, there's the picture."

Jessica pointed out the picture which accompanied the article. There was Glenn, leaving the store, clutching a flower.

Jessica took the newspaper back.

"He needs to be here, you know that…"

"I know that."

"He needs to confront that personal demon of his and get rid of it. It's been bottled up inside him and it's time to let it out."

Zeke looked at his wife. She was right… as usual.

"Besides, he's what this town needs to survive. He can do it, you know."

"That's pretty much what I've been trying to tell Jack. I'm wishing that I had never brought him in here to consult on the matter."

"The consulting fee you've been paying him has been a Godsend to him. You're doing him a good deed."

"I'm still worried that he'll turn the place over to Big Thicket if he has half a chance."

"That's why you're looking at Glenn," Jessica reminded him. "You should at least give Glenn the right of first refusal."

"I'm thinking that way, too."

"I know, love. We both know that your time is short. You need to make a decision about what happens here and you need to see it through. Both of us know that Jack can't handle managing the properties and the businesses. He's sure to make a mess of things when you're gone, so I called Glenn's lawyer friend yesterday and set up an appointment for you to see him tomorrow. He'll help you make the adjustments to your will we talked about. Your first instinct about Glenn was right, you'll see. He'll keep this town from going under."

Jessica went to the other side of the desk to give Zeke a kiss. "I pledged myself to be your wife and your helper. I think I've done a pretty good job of it, too, you old goat."

She put her arms around him and gave him an affectionate hug while he sat… tears starting to well up in his eyes.

"You have no idea how much I love you, Jess…"

"As much as Glenn loved Hannah… no… more."

The Fraternity

It was two on Monday afternoon when Glenn picked up the telephone to at least let someone know that he intended to come to Ohio for a visit.

"Good afternoon, WZEK, how can I help you?"

"Is that you, Becky?" Glenn asked. "Glenn Michaels, here. Is Zeke around?"

"Well, hi, Glenn. Long time no see. How are things in Texas?"

"Not too shabby. How's it with you?"

"Things are still going. Zeke hasn't been well lately, so we've learned to be cautiously optimistic."

"Is Zeke in, now?"

"He's at the house having a nap. You need to come and see him Glenn, before…"

"I understand. Jessica's been keeping me up to date. I need to come up there to wrap up some other business and I thought I might be able to have a long talk with him while I'm there."

"Does this other business have to do with Hannah?"

"Yep…" After a beat or two, he added: "I have business involving Zeke too."

"Are you going to try to do his show?"

Glenn took a deep breath. "Yep… I guess I've reached a point in life when I feel as if I really need to prove that I still have it in me."

"I'll tell him you called… better yet, I'll tell Jessie you called. She'll probably want to set up the third floor apartment for you."

"Thanks…"

"One other thing, Glenn…" Becky's voice lowered a bit. "If you're coming, you'd better come soon. I believe that the station is about to be sold. With the way things are going down here, we may not even be here next month. It's like vultures are circling the place."

"How is that?" Glenn asked.

"We've had visitors here, mostly from Big Thicket Broadcasting, looking the place over; then there's this 'Big Jack' or 'Wild Jack' or something, some guy who's been meeting off and on with Zeke for the past six months or so about something. He and Zeke just had another meeting at the end of last week."

"Is that the same Wild Jack who came in last year after Zeke's heart attack?"

"Same one. I almost think that he thinks he'll be running the place when Zeke quits or dies."

"Do you know if there's anyone in the pipeline?"

"Not that I know of. You know how it is, though."

"I'm sure I do," Glenn told her. "Anyway, just tell everyone that I'll be up the first part of next week."

He paused for a moment after ending the call. He remembered getting calls from Zeke while he was still in the hospital. Zeke was worried about what might have happened when he died, especially after hearing the mess Jack Jay had made of his morning radio show.

Glenn also had a distant memory of hearing about someone called 'Jack Jay', or sometimes 'Wild Jack Jay' who had worked for Truman Howell a few years before he did. Truman owned the radio station in Chillicothe where he had gotten his start. He was hired off the street just after high school, and staying there through two years of junior college.

He worked the college radio station in Athens. Truman offered him a job at his radio station in Parkersburg when he graduated, suggesting that he take a weekend job with Zeke in order to get back in the mindset of commercial radio. He wasn't aware of it at the time, but Truman had actually loaned Glenn to Zeke as a personal favor.

There was a fraternity of people who had worked for Truman Howell. Glenn was part of that fraternity and from time to time he would run into someone else who had worked for Truman, sometime in the least likely places.

Glenn eventually parted company with Truman after working for him in Parkersburg and Fairmont. Truman eventually decided that it was his time to sell his interests and retire. All of the Truman Howell radio stations were eventually sold to Big Thicket Broadcasting out of Tyler, Texas.

Big Thicket brought uniformity to Truman's stations as well as to radio stations throughout most of the country at the expense of being a soulless enterprise which literally ate up any competition which got in its way. Zeke Collins was a holdout. It alone was able to thrive, a small fish in a sea of big fish surrounding it. If the station were to be absorbed into the Big Thicket family, there would be no reason for Glenn Michaels to go back to Magnolia.

Ever.

Glenn thought that taking care of what needed to be taken care of now would be the best thing for him and his continued employment for the Beasley Brothers. Besides, maybe he could be a thorn in the side to Big Thicket – give them at least pause before absorbing WZEK and obliterating Magnolia. Despite the trouble he caused in relation to The Incident (as the locals referred to it), Glenn Michaels had a soft spot in his heart for Magnolia, Ohio. It deserved a fate much better than Big Thicket had planned for it.

Committing to the Trip

"Zeke and I would love to have you come here and stay with us," Jessica Collins was telling Glenn not long after he called the radio station. "When will you be coming up here?"

"I have a couple of chores I need to take care of here, first," Glenn told her. "Right now I'm on my way up to the package store."

"You're not talking and driving at the same time, are you?" Jessica loved playing the part of the mother hen.

"I am but I'm not. I have a hands-free set to use while I'm driving. I'll be leaving here on Saturday and plan to be in Magnolia on Sunday afternoon, probably about three your time. I'll call when I hit Peebles." Glenn noted that he was coming up to the exit he had to take. "Jess, I've got to get going. I'm almost to my exit."

"Glenn, would it be possible to talk for a minute or so more?"

"You know I can't refuse you, Jessie. Go ahead." Glenn had exited the freeway and was coasting down to a stop.

"Zeke's getting worse. I'm worried," she began. "He had that heart attack back last September. The doctors at Ohio State put him back on the road again, but they're concerned."

"How concerned are they?"

"One doctor told me that he thought Zeke has only about a ten percent chance of making it to Labor Day."

Glenn pulled into a parking space in the liquor store parking lot.

"He knows this, right?"

"He knows that he doesn't have long. He's been making preparations."

"Is selling the stations part of those preparations?"

"Its been talked about," she said quietly. "Zeke's been working with John Jankowski and Jankowski's been trying to get Zeke to put him in control of the radio stations when Zeke's gone. The will gives me everything, including control of his business interests, but I can't run things and for that matter neither can Mr. Jankowski. I may end up having to sell everything in the long run."

"Do you know if there have been any offers?"

"Not that I know of. Some people from Big Thicket down in Texas have made the trip here from what I've heard. Zeke's told them to back off, though. He's waiting for something else. All I know is that everyone in town is worried about what will happen here once Zeke passes."

"How about Jack Jay? Is he still interested?"

"He's a little too interested if you ask me. Ever since he filled in for Zeke last fall, he struts in and out as if he already owns the place. Zeke doesn't trust him. I don't either. It would not surprise me to find that he's got another buyer already lined up."

"Why does Zeke keep him around if he doesn't trust him?" Glenn asked.

"Zeke told me directly that Jack was there to help him select someone to take over when he's gone. Jack says he raises horses in Kentucky, but he's also spent a considerable amount of time trying to get me to agree to take care of Zeke's business interests. There's something I just don't trust about his proposed arrangement."

"I presume that you won't take over the stations and run them yourself," Glenn stated.

"No, I won't."

"Tell you what," Glenn heard himself saying, "I'll see what I can do to help Zeke out a bit when I get there. I still know a few people up in your direction who might come in handy in a jam."

"Thank you…"

"For you, my dear, almost anything… by the way, don't say anything to Zeke until I get there, okay?"

"Thanks, Glenn."

Glenn ended the phone then headed into the liquor store. It only took him a short time to find what he needed. He took his purchase back out to the car where he produced a briefcase lined with foam rubber. Nestled in the case were six shot glasses around the space where Glenn placed a bottle of Jack Daniels. He spent a few moments before closing the case and putting it in the floorboard of the back seat of his Fusion.

He had a small pang of regret in his gut for what he was planning on doing. His days of heading to Magnolia were going to be over once and for all after he had done what he intended to do. He would even put Ohio behind him… start fresh… maybe even head out in another direction.

But no, it was right. He would do the right thing. He needed to tick off those last two items and start his life over again, even if it meant ridding himself of old loves and friendships. Right now he was toxic to everyone he knew. They would be better off if he were to just find happiness and ride into the sunset never to be seen in Magnolia again.

Dotting the "T's" and Crossing the "I's"

Greg Fischer almost didn't exit the highway when he drove to Magnolia. He had been in this direction more than a few times, but mostly when he was on his way somewhere else. Magnolia never beckoned to him as somewhere he wanted to go. Had it not been for the telephone call and the promise of a larger than usual fee plus mileage, he would not have been looking for the building housing the homey café and radio station at three on a Monday afternoon.

He arrived, certain that the address was correct. The storefront announced in large letters in the front window and on the antique Pepsi sign hanging off an iron pipe jutting out in the front that he was at Zeke's Café.

"A nice touch," he said to himself.

There was a door off to the side of the storefront marked "WZEK Radio" with an arrow pointing to the right. Offset maybe ten feet back from the original building frontage was a modern brick appendage to the older building with a large front door leading to a lobby and an elevator.

"ADA compliant. Very good…"

Greg rode the elevator to the second floor, stepping out of a side door into a simply stated reception area. To his left, were two radio studios overlooking the street. To his right was an older woman sitting behind a desk working on a computer keyboard.

"Good afternoon! You must be Mr. Fischer! Come on in! Have a seat. I'll tell Zeke that you're here."

A name placard announced that the woman's name was Becky. That was all, just Becky.

"Thank-you, Becky," he said. He took a seat.

Becky slid her fingers on the keyboard in front of her. A few words were spoken into the headset she was wearing and in just a moment, she told the new arrival that he was welcome to go to the second office on the right as he went up the hallway behind her.

Greg thanked her again and went up the hall as he was instructed, arriving at a door with a black sign stating: **Zeke Collins – Enter at your own risk**.

The door was ajar. Greg knocked lightly before pushing the door open.

He entered to find the same sort of hodge-podge encountered by every other visitor to this particular office in the past forty years or so.

"Counselor. Come in. Have a seat." The old man was seated behind the cluttered desk. "Ezekiel Collins… just Zeke to everyone who knows me; and that more or less covers everyone."

Greg sat down in the right hand seat in front of the desk. The other seat was covered with papers of some sort… the sort which really didn't need to be bothered.

"Let me get to the point, young man… I'm at best three months from joining the choir invisible. I have made some decisions regarding my little enterprise here and I need your help in executing those decisions."

Greg decided to keep quiet and listen until the old man ran out of steam.

"I need you to help me sell something to a friend of yours. It's nothing he can't handle and the price is one he can easily afford. He just needs a little convincing and I understand that you might be just the person to convince him.

"I have decided to give this radio station… forgive me… these radio stations, the restaurant downstairs, the building in which we are sitting and a few scattered rental properties to this friend of yours to operate and maintain for as long as he cares to operate and maintain them which I hope will be the rest of his life."

"A friend of mine?"

"Yes, a friend of yours. I understand that you went to school with him and that the two of you still are on good terms with each other. Glenn Michaels."

"Glenn lives in Texas…" was all that Greg could think of to say, having been caught unawares.

"Of course he does. That's where you come in. He'll be up here at this time next week, and I need you to convince him to stay when he gets here. He'll listen to you."

Greg chuckled. Glenn may have listened to him from time to time, but never with any consistency. "I believe that he's pretty well established where he is."

"You heard about what happened to him on Friday, right?"

"The shooting incident?"

"Everyone's heard about it. He called here earlier today, setting up a visit. Magnolia is a refuge for him, you know."

"Didn't he work for you just before he got out of college?"

"He worked for me for a few months back in seventy-six. Great kid… great career, too, until his wife convinced him that he was going nowhere."

"He's pretty well over losing his wife and he seems to be happy where he is."

"And he nearly got shot the other day, too."

"A stroke of luck. The gunman committed suicide instead."

"Michaels is too damn lucky sometimes."

Zeke leaned back in his chair. Greg felt he was being sized up.

"Let me tell you a thing or two… but before I do, I'm going to let you know a ground rule. This is my office. Anything that's said here in confidence stays here."

"I'm in the same business, Mr. Collins."

"I knew that, Mr. Fischer; I just wanted to make sure that you knew that before I told you what I'm about to tell you."

Zeke craned his neck around. Greg assumed that he was checking to see if the door was closed. The old man drew the younger man a bit closer.

"I won't be here at the end of this month. My heart's about to give up, you see. I'm in the process of winding down my earthly affairs… making certain that what I've built will carry on."

"I understood the reason why I'm here when I came, Mr. Collins."

"Zeke. Call me Zeke."

"Okay, Zeke… I take it that the people who work for you are unaware of your condition?"

"Yes and no. Yes, they know that I'm living on borrowed time, but no, they don't know when. They know that I've been looking for someone to take over when I'm gone, but they don't know who."

"I take it that Glenn Michaels is who…"

"Yes, Mr. Fischer… I've thought it through very carefully. I've been working with an advisor for the past few months making sure of my decision."

"Is the person who's been advising you willing or able to take over?"

"He wants to, bad. Problem is that I can't trust the son of a bitch any further than I can spit. The man's a gypsy – a radio gypsy – drifting from place to place for most of his career, usually moving along after getting in some sort of trouble. The reason I'm using him as an advisor is that I feel sorry for him. He puts on airs about being some sort of horse breeder living on a farm outside of Lexington, but the fact of the matter is that he lives in a two room apartment with nothing to his name."

"And he came up with Glenn?" Greg asked.

"Nope – I came up with that myself. I've been thinking along those lines since my heart attack last year."

"Are you certain about your choice?"

"Until the incident on Friday, I was only ninety-five percent certain. Now, I'm one hundred percent. Glenn Michaels needs to come here for two reasons. For one, he's the most qualified. Period. He knows how to run a business and he knows radio.

"For the other, he has a feel for Magnolia and he would be the ideal person to carry on the tradition of the radio station and the café. Let me tell you a little bit about how all this came about."

Zeke leaned back again. Greg sensed that whatever it was that he was about to be told was not really all that confidential.

"The building you're sitting in started out as a hotel. When the market crashed in twenty-nine, it was abandoned. It sat idle through the war.

"After the war, Miss Annie Coggins Darden came to town. Her husband was a doctor who got drafted into the medical corps. He served in Italy and ended up knocking up one of the local girls. He asked for a divorce and she granted it after wiping out his bank accounts and moving here from Bristol, Virginia.

"Annie bought the building, fixed it up, put in an apartment for herself on the third floor, renovated the second floor into rooms she rented out to workmen, and made the ground floor into a café she called Annie's Coffee Cup.

"Before long, the Coffee Cup became a community center for Magnolia. Miss Annie's Biscuits and Gravy became known throughout the county. She did alright by herself.

"I found out about the place in the mid sixties. I'd come up here after working my morning radio show in Portsmouth. It got to a point where I figured that I would be better off just staying here, so, I bought the business, set up a radio station of my own and the rest is history.

"For over forty years, I've promoted Magnolia from the front window of Zeke's Café. People came, people spent money, the town prospered. I want the town to continue to prosper Mr. Fischer. I want Glenn Michaels to come here to continue the legacy."

"You want Glenn in particular," Greg stated.

"Absolutely. He needs to be here, too, because of something that happened twenty-five years ago here in Magnolia. No one talks about it, except to call it The Incident. Glenn Michaels feels that he is responsible for The Incident. It's been his personal demon. He needs to face that demon, stare it down and be rid of it."

"Are you talking about that murder/suicide involving the preacher and his family?"

"One and the same."

"Glenn's mentioned it to me but only in passing."

"Has he ever told you <u>why</u> The Incident happened?"

"No, he just... not really, come to think of it... all I know is what was reported at the time. I take it that there's more."

"There are only three people who know exactly why Reverend Harlan Murphy butchered his family, torched his church and killed himself at a simple traffic stop over by the fairgrounds."

Zeke took another look around them. "You, my friend, are about to be the fourth one."

Greg felt uncomfortable. Confidentiality rides on a razor's edge in some instances. Zeke seemed to know something about The Incident that wasn't known. All Greg knew was that Glenn seemed strangely attracted to The Incident for no apparent reason. Now it appeared that his friend Glenn might be somehow involved.

Zeke watched the lawyer squirm for a few moments. "Let me just start by saying that when the preacher blew his head off, he was headed to see Glenn Michaels with the intention of killing him."

"What!"

Zeke nodded his head. "I'm willing to bet that fellow who blew his head off down in Texas the other day was getting ready to shoot Glenn before he got caught. Glenn knows. When he comes here, he'll be looking for answers. Mark my words."

An hour and a half later, Greg Fischer was back in his car headed north. He had in his notes a draft of Zeke Collins' Last Will and Testament, a check for twice his usual retainer and an agreement (drafted, printed, and duplicated on the spot) of confidentiality. Greg had been told exactly why The Incident had happened. It helped to explain some of the events which happened in Glenn's life over the past twenty-five years.

"That son of a bitch," Greg said to himself as he approached his office. "Of all the people I know, I would have thought that Glenn Michaels would have been the least likely to do what he did."

The Broken Date

Tricia Knox was damn glad that the date she had with Jerry Temples ended when he left her sitting alone in the Colonial in Jackson, Ohio with a $75 dinner check.

"I got us a room at the Inn at Jackson so we can get cozy and spend the night exploring each other," he told her.

"That's nice," she replied in a syrupy voice, "I hope that you enjoy fucking yourself."

His mouth dropped open. "What?"

"You can go and fuck your own self," she stated quite plainly, "leave me the check if you want, but I'm not that kind of a girl."

"If that's the way you want it, bitch, you've got it!"

At least he was quiet about it and didn't make a scene when he left; besides, none of the wine in the bottle had been poured. So, Tricia had the bottle re-corked, paid the tab and headed back to her home five miles north of Prentiss by way of The Cross-State Highway.

"He had a lot of damn gall," she fumed as she passed the turn-off to the short cut she usually took when she was going back home from points east.

It was a first date – something she and… the idiot (he had ceased to be Jerry Temples by this point in the drive) had arranged on the internet. He looked nice, at least his picture looked nice, he was a professional, but his profile didn't mention what he did or that he had an attitude.

"Typical…"

She had almost gotten used to having dates with men who were either stepping out on their wives, or expecting that a divorced fifty-two year old woman would be desperate to be laid. The Idiot just happened to be more blatant about his expectations than most.

She turned on the radio to hear the kid who Zeke had hired to run WZEK on Saturday nights. The sounds of Clarence Clemmons' sax solo on *Born to Run* filled the night air. She boosted the volume. *Born to Run* had always given her shivers of excitement to the point that she found it difficult not to just floor the gas pedal on her Mustang convertible and fly down the highway with wild abandon.

The song ended just as she reached the turn-off to go through Magnolia to head on up to Prentiss and eventually, home. She pulled off the River Highway, electing to take the drive through town. She stopped in front of Zeke's Café. By this time, it was closed for the remainder of the weekend, not to open again until Monday morning.

Tricia parked the car and crossed the street to sit on the end of a bench. This was a special bench. It had a holder welded into the arm on one end which held a single yellow rose every day during the month of July. When one rose started showing signs of wilting, it was always replaced with another just like it. No one ever bothered the rose. There was an unwritten law in Magnolia that the rose would not be disturbed in any way until after Heritage Day at the end of July.

"The rose is a memorial," Jessica Collins had told Tricia a few years ago when she first saw it. "It is there in memory of a woman and her young children who were brutally murdered by her husband, a fallen minister named Harlan Murphy."

Tricia first heard about what the locals called The Incident while she and her boyfriend were working and living together on the east side of Portsmouth.

The Incident was a sordid affair. Brother Murphy had apparently cut open his pregnant wife, decapitated his two sons, went to his church, took over three thousand dollars out of the petty cash drawer and torched the place. He was headed north on the River Highway which went around downtown Magnolia when he was stopped by the highway patrol for having a broken tail-light. As the patrolman approached the car, Brother Murphy produced a gun he had hidden in the glovebox and blew his own head off in front of the officer. It made no sense to the officer as to why the minister committed suicide until he learned about the arson and the murders.

The whole event made no real sense to anyone. There was no motive as far as anyone could tell. One of the reasons Tricia Knox eventually became a writer was that some day she wanted to find out the real reason for The Incident and tell the definitive story which still eluded people in and around Magnolia for the past quarter century.

Summer smells wafted through a light breeze as the sunshine began to wane.

"Finished with your dinner date so soon?"

Harold Richmond, Magnolia's Chief of Police interrupted Tricia's enjoyment of the sounds of a summer evening.

"Hey Harold…"

"So what happened?"

"Nothing, thankfully. The Idiot thought that I'd make a cheap fuck for his sorry ass. Sorry for the f-bomb, but that's all it amounted to. I think I might start carrying an inflatable doll with me just to give idiots like that… whatever his name was… exactly what they want without getting involved."

"Apology accepted. So how's your story on Zeke coming?"

"I'm just about there. I'll most likely file my story with the news bureau on Wednesday so that it can hit the weekend papers."

"Janet and I will look for it."

"So where is Janet anyway? Don't the two of you usually get out around this time on a Saturday evening to take a walk?"

"The kids and the grandkids are in. Officially, I needed to go out on an errand. Unofficially, I needed to get some peace and quiet," Harold chuckled.

"You saw the car and you came over to flirt with me, didn't you?"

"I might consider it, but I'm already taken… you know that."

"And well-deserved, too, Harold. You know that I envy you both."

"I'll take that as a compliment."

Harold bid Tricia a good night before continuing on his walk. She sat and stared blankly at the building in front of her for another half an hour before getting back into her car and heading home for the night.

She didn't like being alone, especially on a Saturday night. She undressed then went outside to her back porch to stand and let the night surround her. Tricia might have allowed the majesty of the night sky to intimidate her into thinking that she was so very small and so very insignificant, but she was Tricia Knox. She was confident enough in herself to know that she could overcome her adversaries… especially the one who was probably trying to pick up some young thing at a bar in Jackson to temporarily be Mrs. Whatzizname so that the money he paid for the motel room wouldn't go to waste.

Spit-Take

Glenn pre-planned every aspect of his trip to Ohio, from where he would stop to refuel to where he would stop for meals. It was an old habit he picked up from his days as a radio announcer. Good timing was good planning.

"Forest City, Arkansas, exit here," he said to himself at around lunch time on Saturday afternoon. The low fuel alarm on his car made its "ping" just as he pulled into the off ramp of the Interstate. "Timed it just right." He was smug about the accomplishment. The car's clock confirmed that he was ahead of his ETA, swelling his head even further.

Memphis, Nashville, then overnight in Bowling Green.

Glenn went to bed somewhat later than he expected, but went to sleep quickly. He woke up in the middle of the night after having had a dream skirt the edge of his memory. He recalled sitting on a bench, holding a yellow rose, then being approached by a woman he felt that he knew. She sat down next to him. He handed her the rose. She took it and put it aside before she whispered in his ear: "C'mon, we have work to do…"

After settling back down, Glenn caught a few more hours of sleep before getting up and heading out. He took advantage of Sunday morning to cut across Kentucky to approach Magnolia by way of Lexington.

It was almost precisely three o'clock eastern time when Glenn pulled up to a familiar three story brick building in the middle of Magnolia.

He looked across the street to see Jessica Collins getting up from a public bench to approach him. She was holding the yellow rose.

"Welcome back home, Glenn," Jessica greeted him as he got out of his car.

Glenn gave the old woman a hug and a kiss on the cheek. "It's good to be back, at least for a day or two. How's Zeke?"

"Still holding his own… right now he's taking a nap. He left strict instructions to have you meet us at four-thirty to go to dinner."

"Still as feisty as he ever was, eh?" Glenn smiled.

"Still feisty. Maybe even a little more ornery than usual."

"Has he found his replacement, then?"

Jessica nodded her head. "He's kept files all these years. He has his replacement in mind, but he hasn't asked him yet."

Glenn opened his car to unload the gear he needed to take up to the apartment on the third floor of the building. Jessica walked back to replace the rose before going back to let Glenn in the front door. Instead of using the elevator to go through the radio station, they went through the restaurant to the back of the building. There was a set of stairs near the back entrance which served all three levels of the building as well as the basement. Actual access to the back stairway was by pass-card only. The second floor housed the offices and studios of the radio stations, WZEK AM and FM. The side elevator went directly to the lobby in the middle of the building. The broadcast studios were facing the street; the offices for the salespeople and Zeke were toward the back of the building. The third floor was occupied with a large, one bedroom apartment which was used by the Collins family for chosen guests.

"You go on ahead and get yourself settled in," Jessica told Glenn when they reached the base of the stairs.

"Any more I'm good for only one trip up to the third floor per day and I've already reached my limit." She handed him a pass-card before going out the back door, through the breezeway and into her house.

The apartment was pretty much like Glenn remembered it. The suite was broad and airy with a good western view of the river and hills beyond the town. Glenn noted the various touches Jessica had completed before his arrival, including leaving an assortment of radio trade magazines, fresh towels and linens and an empty vase next to the night stand.

At precisely four-thirty, Glenn punched the doorbell of the back door of the Collins residence.

"You're fifteen seconds late, Michaels," Zeke growled as he opened the door.

"I'm on Central Time, Zeke… that makes me fifty-nine minutes and forty-five seconds early."

Zeke laughed and gave his protégé a hug. "As I say, there was a time I would smack you for that, young man!"

Jessica made her way past the men to open the green Buick she intended to drive to the Town Lake Club. "Are you going to stand there or are the two of you going to get in?"

The drive up was slow, but uneventful. Zeke filled Glenn in on some of the latest gossip which passed for news in this little corner of the world. When they arrived at the Club, the lot was mostly empty. It was still a little early for Sunday supper. They were greeted at the end of the hall leading to the restaurant and promptly escorted to a table by a window on the upper level overlooking Town Lake.

The Club was a throwback. It was the type of restaurant where many of the patrons were regulars with particular preferences of where they sat or what they would order for their meals. And never, under any circumstances, would any of the servers refer to a group of patrons as "you guys". It was just that sort of place.

"Ah, Mister Collins and the lovely Miss Jessica! How lovely to have you this afternoon!" The server was a young man who appeared to be in his mid to late twenties.

"Hello Thomas," Zeke replied. "We have a guest this afternoon; Mister Glenn Michaels from Dallas, Texas."

"Very good," Thomas replied, handing out the menus. He took drink orders before leaving them alone to read the bill of fare.

"Michaels, I have a problem," Zeke said after they had ordered their dinners. "I have a Doctor who tells me that for some reason he can't cure old age. As I say, I may not have too very much longer to be on this side of the grass."

"Zeke, not yet," Jessica urged. "Can you at least wait until after dinner to have this conversation?"

"I may not have until after dinner, woman, and you know that."

Jessica looked at Glenn and rolled her eyeballs.

"As I say, I'm glad you're here, Glenn. I've decided to give you the radio stations and the restaurant before I die."

"Excuse me?" Glenn sputtered, thankful that he didn't have a mouth full of water with which he would have sprayed on his host.

"Zeke…" Jessica glared at her husband.

"As I say, you are the best person to carry on the business when I'm gone. Since I have no children, I am naming you as my heir."

Glenn took a deep breath. "Oooookaay…" he said as he gathered his thoughts. "I, uh, came up here just to play co-host for a part of a morning and to say goodbye to Magnolia one last time. That's it. I have a life in Dallas."

"What's tying you down, boy? Your woman? Since your divorce, my understanding is that you've fucked your way from bed to bed."

"Zeke... language!" Jessica scolded him.

"So you make some money at that job of yours. What do you do with it? As I say, money is like manure, Michaels. It's useless unless you spread it around.

"Your kids are grown, you have all the skills that you need and, besides, you need a change in scenery. That idiot you work with, the coke head... he's bad news."

"He's dead, Zeke. He shot himself a week ago last Friday."

"I read about it; and good riddance, too. Problem solved. Go get your things next week and come back up to take over the whole shebang."

Glenn looked over to see Jessica covering her eyes and shaking her head.

"Zeke, I'm... flattered. Seriously. But the business has changed. I've been out of it for fifteen years now. I can't go back. All I want to do is to play for part of a morning to show my ex that I can still do radio, take care of some other business and head back home."

Zeke gave Glenn a hard look.

"How soon are you going back?" he asked.

"I was going to be on my way back to Texas on Friday morning."

"Before you say no, I want to have a long talk with you. Can you at least let me talk with you on... say, Tuesday?"

Glenn thought for a moment. "I can do that much for you," he finally told the old man.

Dinner came and talk shifted over to some of the usual minutiae of day to day living. At one point, Zeke excused himself to go to the men's room.

"Is he serious about his offer?" Glenn asked Jessica when Zeke was out of earshot.

"Most definitely," she answered. "If you don't take his offer, I'm told that some big company which doesn't give a damn about our town will come in and take the place over. I'll be okay. If he goes right now, I'm set for the rest of my life, but the radio stations and the restaurant will be at risk. There are a lot of people depending on both of them, Glenn, and if you should decide to walk away, Magnolia may just wither up and die."

Magnolia Revisited

THE LANDSCAPE HAD CHANGED. The wide spot in the road at the intersection of two highways wasn't quite the same as it was when Glenn worked in Magnolia nearly thirty-five years earlier. There really wasn't a "downtown" any more, except for hangers-on like the former hotel-turned-café and radio station where Glenn was staying, Ed's Church and Grill, The Bank of Pomeroy, and Village Hardware. Everything else seemed to have moved to an extension of South Street, hoping to catch traffic as it exited one highway as the other ran north, or traffic from the north headed south, east or west.

After returning from the early dinner, Glenn went for a walk to get his bearings. Magnolia on a Sunday night was quiet; the only sounds the occasional barking dog or the murmur of preaching through an open door at the Community Baptist Church. Glenn stopped at the church, wandered in and stood at the back for a short while. The Reverend John Kellough was at the pulpit as he had been for over forty years, now.

"He's got to be pushing eighty, hard," Glenn thought as he listened, "but hasn't changed a bit."

During Glenn's short tenure at WZEK, the Reverend Kellough would come in the early morning to preach "The Word" on the radio before going to Community Baptist to conduct his regular Sunday morning services. He would come in before his assigned slot, have a word or two with Glenn, referencing the Bible, do his show and leave. Glenn would feel at peace after Reverend Kellough would make his weekly appearance: he was one of the only islands of comfort and sanity in the parade of dog and pony shows preceding or following.

Glenn slipped out of the church un-noticed to continue his walk.

"I know you, I think…"

The only other person Glenn encountered during his hour-long walk was a man who approached him as he sat on the bench across the street from the radio station where Jessica had waited for his arrival several hours earlier.

"You used to work there, didn't you?" the man said, pointing to the building across the street. "Saturday and Sunday afternoons. I was a senior at the high school and I'd come up to watch you once or twice. Steve Mulligan, by the way. You're… let me see if I remember… Glenn, wasn't it?"

"Glenn Michaels, and it still is. You remember back that far?"

"You betcha. Best years of my life up to that point."

"I take it you still live here in Magnolia?"

"I haven't always. I lived over in Beaver for a short while. That's where I met my wife." He chuckled. "She wanted to move to the big city."

"So what keeps you in Magnolia?"

"I own half the town. Village Hardware, Millie, my wife, she runs that. Ed's Church and Grill – I bought it about ten years ago when Ed retired. Then there's the pizza shop – Father Linguini's Most Excellent Authentic Italian Eatery. I got that name from you, you know, you once had me in stitches doing a Godfather imitation, saying that you were Father Linguini. And there's the IGA down on South Street, too."

"You're keeping busy, I take it."

"Me, two sons, a wife and a daughter. We distribute the load. Tell me, what brings you back to our little burg? You still on the radio?"

"I quit the business fifteen years ago. I manage a store for a small chain of appliance stores down in Dallas, Texas."

"That's too bad. I remember listening to you from time to time when you worked out of Cincinnati,"

"That was a good gig. The wife didn't like it, though. Come to think of it, she didn't like any of the gigs I had, so we settled down in Dallas."

"Did you bring her with you this trip?"

"Nope, I've been divorced from her for ten years."

Steve stayed silent. Both men sat on the bench, watching the building across the street. After a minute or two, a figure emerged from the building, fired up a cigarette and stood there urging the death stick to hurry up.

"Fool kid. Punctual, though. That's the only reason Zeke keeps him," Steve confided. "He does the evening show Sunday through Friday. Six to sign-off at midnight."

The figure disappeared back into the building.

"You heard about Zeke, right? I assume that's why you're here."

"His heart condition? Yep. I've heard. Had dinner with him and Jessica this afternoon."

"Town Lake Club, I'll bet."

"Yep."

"Tradition. He and Jessica go up there every Sunday afternoon, sit at the same table and order the same thing. Every once in a while, he'll have a guest. Millie and I have been Zeke and Jessica's guests a few times. That old man is full of stories. I've never heard him repeat a one of them."

"He hasn't changed, let me tell you."

"We're gonna miss him. He was sayin' to me that he might have a replacement when he goes, but he won't never be as good as Zeke."

Glenn smiled and nodded.

"You're not the replacement, are you?"

"Nope, I'm just up here on a visit before he shuffles off."

"Too bad," Steve sighed. "I'm just afraid of what will happen when he goes. No replacement, no Magnolia. Most everyone here in town is worried about what will happen."

"Something will work out; always does."

"I sure hope so. I may have to end up eating my wife's cooking for breakfast on Monday mornings!"

"Mondays?"

"Yeah, me and most of the other people who run the village meet here regular on Monday mornings to have breakfast.

"We listen to Zeke before we get going for the week. You'll see what happens, supposing you'll be there with Zeke in the morning."

Steve got up and shook Glenn's hand before going back up the street toward home. "Good to see you again, Mr. Michaels. See you in the morning!"

Glenn stayed tied to the bench for another hour as the light dwindled, signaling the transition from day into evening into night.

"Something will work out, it always does," he kept telling himself.

He was just having a hard time believing it at the moment. At the same time, he was hoping like hell that the solution wouldn't include him.

The Texan

TRICIA KNOX FELT COMPELLED TO go to Zeke's on Monday morning, acting more on a hunch than on good sense. She didn't have to go. She had finished the research on her story and was about an hour away from finishing and sending it to the bureau. She rolled out of bed, completed her morning abolitions and was out the door by five-forty-five.

Traffic was light. She made it to the back parking lot just after six and was in place when Zeke started his usual morning banter after the network news at five after. He looked as if he had had a rough weekend and seemed to struggle a bit more than usual to keep up with the demands of his job.

"Think he'll make it through the week?"

Steve Mulligan pulled into the booth opposite Tricia.

"Looks iffy. What do you think?"

"Don't know, but the Mayor and Town Council are getting anxious about the situation."

"Any idea who belongs to the red Fusion with Texas plates in the back lot?"

Tricia craned her neck around to see if she could spot a Texan, fully expecting someone with boots and a cowboy hat to jump out at her.

"Probably belongs to this guy who used to work here named Glenn Michaels. I met him last night out walking. I used to listen to him when he worked out of Cincinnati."

"See him in here?"

"I didn't notice. I'll assume he's staying on the third floor as Zeke's guest, though. He may come down after a while."

Tricia decided to wait and see who this Glenn Michaels was. He might be someone with insight who she could interview so that she could add a little bit to the story she had been writing.

It was seven-thirty before the Texan came whisking by her and marched up to Zeke's desk in the front window of the restaurant.

He looked to be somewhere in his mid fifties. Dark head of hair with a whisper or two of grey, looking a little out of control, perhaps due to the summer weather. He wore a simple collared shirt with some sort of a logo along with khaki pants and a pair of casual walking shoes.

After the newcomer had introduced himself (she had already written down his name: Glenn Michaels) and had traded a few lines with Zeke, he seemed to fit in with what Zeke was doing. He actually seemed to give Zeke the added boost of energy he needed to get through his Monday morning.

"My God," she thought just after the show resumed after the nine o'clock news, "he's Zeke's replacement."

She twisted around to look to her right to what was known as the family table. It was where Town Council usually met (informally) on Monday mornings and on other occasions when needed. They were discussing among themselves in whispers and asides.

Maybe they were thinking the same thing.

Zeke's imminent departure from among the living had been a constant source of speculation since the previous September when Zeke was absent for a week, hospitalized due to chest pains. Tricia had not paid much attention to Zeke's enterprise until about a month after his return. A friend of hers suggested that she might want to go and observe Zeke's morning show, perhaps even do a little more research and maybe write a book about what she found.

Tricia visited sporadically for the next several months, coming to the conclusion that the fortunes of Zeke Collins and Magnolia were tied together.

What Tricia found most interesting was that Zeke's reign as the Morning Mayor of Magnolia, Ohio came about because of his love of biscuits smothered in home-made sausage gravy.

"Zeke came to town originally because of the biscuits and gravy served up by Annie Coggins," she wrote. "Annie had come to town just after the Second World War with a settlement gained by a divorce lawyer from her cheating ex-husband."

Tricia's story went on to explain that Zeke came to Annie at about the time she was ready to pack it up and head back to her home in Tennessee. Zeke already had an audience for a radio show he had in Portsmouth and eventually purchased rights to radio frequencies granted to Fuller County. He built up Annie's restaurant business on the first floor, modified the second floor for the radio stations (once used as housing for workers at the energy plant down the road) and kept the third floor apartment; living in it at first, then, using it as a "guest facility" after he and his wife purchased the house across the alley.

"Zeke's fame followed him," she continued, "and the businesses and the town of Magnolia have both benefitted."

Ever since Zeke's heart attack, rumors of what would happen spread through town like wild fire.

"He's good; really good." Harold Richmond, Magnolia's police chief came by and broke Tricia's concentration. By nine-thirty, she found herself totally captivated by the Texan's voice and personality.

"I sort of think so, yeah."

Tricia caught herself talking as if she was a schoolgirl with a crush.

"What's more important is that Zeke thinks so. Him and Wild Jack are maybe going to make Mr. Michaels an offer."

"Knowing Zeke, an offer may already have been made," Tricia mused. "Jack Jankowski probably didn't have any voice in the matter."

Tricia had picked up on Zeke's reluctance to hand over the keys of his radio stations to the former disc jockey living in Lexington. She had talked with Jack on several occasions and felt that he hadn't been entirely honest with her. There was something more to his story.

"He does seem to have Zeke's act down pretty well," she continued.

"Zeke ain't no act," Harold reminded Tricia. "He's as real as they come. Michaels was that way, too when he was in radio…"

"You mean he isn't?"

"He's been doin' something else these days… sellin's what I hear, but he sure hasn't lost his touch."

"I couldn't tell that there was any time he wasn't on radio."

"He almost quit a couple of times, 'specially after The Incident."

Tricia perked up.

"You're talking about the Murphy killings…"

"Uh… no… it was something else."

Harold Richmond was lying. He never was a good liar. She could tell.

"Mulligan told me that Michaels used to work in Cincinnati."

"Yeah, he did."

"He visits Zeke."

"So?"

"I've heard rumblings that Zeke maybe knows more about The Incident than he's ever let on. Maybe there's something he'll be taking to the grave with him… or maybe there are people in this town who know what Zeke knows and are hoping that the whole thing will pass once he does."

"I wouldn't be looking too hard, young lady. Fact is there were a lot of hurt feelings because of what happened and if you went to diggin'; you might not like what you find."

Harold left without another word.

Tricia sat and waited for the show to be over. She always suspected that Harold may have known something; now she was almost certain. Maybe Glenn Michaels knew something, too.

Trying it on for Size

Glenn spent a restless night in the queen-sized bed on the third floor of Zeke's. He woke up, showered, dressed and wandered down the back stairs to the restaurant where Zeke Collins held court as the Morning Mayor of southern Ohio. He was rather amazed at what awaited him when he came in through the back of the restaurant. Most everyone was transfixed on Zeke, sitting in the front window, telling some story or other and entertaining his audience.

There was quite a crowd. Most of the booths were filled, the majority with farmers loafing before having to go out in their fields to put in a hard day's work. There was a woman in a booth near the back of the restaurant who seemed to be taking notes as Zeke's words wove around eventually giving a plug for one of his sponsors.

Zeke spotted Glenn at about the time an announcer from the studio upstairs was reading the local news. He waved Glenn to come and sit with him in the front window.

"You're late, son… it's seven-thirty…" Zeke started in.

"Six-thirty Central, Zeke," Glenn shot back lightheartedly. The PA system was still on so there was a slight chuckle from the audience.

"You just sit right up here and show me what you've got, okay?" Zeke shoved some papers in Glenn's direction. There was a program log and several sheets of paper with basic outlines on them for live commercials.

Slowly at first, then with more gusto as time went on, Glenn spent the next two and a half hours running the morning radio show on WZEK with Zeke Collins. There was a definite ebb and flow of people coming in and out of the restaurant throughout the entire time of the program. Most of the customers would come by to say hi before leaving the place. The people in the restaurant belonged to Zeke. There was no doubt about it in anyone's mind. Zeke Collins' morning show was a Magnolia tradition.

Glenn felt pretty darn good about himself at ten when the show ended. He finally headed to the back of the restaurant to go upstairs to freshen up before starting the business of the day. The woman whom he had noticed on his way into the restaurant at seven-thirty was still there when he was on his way out.

He walked past her, avoiding eye contact. He found her attractive, but he didn't want to be trapped. He didn't want to poison another life. More importantly, he didn't want to have any extra baggage to take back to Dallas.

When he came downstairs twenty minutes later he went out the back door to find that the woman from earlier that morning had propped herself against his car.

"Mr. Michaels?" She appeared to be in her late forties to early fifties. She carried herself with an air of self-confidence. He didn't notice her wearing an excess of rings or jewelry, the only piece she seemed to have was a simple necklace with a small gem attached. Her hair was starting to show just a touch of grey making the pony tail emerging from the back of her baseball hat just a little more interesting. She was dressed modestly in a pink pull-over shirt and blue jeans which did not seem to be painted on like they had been on some other women he had known.

Glenn hesitated for just a moment, stopped by her piercing green eyes.

"Hi," he said. He was trapped for the moment and he knew it.

"Hi. Patricia Knox. I prefer Tricia. I'm a free-lance writer. You've done this, the morning show, that is, before, haven't you?"

"Once or twice..." Glenn tried to tear himself from Tricia's eyes.

"Could I get you to sit down with me for a minute or two and talk?" she indicated the back door to Zeke's.

"There's no story here, sorry." For some reason, Glenn hesitated instead of shooing her off his car so that he could do what he had planned to do.

"How about a drink, no strings attached, sometime?"

"I guess I could do that. I'll be around for a day or two, at least. I have some other business to attend to."

"Then back to Texas?"

"How did you know?"

"Red car, Texas plates parked in the back lot sort of tipped me off. You mentioned living in the central time zone for another. I'm guessing you used to live here."

"A long time ago, yes. I worked here for a few months back in the mid seventies while I was finishing up my degree over in Athens. Zeke and I have kept in touch ever since."

"What do you know about Zeke's health?"

"I'm not a doctor, I can't really comment."

"I'm doing a story on him and I would like some input from someone who doesn't live here now."

"There's something I have to settle between Zeke and me, first. Maybe, tomorrow some time?"

Tricia nodded. "Tomorrow will be fine," she said.

Glenn finally was loosened from the grip she had on him with her eyes. "Tricia, right?" he called after her as she started to step away.

"Yes, Tricia. Tricia Knox."

"I have something I need to do tomorrow morning, probably between ten and eleven. It has to do with something that happened a few years after I worked here and I was wondering if maybe I could get you to come along."

Glenn was surprised to hear himself say it and almost took back the offer as soon as he made it. He was going to head out towards Jumpstart to visit Hannah Smith's grave. "What kind of a person would take a woman to a dead woman's grave?" he asked himself.

"Sure, why not? I'd like that. I'll tell you what; I'll take you to lunch afterwards."

She looked him in his eyes again. "See you tomorrow, Glenn."

Tricia turned to enter the back door of Zeke's. Glenn watched her as best as he could as she wound around the patrons to head to the front door.

Reality hit him again. He had just set himself up on a date. He had no idea why he had stuck his neck out to ask a perfect stranger out to a cemetery in the middle of nowhere, but it was apparently a done deal.

"It's only a spur of them moment thing and she'll probably be suddenly unavailable. I promise not to get involved," he thought.

Anyone observing would have noticed a spring in Glenn's step as he momentarily forgot what he had intended to do and went back up to the third floor apartment.

Back to the Stomping Grounds

Glenn eventually drove up to Chillicothe to keep a promise he made to himself to visit his parents' gravesite in Grandview Cemetery before leaving Ohio forever. He thought that he should pay a final visit with no promise of a return.

He drove up to the ridge at the top of the cemetery overlooking Paint Creek as it flowed east on its way to the Scioto River. He stopped the car and rolled down the windows when he arrived, then sat for several moments to contemplate exactly what he would be doing next.

Glenn retrieved the briefcase which he had carefully packed before he left from the foot well of the back seat, took it over to his parents' marker and set it on the ground. He sat down and offered a brief prayer before opening the briefcase to extract two of the glasses and the bottle of Jack Daniels. Carefully, he poured an ounce of the whiskey into each of the glasses. When he was finished, he stood up, put one of the glasses on top of the marker and held the other up in a salute to his parents.

"I know that this is probably more whiskey than you ever had when you were living, but it's like you always told me. 'Try new things,' you said. So here's to you. Bottoms up." With that, Glenn emptied his glass before he took the glass from the monument and emptied it on the ground. He then replaced the empty glass on the grave marker before placing the glass he had used and the bottle into the briefcase.

Glenn tarried ten more minutes before packing up and heading downtown for an early lunch.

"You, sir, are a predictable creature." The voice coming from behind him as he sat at a table in the Cross Keys Tavern sounded familiar. Glenn turned around and found himself face to face with Bill Preston, an old friend who used to work with him at the radio station when he was just getting started.

"I heard you on the air with Zeke this morning and I figured you'd be here eating lunch after visiting your mom and dad," Bill stated as he sat down opposite Glenn.

"Am I really that predictable?"

"Let's just say that there are times when I could set my watch by you, Michaels. Tell me. How the hell have you been?"

"Not too shabby. How about you, you old coot?"

"About the same," Bill replied. "Still hanging your hat at the appliance store, or are you thinking of getting back on the air?"

"Appliance store. I'm on an extended vacation. One of my sales guys went berserk and put a bullet in his brain in our parking lot a little over a week ago. I had a problem dealing with it because of what happened down in Magnolia a few months after Dad's funeral, so I came up here with the notion that I was going to put some of my baggage behind me."

"So that <u>was</u> you I read about in the paper. I thought it might be. How does it feel to be famous, again?"

"It's not all that it's cracked up to be, believe me."

A server came by with a cola for Glenn then asked Bill for his order. When she left, Glenn continued: "I'm here on business then I'm leaving Ohio for good this time. No coming back. I'm going tomorrow to say another goodbye, then I'm headed back home to Texas where I belong."

"You still have that list, right?"

"Yep. Tomorrow I finish it."

"The show this morning was number nine if I remember correctly."

"Tomorrow I'll tick off number ten."

"You mentioned ridding yourself of Hannah Smith and cutting your ties to Magnolia, right?"

"Yep. I came to the conclusion that I have to get her out of my system and say goodbye for good. That's what I'll be doing tomorrow. She's getting in the way of any hope I have of settling down and leading a normal life. No woman wants to live with a man and his pet ghost."

Bill chuckled briefly and took a drink before he put his hand over his mouth to keep his lips from being read. "Don't look now, but Randy Green just walked in the front door. He'll likely be back here in a moment. Watch what you say."

"Hi, Bill," Randy said as he approached the table where Bill and Glenn were sitting. He looked over at Glenn then grinned ear to ear. "Well if it isn't the late, great Glenn Michaels! We heard you this morning with Zeke. What's the occasion?"

"No occasion, Randy. Just visiting, that's all."

Randy occupied the chair next to Bill so that he could look directly at Glenn.

"Are you sure you're not auditioning to take Zeke's place when he finally keels over?"

Glenn felt uncomfortable in Randy's presence. It wasn't always so. He remembered a time when Randy, Bill and he would sit around a case of beer and talk for hours on end about the radio business, solving problems with a snap of the fingers.

Then, reality set in. Big Thicket Broadcasting came to town, swallowing up and spitting out people and traditions. Randy decided he wanted to join in. He had a family. He found security. He became distant.

"Nope, just in for a visit. Zeke and Jessie are letting me use their apartment while I'm there."

"Word on the street is that Zeke won't be around much longer, you know."

"Really? He seemed just fine when he took me to dinner last night and he seemed to be quite well this morning. I'm looking forward to being here when he has his hundredth birthday show."

Randy forced a laugh as he often did. Glenn remembered that one of the reasons he really didn't like Randy after he joined up with Big Thicket was the forced laugh. His natural ebullient personality disappeared when he joined the corporate world.

"Big Thicket is looking at buying Zeke's stations from the estate when he's gone, you know."

Glenn smiled. "And I'm sure they have plans to make it into the same kind of whorehouse that Big Thicket has made of every other radio station they've ever taken over."

Bill lowered his eyebrows in disapproval.

"You could have been part of it, you know. You're getting to the age where you might want to consider retiring. A good pension from a good company would be an awfully nice thing to have when you get older."

"I'm sorry, Randy, but if I go to work just to get a pension, I may as well shoot myself instead of stepping in Big Thicket's stench. I like you, Randy, but I'm not now and I've never been comfortable with Big Thicket. As a matter of fact, I'm damn glad to be out of the radio business the way it is these days."

Randy showed signs of being irritated with Glenn. The server interrupted by bringing sandwiches for Glenn and Bill.

"Well, I guess you guys are eating, so I'll mosey along... ha! Get it Michaels? Mosey along. Just like a Texan, you know!"

"Sure. I'll be glad… to…" Randy left before Glenn could even finish what he was saying. "He's still as fucked up as ever since he went to the dark side, isn't he?" Glenn asked Bill.

"He's become what I like to term as a patented bastard, too," Bill told Glenn. "I'm still under contract, but I don't do much work anymore. It all goes through this guy Randy was told to hire from his higher-up in Pittsburgh. Hell, he has to get permission from Pittsburgh to even fart these days. No one's 'live' any more either, except for Rick and Ray - and they're running a poor second to Zeke in audience, even up here."

"So I take it that when Zeke goes, Rick and Ray will have a monopoly."

"Pretty much… actually, when Zeke goes, word on the street is that WZEK goes off the air. Randy and the big wigs at Big Thicket have been working on plans to move the FM to Huntington. The AM station will just be a repeater of Big Thicket's usual talk show dreck."

"Who knows this?"

"No one outside of Thicket, except you."

Glenn ate in silence for a few minutes. "Suppose that Zeke were to sell the place to a third party before he died. What would happen to Thicket's offer?"

Bill gave Glenn a puzzled look. "I never really thought of it before. The biggest problem that I see is that Zeke's departure would put a hole in the station it would never recover from. Anyone thinking of buying the place and making a go of it would think twice before putting money into the station without hiring a host with the appeal of Zeke Collins."

Bill stopped and opened his mouth for a moment as a light seemed to come on. "You aren't thinking of buying the place from him, are you?"

"No," Glenn smiled. "But I was offered it as a gift."

"No shit?"

"Free and clear. The whole shebang. All I need to do is want it."

"How soon will you take over?"

"Never. I told you before. I'm through with radio and I'm through with this burg."

"You're sure about that?"

"I'm meeting with Zeke tomorrow afternoon to listen to his pitch one more time. I'll politely decline the offer then I'll move on with my life."

Bill finished his sandwich, leaned back and took a good look at his friend. "Michaels, you're too damn predictable. I'm betting twenty dollars that you will come up with some crazy, hare-brained scheme to take Zeke up on his offer by the end of this week."

Glenn reached in his back pocket, pulled his wallet out and pulled out a twenty. "I say you lose. For old time's sake, I'll give you the money you expected to win." He put the money on the table. "So you get to pay for lunch." With that, Glenn got up and left the Cross Keys. He had a few other old hang-outs to visit before heading back to Magnolia later that afternoon.

Key to a Mystery?

SHE WAS SOOO CASUAL ABOUT it, she couldn't stand herself.

On the other hand, she wondered why she felt sooo casual. She found that she had some of the same feelings she had before she met Donald.

Tricia walked back through Zeke's hoping to find someone who could give her some background about Glenn Michaels. Unfortunately the regular crowd had dissolved into the usual tourists who came looking for the local color they had heard about on the radio.

She exited Zeke's and looked over at the bench with the yellow rose. Empty.

She went to the side of the building to take the elevator to the reception area of the radio station. Maybe Becky Walters would help her out… give her some information. There were already people in reception waiting to see one or another of the staff. Becky gave Tricia a wave as she entered while at the same time talking with a man who insisted on seeing Zeke as soon as possible.

Tricia's heart froze. She knew the voice. "Shit!" she thought. "It's that oversexed jackass from Saturday night!"

"Well, you tell Mr. Collins that Jerry Temples was here, would you? Tell him I have some important business to discuss with him."

Tricia turned around and pretended to read a magazine, hoping that the man wouldn't notice her.

"I'm sure you do, Mr. Temples, but Zeke needs some time to rest after doing a show. Would you like to come by on Wednesday, say, around one?"

"Just tell him… I'll be back on Friday on other business."

The man turned and stormed out of the lobby.

"Idiots from Big Thicket…" Becky said out loud. She saw Tricia and smiled. "If you want to see Zeke, he's not in. Not feeling well."

"He didn't look too well this morning, at least until after that fellow Michaels came in. Who is he, anyway?"

"Glenn Michaels? He used to work here part-time a long time ago. Nice guy, really. I think Zeke and Jack want him to run this place after Zeke passes."

"Which Jack?"

"I'm not sure which one. Chances are that Glenn won't take the job anyway. He has a nice job in Dallas."

"Does he have ties, here?"

"No. No family to speak of. He just worked here back… hmmm… it's been nearly thirty-five years ago… part-time on the Saturday night/Sunday morning gig. He ruffled a few feathers and he had a job waiting for him in Parkersburg, so he left. He and Zeke became close for some reason, though, and he's been back pretty regular since."

"Was he involved in The Incident?"

"No one talks about The Incident," Becky said in a whisper drawing Tricia closer. "Everything you need to know about it was in the newspapers. That's all."

"There was one question the newspapers never answered. Why."

"No one knows that, except maybe Zeke."

"Did Michaels know her?"

Becky's face showed that she was troubled by the question. After a moment or two, she drew Tricia even closer.

"The person whose feathers were ruffled the most by Glenn Michaels was the girl's mother, the one who ran her car into an abutment after the funeral. You didn't hear that from me."

"From all accounts, that was an accident."

Becky nodded her head. "Yes. At least it looked like an accident."

"Was the girl's father involved? I never saw or heard of any mention of him."

"No one knows who the father was. The mother was single; from all accounts she came from Kentucky. There are a lot of unanswered questions about The Incident. Maybe they would be best left alone."

Tricia wasn't satisfied with the answers she was getting, but decided not to press the receptionist any further. It was time to do a little more research. Her story on Zeke was just about finished. It was time to see if she could re-start her investigation and write the story about The Incident.

Twenty minutes later, Tricia was in the town library looking for clues which could tell her about why The Incident took place.

The headlines were pretty much the same: **Local Preacher Brutally Murders Wife - Kills Self**

There were sidebars about the fire that the Reverend Murphy set at his church before driving into town where he was stopped by an officer from the Ohio Highway Patrol. Apparently, Harlan Murphy probably thought that the patrolman was aware of the mayhem he had left behind at his house and his church and so shot himself before he could be questioned.

Tricia read and re-read several accounts before coming to a dead stop.

She did a double take.

According to one account, Reverend Harlan Murphy was pulled over by a rookie Ohio State Highway patrolman named Harold Richmond.

Tricia Knox made a copy of the newspaper account of Harold Richmond's part in The Incident before going out to try to find him. He was easily found, finishing lunch at Zeke's at the Family Table.

"Becky said that you might try to come and find me later on today..." Harold carefully wiped his mouth with his napkin.

"She said that for some reason you might try to ask me again about my part in The Incident."

"It <u>was</u> you, then."

"It was me. Never saw a man blow his own head off, hope to never see it again."

"Did he say anything before he pulled the trigger? Did he say why he did what he did?"

"He didn't say much… he was largely incoherent. No one had any idea at the time of what had happened at the house or at the church when I pulled him over."

"What did you do?"

"Well, I lost my breakfast, to put it politely. I spent a good five minutes by the side of the road being sick before I called the dispatcher. There was another cruiser and an ambulance there within ten minutes. About the time they came, the County Sheriff called in the fire. The bodies of the woman and her kids were found not long after that."

"Where was Murphy headed?"

"I can't say."

"You can't or you won't?"

"Yes."

Harold folded his napkin, put it on his plate, pulled out a ten dollar bill for a five dollar lunch, put it on the table with his check then left without saying another word.

Tricia sat there dumbfounded. Harold Richmond knew something; something he had no intention of sharing.

Getting Grilled

After Glenn returned to Magnolia, he decided to have dinner at Ed's Church and Grill. It was an easy walk over and, depending on his mood and his alcohol intake, a moderately easy stagger back to the apartment on the third floor of Zeke's. The place was just like he left it back in the day, although it seemed to be cleaner now. Ed's was an institution unique to Magnolia. It started out as a small church in the middle of town. The congregation eventually outgrew the building, selling it to Ed Palmer who gutted it and established it as a watering hole for thirsty workers at the government project south of town. From time to time, Ed took a fancy to be a minister on Sundays; so it doubled for the best part of twenty years as a church on Sundays, which didn't sit too well with the local authorities.

Glenn had just sat down when a voice behind him said: "Are you here to collect the drink I offered earlier?"

Tricia Knox came around the table and sat down opposite him. "Busy day?"

"Moderately. I went up to Chillicothe to see my parents' resting place; saw some old friends and visited a few old haunts. How about you? Gotten anywhere with what you're writing about Zeke?"

"I have this problem. It seems that Zeke's star pupil showed up this morning in the front window of the cafe and most everyone's talking about him and not Zeke."

"Really. What's he like?" Glenn tried to act casual.

"From the information I was able to gather, he's an interesting character. He worked here for about three and a half months back around 1976 before graduating from Ohio University and taking a job working overnights in Parkersburg."

"Hmmmm. This person sounds familiar. I have a feeling I may know the guy."

"I hear he's worked in a few places… Cleveland, Cincinnati, Louisville and St. Louis and then he dropped out. He became the manager of an appliance store in suburban Dallas and hasn't been heard from since."

The server came from behind the bar and interrupted them. After placing an order for the 'special', Tricia continued: "I'm starting to get the idea that this guy was involved somehow in something the locals call The Incident. It was a murder-suicide that happened in Fuller County about twenty-five years ago this month."

Glenn stayed silent.

"It was big news. Made all the papers. I had just met the man who's now my ex-husband when the story broke. Jessie Collins reminded me. She said that you may have known the parties involved, that's all."

Glenn folded his arms across his chest. "Maybe I did. What did Jessica tell you about any possible involvement I may have had in this… incident?"

"Not much, really, except to say that you might have known the parties involved, that's all. I thought that you might be able to shed some additional light on what happened."

"No one talks about it anymore. It's ancient history. Just so you know, if you haven't learned already, I knew the victim and I knew the man who killed her. I met them both when I worked here and I have gone to the victim's grave when I've been in the area. That's where we're going tomorrow."

Glenn was relieved, but at the same time, he was irritated that this woman had deliberately stepped on a raw nerve. He was distress that he had revealed that part of himself which had remained hidden for so long.

He didn't know why he did it, and for that matter, why he did it in front of this perfect stranger. But it felt good to open up, even just a little bit to someone else. He was still apprehensive about letting this woman he had just met know more than he had told almost everyone else in Magnolia about The Incident.

"Tell me, where were you working when the story broke?" Glenn tried to shift the direction of the conversation.

"I was working in a furniture store in Portsmouth."

"So you haven't always been a writer."

"No. I worked in retail for twenty years. The husband did, too. We made the mistake of working at the same time in the same building. He found another job working for a woman with big tits at another store in Ironton. He started to fuck her and ditched me. It was good riddance. I moved to Athens, earned a degree in Journalism then came down here to work as a stringer for a news service."

"You probably did some research on The Incident today, didn't you?"

"A little, yes."

"You talked with Harold?"

"He said he witnessed the suicide."

"Did he tell you anything else?"

"Nothing. In fact he left rather abruptly when I started to probe."

"He probably didn't know much else, anyway, at least nothing he ever told me."

Glenn watched Tricia's face. He had just lied to her and he was trying to see if she had a reaction. He had either gotten away with the lie, or Tricia was someone he didn't want to play poker with.

Glenn and Tricia spoke of unimportant matters for the rest of the meal. The entire time, he couldn't help but think that there was something about her… something he needed to know or something he would soon know. He shook off the feeling. She was just a reporter doing her job. That was it. He was resolved not to get involved. He was toxic.

In a larger sense, though, it didn't matter. The ice had been broken and two not quite strangers left Ed's Church and Grill at a decent hour to go home and get some rest.

"He lied to me. I know it," Tricia told herself as she drove back to her rented house a few miles north of Prentiss.

"He expects me to believe that Harold never said anything important to him. They're all hiding something from me."

Tricia had done numerous interviews that afternoon between the time Harold Richmond walked out of Zeke's paying ten dollars for a five dollar meal and meeting up with Glenn at Ed's Church and Grill. Jessica Collins was the most talkative, but the best she could do was to fill her in on where Glenn had worked when he was in radio and to confirm what she already knew about his marital status. For the most part, she got the impression that Glenn was well-known and well-liked in Magnolia, despite only having worked there for only a few months many years back.

There was one other thing that bothered her… the one thing which did not come up while she was conversing with Glenn at the dinner table. He did not once mention any plans he might have regarding replacing Zeke when he passed on. Yes, there was the talk around town, especially at Zeke's, but Glenn gave every indication that he was merely passing through.

Glenn had glossed over sitting in for the majority of Zeke's radio show that morning, mentioning it only once in their conversation as part of a passing reference to his ex-wife.

Back to The Incident.

It still bothered her. There was something being covered up.

She got home, undressed then went out to the hot tub on her back porch to contemplate and look at the stars.

"Maybe tomorrow will bring some new answers," she thought.

Half an hour later, she got out of the tub, dried herself off and settled into bed.

"Maybe tomorrow…"

Call To Glory

"Ezekiel."

The voice was quite clear.

Zeke recognized it as the same voice he had heard several days earlier.

"The time has come."

"I'm ready."

His voice was clear as a bell. He couldn't remember the last time his voice had been that clear.

He became aware of his surroundings. Zeke was in his bedroom, looking down on the bed he shared with his wife for over sixty years.

She rustled slightly, shifting her position to be closer to the now lifeless shell which had been Zeke Collins.

"Yes, you may bid her goodbye."

The voice answered the unasked question. Zeke sensed that he would be able to bond somehow with Jessica – connecting with her – sad that what they had shared for so many years was over.

"I love you with all of my heart and all of my soul, Jessica."

"I love you, too, Zeke." Her voice came from her body, soft, quiet. An observer would have thought that she was talking in her sleep. "I will miss you, but only for a little while."

She smiled, rolled over and kissed his shell.

"Have a pleasant journey, Zeke. Be careful."

"You, too, Jess. Be careful."

He watched as she became completely awake and aware of the situation. When she saw that his heart was no longer beating and that he was no longer breathing, a tear started running down her cheek.

Zeke reached out to her the best as he could. For an instant, she was the same woman he had chosen to spend his life with, now mourning her loss.

"I know that you wish you could stay with her. She will be joining you soon enough."

The voice comforted him.

Jessica picked up the telephone by their bedside and dialed. Zeke could no longer hear her voice, but he knew what she was saying.

"You have prepared well," he heard the voice again, "you should be proud."

He beheld his accomplishments in a collage of images… the endeavors of a life well spent.

"Will it continue? Will Magnolia thrive?"

"Yes, it will. The seed has been planted and is ready to grow. The legacy begun by Miss Annie will continue for the foreseeable future."

Zeke felt a sense of peace surrounding his being. He watched as Jessica put the phone back in its cradle, then reached over to the shell to give it one last kiss on the forehead.

Jessica faded out, replaced by what seemed to be a slight breeze on Zeke's face as he felt himself being propelled toward an aura… a light which beckoned, promising complete peace and freedom from the cares of the living world.

He took one last look backwards to see Magnolia… his Magnolia, alive, vibrant, coming awake on a Tuesday morning, as of yet unaware of the passing of its favorite son.

Dreaded yet Anticipated

The dream came back to Glenn again late Monday night going into early Tuesday morning. He was in a church, at sunset, the colors streaming across the church, highlighting the bride. He approached her, ready to melt into her arms in a comfortable embrace. He knew the dream. He would end up recognizing some romantic fantasy of his involving a woman he knew when he was much younger. It was the same dream he had had for the first time in over a decade when he was on his way to Magnolia. She turned before he could see her face, confirming who he thought she might be. Her wedding dress had become a pair of jeans and a t-shirt. "C'mon," he heard her say, "we have work to do." Her voice was immediately followed by an insistent knocking and someone calling him through the front door of the apartment.

"Mister Michaels!"

"Mister Michaels!"

Glenn rolled out of bed and went to the front door of the apartment. "What?"

"It's Earl – Earl Peters from the station. I run the board for Zeke in the mornings."

"Why the fuck are you banging on my door at… what time is it anyway?" Glenn opened the door just a hint. He was naked, just out of bed.

Glenn saw panic in Earl's eyes. "Zeke's dead. Jessica found him and called the ambulance about forty-five minutes ago. We're on the air in less than five minutes and there's a room filled with regulars expecting something… anything. We need you downstairs, now."

"I take it everything's ready… I'll be down… I'll be down in a minute or a little more. Let me throw on some clothes."

It took Glenn only three minutes to toss on a shirt, a pair of slacks and head downstairs. The patrons in the café hushed as he mounted the platform at the front of the dining room in the place of the café's namesake. They expected the news, whatever it was, now that it was apparent that Zeke was late.

Glenn glanced at the clock on the desk. Six after six. He put the set of headphones on and noticed that his microphone was live. He was on-the-air. "Hey everyone, looks like we're getting started just a little bit late this morning…" He looked around to see a sea of somber faces. "…but if you recall from yesterday, I'm set on central time, so we're really in here almost an hour early."

The live audience did not react. They knew that something was up.

"In case you missed it yesterday, I'm Glenn Michaels sitting in for Zeke Collins. It's good to see everyone here this morning," Glenn continued. He scanned the desk to see if there was any clue as to what came next and when. "I'm here a little unexpectedly. Earl up in the control booth upstairs woke me up to tell me that Zeke would be unable to make it here on time this morning and asked if I would be able to fill in for him."

"We saw the ambulance at the house, how is he?" came a voice from two tables away. There was a hubbub of agreement.

"There's nothing official, yet. All I know is that Zeke was taken to the hospital in Prentiss. When we get more news, we'll pass it along."

Panic welled up inside of him. He had no idea what came first or what came next. There was a rudimentary log along with pages of handwritten notes which Zeke used every day; some of the notes had been used, apparently, for years.

There was a program wheel. Glenn remembered program wheels. He was able to fake his way for a few minutes until the first commercial break.

"What do you have that can be put on a laptop, Earl?" Glenn was on the intercom the moment the commercials started airing.

"You have a laptop with you?"

"I have one in the apartment."

"There's a few things we have which can be made available on the local network, we do have wi-fi…" Earl tended to talk slowly.

"Give me three minutes till I get back. Stall… throw in a PSA if you have to." Glenn was out of his chair and on the way as he spoke. Glenn was back in less than three minutes, much to his relief. He opened his notebook and was in the process of booting it when he was given the cue to get back to the show.

When the computer kicked in, Glenn had a wealth of information available to him so that he could do the show while organizing on the fly. "Just like riding a bicycle," he thought in one of those moments he was actually able to think.

The dreaded news came in at 7:15. Pastor Ezra Kellough came in to make the announcement to what was now a packed house. Word of the ambulance at Zeke's house early that morning spread faster than the speed of light, it seemed. When the pastor stepped over to the broadcast table, the room became silent. Everyone had anticipated what was coming next. Even the usual noises from the kitchen were stilled. Pastor said what had to be said then offered a prayer. There was not a dry eye in the house.

The stretch until 10am was one of the slowest Glenn had ever worked. As he gathered his laptop to take it upstairs, he noticed Tricia Knox waiting for him in the same booth she had inhabited the previous day.

"Good job this morning," she commented. "You've obviously done this before. I would have cracked under the pressure."

"Thanks," Glenn smiled at her. "If you don't mind, I'm overdue for a clean-up and maybe a stiff drink."

"That's understandable," she told him. "Mind if I come up with you to ask a few questions?"

"Suit yourself. If you're easily offended by a naked or semi-naked man, you'd best not come."

"No offense taken. All I want is a word or two before the storm hits."

"What storm?"

"You may not want to know. Chances are you'll be busier than the proverbial one legged man at an ass kicking contest here later this morning."

"I think not," Glenn told Tricia. "My plan is to shower, pack and get the hell out of Dodge. I suppose that Jack Jay, or whoever he is, has been contacted and is on his way up here to do the show from here on out."

"Says you," Tricia shot back. "I talked with Becky in the office while you were in your last segment. Zeke's lawyer needs to talk with you. He'll be in at 10:30. There are at least a dozen other requests for your time this morning into this afternoon which you can handle any way you want to. But at the very least you'll have to talk to Mr. Fischer before you do anything else."

Glenn perked up slightly. "Would that be Greg Fischer?" he asked.

"Yes. I take it you know him?"

"Greg and I were running buddies back in high school."

"That would explain something."

"What's that?"

"Zeke only hired Fischer a week, maybe two weeks ago. Before that he's had the same lawyer here in town for years."

Tricia followed Glenn up the back stairway as they talked. They went into his loaned apartment where Glenn set down the notebook and the papers he had been working with.

"It might have had to do with the offer Zeke made on Sunday."

"What offer was that?"

"Zeke - offered me the radio stations."

Tricia was stunned. Glenn started to take off his shoes and his shirt.

"The radio stations?"

"Yep. He and Jessica offered to give me the radio stations to run as I pleased, as well as the café and some rental properties he has in the county."

Tricia pulled up a chair while she prepared her pen and note pad.

"I'll leave the door open so that you can talk to me while I'm in the bathroom."

Glenn dropped his pants in front of her, partially for the shock value and partially to see if she would be offended and finally leave him alone. "You can come in while I shave and shower. I'll spare you the time I spend on the throne."

"That would be appreciated," she told him.

"Do you have any idea why Zeke would have offered you his stations, or did you have an idea that he would do that when you came here?"

"Those are two questions. As to the last question, I had no idea that he would make such an offer. I came to see Zeke. He's been a friend and a mentor for… well, ever since I was in college. That might be the answer to the first question. He was always telling me that I looked better on the radio."

"I had the impression that you hinted last night that you didn't come all the way up just to see Zeke."

Trisha heard the sound of water running as Glenn started to shave.

"Well, I'm not here strictly just to see Zeke. I'm here to rid myself of a pair of albatri."

"Albatri?"

"Plural of albatross - as in the *Rime of the Ancient Mariner*. There's some excess baggage I need to be rid of so that I can continue with the rest of my life."

"You made that word up," Tricia protested, smiling.

"Indeed, yes I did," Glenn admitted. "I've made up other words, too." He peered around the corner. There was still a little bit of shaving cream on his face. "I'll bet you've made up words, yourself."

"Sorry," she apologized. "I gave up my poetic license when I took up the mantle of a journalist."

Glenn started running water for his shower. Momentarily, he came out. "Fair enough," he told her. He rummaged in the suitcase at the foot of his bed. He pulled out a pair of underwear. "I came to Magnolia for two reasons. One is a woman; the other is to prove myself…" He paused. "Give me a couple of minutes, Will you?"

He went into the bathroom without another word to take his shower. Tricia waited.

A few minutes later, Glenn emerged wrapped in a towel. "We're going to see Hannah Smith, the victim of The Incident."

He dropped the towel then walked over to his suitcase to choose a shirt, a clean pair of slacks and a pair of socks. "I was young, she was younger. We met here, actually downstairs at the radio studio.

"I had just turned twenty-two. I came here to work for Zeke on weekends while I was wrapping up my bachelor's degree at Ohio University. Zeke had heard of my work at the radio stations in Chillicothe for a couple of years while I was taking classes at the Branch, so he was happy to have me.

"He had me working the "God Squad" on Sunday mornings in exchange for letting me do whatever I wanted to do on Saturday nights and on Sunday afternoons. I stayed in this apartment on Saturday nights just to keep from having to make the drive to and from Athens early on Sunday morning.

"The last preacher every morning was a fellow called Brother Murphy. Harlan Murphy. He was a sight. He looked like someone off the cover of a late fifties country music album. You know, with a pompadour and wearing a bowling shirt."

Glenn had pulled on the socks and a Beasley Brothers shirt.

"Brother Murphy came in with a retinue. One member of his usual crew was this girl who usually sat down in one corner.

"She was pretty, despite the old fashioned dresses she had to wear. About six weeks into my job here, I started to notice that this girl was noticing me. On the day I _really_ noticed her, I got a phone call from a girl at about three in the afternoon. The voice on the other end held my attention long enough that we had a decent conversation. A couple of weeks and several conversations later, the voice on the phone had aroused my interest. She mentioned the shirt I had worn that morning and all of a sudden I made the connection. The girl on the phone was the girl who was coming in week after week with the Reverend Murphy and his God's Army."

Glenn finally pulled on his slacks and adjusted his belt.

"I found out more out about this girl. She was fifteen, almost sixteen, in high school and really smart. We made dates with each other on the phone and eventually spent parts of Saturday and Sunday afternoons in conversation on the bench across the street from the station."

"The bench with the yellow rose…"

"Yes… but that part came later. Anyway, we kept our contact limited at Zeke's suggestion. He knew what we were up against, both with her mother and the good Reverend Murphy."

"What about her father? Was he involved?" Tricia asked.

"Hannah told me that she didn't know her father. Scratch that. She knew who her father was, but she wasn't allowed to tell anyone. They had a clandestine correspondence going on."

"Okay."

"Anyway, about three weeks before I was going to graduate from Ohio U, Zeke approached me about the relationship I was having with the girl.

"It seems that some of Reverend Murphy's flock saw the two of us having a conversation and made the assumption that we were… well, put another way, her mother found out and lit into Zeke about his allowing her daughter to associate with that 'unchristian older man from the radio station'. Zeke quietly suggested that I filter out of town before he and Hannah caught too much hell from everyone concerned. I left on good terms with Zeke, letting him off the hook with Hannah's mother."

Glenn bent over to slip on his shoes.

"I took a job in Parkersburg, just like I planned, and wouldn't you know, I started getting letters from Hannah through Zeke. She would write and slip her letters into the station's IN box, retrieving my replies when she came back the next week. For nearly a year we wrote back and forth clandestinely, then the letters stopped. I mentioned something to Zeke… he found out that she was told to marry Harlan Murphy.

"She had just turned sixteen and was pulled out of school to become the wife of a man who was almost three times her age."

By this time Glenn had finished dressing and was sitting down on the edge of the bed facing Tricia. He paused for a few moments to collect his thoughts.

"I went on with my life," he finally continued. "I found this woman, Alice, who seemed to be a good fit. We got married: I continued what was to be a fabulous career and life was good, for a while.

"I started getting letters from Hannah again. They were filled with despair and darkness. By the time she was twenty, she had produced two sons, much to the delight of her husband. The last letter I got from her was twenty-five years ago this past May. She still wasn't entirely happy that she was the teenaged bride, but she had learned to live with it. She expressed regret that she didn't run away to join me in Parkersburg when she had the chance. She had hoped that some day we would meet as adults and explore the possibilities of a relationship when we were both free to love another."

Glenn paused again. What he was about to tell this stranger had weighed heavily on his mind for decades.

"I was working in Cleveland. Just as I got to work one morning, I got the phone call from Zeke. He told me that the Reverend Harlan Murphy apparently flew into a rage when he found out that Hannah was pregnant and carrying a girl. He butchered her and cut the child out of her mother's body before killing his sons. He drove out to the fairgrounds and then took his own life."

The room was quiet except for a barely discernible drip from the bathroom sink. Tears started to flow from Glenn's eyes. Tricia waited to see if there was any more to the story. Glenn finally regained his composure then he resumed:

"I came down to Magnolia as soon as I heard. As far as I know, Alice never knew. Hannah's mother accused me of killing her daughter by continuing my unholy relationship with her after she had been married. The Sheriff had to restrain the woman. When that wasn't enough, she was put in jail until after I left town. The woman had an accident less than three months after the funeral. At least it looked like an accident.

"I've made it a point to come back on a regular basis ever since."

"The yellow rose?"

"My memorial."

He paused again.

"This year, I had decided that I would put it all behind me. I had plans… I still have plans to head out to the cemetery this afternoon to say goodbye for the final time."

The quiet resumed for a minute and a half.

"It will be my honor to go with you," Tricia said in a very small voice.

"I'll call when I'm ready," Glenn replied.

Tricia got up to give Glenn a kiss on the forehead. She left the apartment, leaving him alone. Glenn closed his eyes after she left. He was thankful that Tricia Knox didn't pursue her line of questioning any further. He was just as thankful for the kiss. Somehow that simple kiss on his forehead fortified him for what he needed to do for the rest of his day.

New Plans for Old Business

John Jankowski's original plan for this Tuesday morning was to have a leisurely breakfast at the Senior Center before loading up the station wagon to take the three hour drive up to Magnolia. He figured that he would get there at about one to meet with Zeke and Glenn Michaels before enjoying a free lunch.

His plans changed just as he was about to leave his apartment. Becky Walters was on the phone telling him about Zeke's passing earlier in the morning. He thanked her for the news, told her that he would be up later that day and hung up.

The moment he was off the phone to Magnolia, wheels started turning. In an instant, he was back on the phone.

John Jankowski's life had been spent in radio. He went back and forth across the country working one place for a while until getting the itch and moving on to the next town. His nomadic lifestyle gained him a large number of contacts which led to a second career as a wheeler-dealer. He knew who was where, who wanted what and was able to put deals together for equipment, for people, or even entire radio stations.

One of his contacts, Brian Thompson in Tyler, Texas was president and CEO of Big Thicket Broadcasting. John Jankowski had met him twenty years previously while John was working at a radio station in San Angelo. The two hooked up, with John making the deals which allowed Brian to create virtual monopolies in broadcast properties in several areas of the country.

There was one more deal in the making. It was one deal which Brian Thompson wanted to make, not because it would make him more money, but for the sake of nostalgia.

Brian Thompson's first full-time job on the radio was at a small radio station in Magnolia, Ohio run by a fellow named Zeke Collins.

John Jankowski listened as Brian Thompson's phone rolled over to voice mail. He waited through a greeting designed to confuse the casual caller into thinking there was something wrong with the connection.

"Brian… John Jankowski, here… I just got a call from the receptionist at WZEK up in Magnolia. Zeke passed this morning and the state of the station's ownership is up in the air.

"I'll be heading up there in about an hour to see if the kid Zeke wants to take over the place would be open to an offer from me. I'll update you later this afternoon."

John hung up the phone before heading out the door for breakfast. He needed the energy to make the drive; besides, it would be a free meal.

He checked his wallet as he was walking. His corporate credit card and the fading picture of the daughter he lost were in there and that was all he was concerned about.

Actually, his daughter was what the deal in Magnolia was about for him. Once the acquisition of Zeke's properties was complete, John would have enough money to have a comfortable retirement in Magnolia. He wanted to be close to his daughter while he waited for his final reward.

His only obstacle was the man Zeke Collins deemed worthy of passing on the mantle of Magnolia's Morning Mayor; someone deemed more worthy than he was of caring for the legacy passed on to Zeke from some woman he barely knew. That other part of him, Wild Jack Jay, was determined to keep Glenn Michaels away from Magnolia, no matter what it might cost him. Glenn had already cost him the daughter he loved, despite everything John had done for him behind the scenes. The time of reckoning was coming. Hannah Smith's death needed to be avenged.

Reality Check

"Well, it's about time you showed up!" Becky Walters, Zeke's office manager and receptionist looked as if she were on the edge of going completely nuts. There were at least fifteen people in the reception area who were waiting for Glenn, or Zeke, or news, or something. The jabber picked up as soon as Glenn entered the room.

"I understand that Greg Fischer is here."

"Yes, Mister Fischer is in Zeke's office waiting for you."

"Thanks. I'll, uh… who are these people?"

"Some of Zeke's friends. They're holding a vigil."

"Oh." He looked at the people who were waiting. "Folks, look… I need to get some things straight with Zeke's lawyer before… whatever it is you are waiting for."

"When's the viewing… when's the funeral?" several voices asked at once.

"I'm sorry. I just got off the air. I have no idea. You'll be informed the moment we have any information, okay?"

There was general agreement among those in the room to wait for a while. Glenn went down the hallway to Zeke's office.

Zeke's office was as homespun as Zeke himself. Some would say it was disorganized with scraps or heaps of paper extending in every conceivable direction… even on the ceiling. There were awards of nearly every description. Pictures of Zeke were everywhere, showing Zeke with a veritable galaxy of stars from every corner of the media. One of Glenn's favorites was a cartoon showing Zeke and the Pope waving to a crowd at the Vatican – with two nuns wondering "Who is that standing up there with Zeke?"

Greg Fischer was looking at some of the mementos as Glenn walked into the office.

"Just how did you get involved in this mess, Greg?"

"I was about to ask you the same thing, you son of a gun… how the hell are you?"

The men spent several minutes catching up on each others' lives before the inevitable business came to the forefront.

"So you're the new Zeke," Greg remarked.

"I was this morning… tomorrow it will be someone else's turn."

"It may not be as easy as you think. You are now the caretaker of the radio stations in this building." Greg opened the briefcase which had sat unnoticed on top of Zeke's desk. He produced a folder which he handed to Glenn.

"The last Will and Testament of Ezekiel Everett Collins," Greg announced. "According to this, you are now the proud owner and operator of WZEK, WZEK-FM, Zeke's Café downstairs and all of the real property owned by Zeke including his rental properties and the building you are now standing in."

"What about Jessica and their house on the other side of the alley?"

"She's taken care of. Jessica told me to tell you not to worry about her. Zeke had set aside a fund which will take care of any need Jessica has for as long as she lives. While technically you own the house, Jessica has been promised that she can live there for as long as she cares to without having to pay rent. When she passes, the house and the remainder of the estate will revert to a scholarship Trust."

"There must be some kind of mistake. I'm going back to Texas. I have unfinished business here which I'll take care of later this afternoon. But other than that, I'm done. I told Zeke that on Sunday night when he made me the same offer."

"I know it sounds crazy," Greg sighed, "but before you walk out that door to head back to Texas, let me tell you something. Zeke went to a lot of trouble to seek me out and hire me so that I could get you to accept and care for his legacy. That's what this place is, Glenn; it's a legacy. The people of Magnolia depend on Zeke's operations. They draw people in from out of town. They come, they shop, they leave their money and the town thrives. Before Zeke came to town, there was just the Coffee Cup. This isn't just a business; it's the life's blood of this town. Everyone here wins when Magnolia thrives, Glenn.

"Zeke knew this. He knew that he was about to die and he wanted the best possible caretaker for what he had built over the past fifty years. I spent a few hours with him on the fifth of July. He explained everything – including the reason why you are the only person he wanted to take over his operation.

"Honest to God, Glenn, we've known each other for what… forty years?

"I thought the man was crazy when he called me down here, but I've become convinced that your acceptance of Zeke's legacy would benefit everyone involved… especially you. If you pass on this deal, the stations here and Zeke's Café will be up for grabs. I'm willing to bet that right this instant Randy Green is on a conference call with Big Thicket Corporate, or at the very least with the Northeast division manager in Pittsburgh. I look for Randy or someone like him to be here between two and two-thirty today to scope out the operation and make an offer to buy, if they haven't been here already."

"As far as I'm concerned, they can have this headache. Sell it. Give Jessica the money and God bless her for her good fortune. All I did was to I come up here with the idea that I wanted to see if I could handle a radio show just one more time. I did it. All I have to do is to pack my bags, wrap up one more piece of business and head back to Texas."

"Okay, that's fine, go ahead…" there was a sign of resignation in Greg's voice. "I guess the only reason you wanted to be on the radio in the first place was to prove Alice wrong."

"Alice supposedly has her own problems, but yes, part of the reason was to prove Alice wrong."

"Alice's bitching wasn't the only reason you quit the business, Glenn." Greg's statement was firm, yet quiet. "I remember you telling me that you detested The Monster and the whorehouse it's become. Big Thicket Broadcasting is that monster, isn't it, Glenn?"

Greg continued while Glenn stayed silent: "I remember your tirades against The Monster for a solid year before you moved to Texas from Missouri. We've had conversations since then about The Monster. You wished that you could do something about it. Well, buddy, here's your chance. The Monster, Big Thicket, is poised to come into Magnolia and rape this place now that Zeke is gone. You are the only person with the power to keep that from happening. If you leave now, you'll be handing Big Thicket the town of Magnolia on a silver platter. You know as well as I do that they won't give a shit about what happens here."

Glenn stayed silent for a few moments while he digested what Greg had just told him. "Are you sure that no one else can do what Zeke did other than me?"

"I honest-to-God don't know, Glenn, and I really don't have the time to find out. There will likely be a hearing in Probate Court, maybe as soon as Friday because of Zeke's decision to hire me in the place of his usual lawyer less than two weeks before he died. If you are not on the air between now and Friday morning, and if you do not make it to court, Big Thicket or someone working for Big Thicket may just be able to take over Zeke's operation here without you or Jessica Collins collecting one thin dime."

Glenn took a deep breath. "I suppose I could hang in there at least until Friday. It might give someone else a chance to make a bid on the place, or I might be able to find someone else more willing to do what needs to be done here."

"I believe I can hold off the bastards until then, Glenn. Can I count on you to do Zeke's show for the next three days?"

"Sure, why not," Glenn agreed. "It's bound to get easier, isn't it?"

After spending a few minutes more with Greg going over some details, Glenn left Zeke's office to discover that Tricia Knox was right about this becoming a busy day. He went back out to the reception area to discover that there was a fistful of notes from people who had called in and wanted a call back right away. There was an entirely new group of people in the waiting area wanting "…just a minute or two of Mr. Michaels' time…" as well as several staff members who had come in just to see if they still had jobs after the demise of Mr. Collins.

Glenn pulled his cell phone out of his pocket to find that there were several messages awaiting him on his voice mail. Scanning some of the various messages, he instructed Becky to tell any new callers to the radio station that he would not be available for the rest of the afternoon.

The people wanting "… just a minute…" were told that there were no changes being made for at least the next several days and that the morning show would continue as it had at least until the end of the week.

The rumor mill in Magnolia was buzzing for the remainder of the afternoon.

The staff was collected in the reception area for a short meeting. Glenn thanked them for their patience, promising nothing more than to keep his hand on the tiller for at least the next couple of days. Pizza was ordered from Father Linguini's, arriving with a note from Steve Mulligan stating that there would be no charge, considering the circumstances. Glenn saw to it that $25 was taken out of petty cash to tip the driver. While the staff was eating lunch, Glenn and Becky sorted through the phone messages to select which messages would be answered in what order.

For a solid hour, Glenn barricaded himself in Zeke's office returning phone calls from a number of locals, each wanting to know the same thing about what was going to happen to the radio stations. Glenn gave each of them the same standard answer: "We will see what happens later this week." Becky did let through a call from Jessica Collins while he was on the phone. For ten minutes, they went over several details regarding the funeral. Apparently Zeke had informed his wife that she could rely on Glenn immediately after his passing.

At about one-thirty, traffic at the radio station had settled down to a dull roar.

Greg returned by prior arrangement to fend off any inquiries by representatives from Big Thicket if they showed up.

Glenn went back to the apartment to freshen up a bit before calling Tricia Knox.

"You were right about the circus at the station this morning," Glenn told her after she answered. "I'm headed out to see Hannah Smith. Can you meet me in the parking lot behind the station in, say, ten minutes?"

"Make it about twenty-five. I'm at my house," she answered. "This won't be a formal dress party, will it?"

"Come naked if you'd like, the guest of honor is beyond caring at this point."

Glenn finished making preparations for the trip he was going to make with Tricia. He checked the briefcase before he headed downstairs to his car. There were five glasses left. He would decide how they would be distributed when he got to Hannah's resting place.

Persistent Questions

THERE WAS STILL SOMETHING MISSING from the equation.

Tricia wondered about Glenn's story while she drove herself back home. While the pieces fit into what she had previously heard regarding the Murphy murder/suicide, there was still the overwhelming question of why. What bothered her the most was how a country preacher was able to determine that his young wife was carrying a girl.

Yes, ultrasound was in use at the time and, yes, there were doctors who could easily determine the gender of a child by using it, but the vast majority of the doctors who were using ultrasound at that point in time were not the general practitioners available to patients living in rural Fuller County.

How would a country preacher know that his wife was carrying a girl? More importantly, why would he fly into a rage, cut out the child, kill his own children, burn his Church then head toward town only to commit suicide when he was pulled over for having a busted taillight?

Something just didn't fit.

Another thought crossed her mind as she parked the car to head inside her house.

"How would anyone know what the Reverend Murphy's reasoning for his rampage was when the only witnesses were dead?"

The coroner visited both scenes on the day of The Incident. Tricia had seen the reports. In fact, she had made copies as part of her research.

She marched straight into her study and headed to a file drawer next to the simple desk.

Minutes later, she found what she was looking for… a file with the coroner's report on the death of Hannah Murphy.

Tricia devoured the report for what seemed to be the fifteenth time. There was mention of a fetus being found apart from Hannah's body; there was no mention of the gender of the fetus.

"He made it up. Glenn Michaels made it up… possibly to cover his involvement with Hannah Smith after she was married. Maybe that's why Hannah's mother made the accusation that Glenn Michaels did something to kill her daughter," Tricia speculated.

She put the file away, closed the drawer and stood there, propping up the file cabinet.

Maybe she needed to divert her attention for a little while. The usual jeans and shirt came off, were carefully folded and put on her bed for use later that day. She then went into her closet to choose a nice summer dress to wear for her trip with Glenn later on in the afternoon. She staged the dress by the front door so that she could slip it on as she left the house.

She puttered in her vegetable garden, doing a little watering and light weeding until about half past one.

Her phone rang. It was Glenn.

"How should I dress?"

"Come naked if you'd like, the guest of honor won't care very much at this point."

She bit her lip and smiled to herself. Glenn might be in for a shock if she didn't at least toss on the dress she had by the front door… maybe not. For some reason, despite the lie he had apparently told to protect himself, she felt as if she could trust him. Yes, there was a truth hidden in what little Glenn Michaels had told her. It would eventually come out and she could possibly have a juicy side bar to the story she was writing about the changing of the guard at WZEK.

Upsetting News

The Golden Triangle would have been the perfect scene outside of Joe Campbell's office in Pittsburgh, Pennsylvania. He would have preferred it, but, unfortunately his office was in a soulless building in another section of town. His office had no windows. He was Vice President of the Northeast Division of Big Thicket Broadcasting, yet he had an office in an outlying neighborhood of the city he loved. The office was away from downtown, away from the Triangle and away from any windows connecting to the outside world. He wasn't too far from retirement. He would eventually be able to move out of that goddamned office to live somewhere where he could actually enjoy the scenery. He often wondered if he would be able to afford a place on Grandview Avenue, a street that truly lived up to its name with its unrivaled view of the beloved Triangle.

Joe was in a grumpy mood when he arrived at work and was prepared to be grumpy all day long. After all, it was July, it was warm and it would be a good day to leave the office to take a walk. Instead, his arrival was greeted with a phone call from his boss in Texas.

"Joe… you need to listen to what's going on over in Magnolia this morning. Zeke Collins apparently died and there's this guy named Glenn Michaels winging it as we speak."

Joe's attitude instantly soared then just as quickly crashed in the space of the sentence he just heard from Brian Thompson. The place he wanted on Grandview Avenue could possibly be within his reach because of a bounty offered by Thompson for the executive responsible for the acquisition of any new radio station within their division. At the same time, he remembered the name Glenn Michaels, wondering if this was the same upstart who cost him his job in Parkersburg.

"Glenn Michaels." Joe repeated. "Do you have any idea where this guy is from, Brian?"

"Randy Green in Chillicothe tells me that this Michaels guy used to work in the area. He apparently worked for Zeke for a short time after I was there."

Joe bit his lip and said nothing. "It might not be the same Glenn Michaels," he thought.

"He said that later, Michaels worked in Parkersburg for a while. You worked in Parkersburg for a while, ever run into him?"

"Sorry, can't say that I have," Joe lied.

Hatred welled up inside him. "It's that same son of a bitch!" Joe Campbell knew exactly who Glenn Michaels was.

"Well, whoever he is, he sounds damn good in what's probably a pressure cooker this morning," Brian continued. "Joe, can you do me a favor? I need you to drive over to Magnolia tomorrow or Thursday and talk to this Michaels fellow. If he's as good on the air every day as he is today, we could use him."

"Yes, Mr. Thompson." Joe was able to refrain from expressing any emotion in his voice, deciding to be properly professional until this phone call was finished.

"I'm making plans to fly into Cincinnati on Thursday night so I can be there when he does his show on Friday morning."

"Yes, Mr. Thompson." Joe Campbell felt his blood pressure rising. The last thing he wanted was to have loose cannons like Glenn Michaels around questioning his authority, perhaps even getting him fired again.

He particularly didn't want any waves so close to retirement.

"You and Randy get together and see what it would take to get this Michaels working for us and get back to me later today."

"Certainly, Mr. Thompson."

It was all Joe could do to keep his feelings about Glenn Michaels under control until after he ended his phone call to Brian Thompson.

"**SON OF A FUCKING BITCH!!!**" he thundered as he hung up the phone.

Joe stormed out of his office invoking a curse every other step. He didn't much care that everyone in the office was staring at him open-mouthed. He was in a rage. He didn't much care who knew it. He threw off his jacket and his tie, dumping them on the receptionist's desk as he left. He ran to his gym half a mile away where he spent the next hour working off three decades of hatred directed toward Glenn Michaels.

It was a quarter after three before he had calmed down enough to organize a trip to southern Ohio to see if there was a way to short circuit the changing of the guard in Magnolia.

Tribute

Tricia arrived dressed in a light summery dress which seemed more appropriate for a picnic than a trip to a cemetery. Glenn was quiet for most of the trip, preferring to listen to the Bruce Springsteen CDs he had loaded into the car's entertainment center. She followed suit by keeping quiet, listening and observing while he took advantage of the time to gather his thoughts. Toward the end of one of the songs, Tricia looked over at him.

"This is the secret you want to cut loose, isn't it?" Tricia asked between tracks. Glenn nodded his head to affirm her supposition. There was a secret other than the one she supposed. He just wasn't ready to cut it loose… not quite yet.

She settled back to watch the scenery for the rest of the ride.

The cemetery was small and out of the way. Most of the monuments were older, although there were signs of more recent burials. Glenn drove three quarters of the way toward the return loop then stopped the car. He cranked his window open. She followed suit, allowing the hot, humid, breezeless summer air to seep into their air-conditioned cocoon.

Without a word, Glenn opened the trunk of his Fusion to extract the briefcase he had brought with him. Tricia followed, but not too closely, sensing that he was about to be involved in an extremely private moment.

It took him about a minute to set up the contents of his case. He motioned for Tricia to come over to him.

Glenn very carefully filled three of the glasses with the liquor he had extracted from the briefcase, setting one of them on a simple monument reading:

Hannah Smith
1961 – 1985

Glenn handed Tricia one of the glasses, placing the third one on top of the gravestone. "Now that Zeke is gone, I needed to let at least one other human being know about the pain I have borne because of Hannah's murder. I also needed a witness to this last goodbye."

Glenn crossed himself before raising his glass toward the monument. Tricia did the same, consuming the shot of liquor after Glenn had emptied his glass. He then took the glass on top on the monument and poured the contents onto the ground.

Glenn placed the glass back on top of the monument before replacing the remaining items into the briefcase.

Moments later, Glenn and Tricia were in the car about to pull onto the road leading to the cemetery. "You crossed yourself back there," Tricia remarked. "Are you Catholic?"

"No, Episcopalian," he answered. "Cradle… the worst kind…" he added.

"Have you made a Cursillo?"

"Yes," he answered, "Dallas Fort Worth, five years in September."

"Southern Ohio, seventeen years in October."

"It was a hell of a weekend, wasn't it?" Glenn remarked. "It brought me back to my roots in the church. I'm ashamed to say, though, that I really haven't followed through as I should have."

"Cursillo at least served its purpose as a renewal – at least it did for me. You show signs that it worked on you."

"Well, it seems that I took the right person to go with me, then, didn't I?" Glenn smiled for the first time since they got into the car at Magnolia.

They drove for a couple of minutes before either of them spoke again.

"I sort of get the impression that you're going to go back to Texas," she said.

"I sort of think you're right," he told her. "I have no desire to stay here and run a business which I left fifteen years ago."

He looked over to her briefly before concentrating on the road again.

"You said that you run an appliance store… how could that be any different from taking over a business selling… well, selling Magnolia on the radio?"

"It's a lot different," Glenn explained. "For one thing, the radio business is dominated by big corporations who care about nothing more than making money."

"I sold furniture for a mom and pop store in Portsmouth. Even when the big guys came into town, the store I worked for still did alright," she countered. "Not everyone wants to buy from the big guys."

"Beasley Brothers Appliances does alright, too, considering that there are only three stores in the chain."

"Zeke's lived pretty well off of being a little guy," she resumed. "Big Thicket should, by being a big guy, be eating Zeke's lunch. You do know who Big Thicket is, don't you?"

"They're the bastards who bought out the radio stations I started working for in Chillicothe."

"They already have a hammerlock on most of southern and central Ohio, as I understand it."

She waited for a reaction.

Glenn reflected for a minute or so while he continued to drive toward Magnolia.

"I told people that I would stay and do Zeke's show until the end of the week, then I have other plans."

"What would those other plans be, Glenn?" Tricia asked pointedly.

"I'll make them up as I go along."

"Would you mind if I tagged along with you while you're still here?"

"I'd like that. I could use an escort, but I need to warn you, I'm poison." Glenn was surprised at what he just said.

"What do you mean?"

"I don't do well in relationships. I'm just being honest, you see."

"I'm not good in relationships, either. The only reason I asked to tag along was that I thought that you might like some insight… some input as to what might be expected of you in the next few days."

"Expected of me?"

"Well, there's a certain order of ceremony revolving around being in the front window of Zeke's on any given morning. As the new guy, you'll have certain obligations… ways you will need to assure Zeke's people that the traditions he had established would be carried on."

"I hope that they won't be disappointed if I call it quits after Friday's show…"

"They may be, but if you do it right, the person who'll be the new Zeke will find that his audience will be more receptive. There's also the matter of a suit for the funeral. You would be expected to attend."

"Yep… you're right about that."

"Are you going to be high maintenance?"

"I never thought I was."

"Right…"

By this time, they had arrived back in Magnolia. Glenn parked the car, retrieved his briefcase then turned to say goodbye to Tricia. He put down the briefcase to thank her with a hug.

"Be careful," she told him.

"Be seeing you," he told her.

She watched him take half a dozen steps toward the back of the radio station when something stopped him. He turned as if he had forgotten something. Their eyes met. She sensed that in a brief moment, a bond had been created between them for better or for worse. There was definitely something going on between them.

She smiled.

He smiled back.

Yes, definitely something.

The Unknown Ally

THERE WAS SOMETHING IN WHAT Tricia Knox said which aroused a part of Glenn which had not been aroused in quite some time.

"Be careful," she said.

"Be careful."

It was his mother who had always said that. His mother told him to "be careful" at times instead of saying "I love you". He had passed on the tradition to his own children before they became estranged from him.

This woman, someone he had met only the day before, had somehow reached into his very soul.

His heart was much lighter as he climbed the stairs and entered what had become a hornet's nest of activity since the demise of Zeke Collins earlier in the day.

"Mister Michaels, I'm Ray Davies." The short man with the cherubic face extended a chubby hand in Glenn's direction almost as soon as he walked in the door of the radio station. "I'm with Big Thicket Broadcasting based in Tyler, Texas. Perhaps you've heard of us."

"Somewhere, I'm sure, Mister Davies." Glenn was less than thrilled at the appearance of his uninvited visitor. "I live outside of Dallas."

"I heard your show this morning. I operate Big Thicket's property down the road in Portsmouth. I listened this morning and, quite frankly, I was impressed. You must have been under a lot of pressure. Your performance was extraordinary, Michaels, simply extraordinary."

"I'm glad you liked it. Personally, I lost a mentor and a good friend."

"Mr. Collins. Yes. We're sorry for your loss. We've already sent flowers to his widow."

"Word travels fast around here."

"There's the power of radio for you. I just wanted you to know that our family is here to help your family in your time of need." He handed Glenn a business card. Glenn took it and put it in his shirt pocket.

"Thanks, Mr. Davies, I appreciate your concern. We'll be in touch."

"Any time, Michaels, any time."

Ray Davies seemed to ooze out the door.

"Schmuck," Glenn commented when the man was out of earshot.

"So… who exactly was he anyway?" he asked the receptionist.

"Ray Davies runs the Big Thicket stations in Portsmouth. He's one of several Big Thicket people who run in here now and then," Becky told him.

"What's the deal with them?"

"We seem to be the only island of independence between Columbus and Portsmouth, or for that matter, much of southern Ohio.

"Changing the subject, John Jankowski is in Zeke's office waiting for you."

"John Jankowski?"

"He's been working with Zeke on some sort of project."

"Yes, something's been said about the consultant."

"I guess you could call him that."

"Thanks, Becky. I'll see what he wants. Hold my calls… presuming that I'm still getting calls."

Glenn went back to Zeke's office to find an older man with thinning hair going through a file drawer next to Zeke's desk. He laid some files down and closed the drawer when he heard Glenn come in.

"John Jankowski?"

"Glenn Michaels. You look a lot like your picture, at least the one that Zeke has on file for you. Come in and sit down. This is your office, now as I understand it. Sit. Let's talk."

John Jankowski slid over to one of the guest chairs facing Zeke's desk. Glenn deliberately sat down in the other chair on the same side of the desk.

"This is still Zeke's office. I'm the temporary help."

"I was under the impression that Zeke's new attorney, Fischer, was in here this morning shortly after you got off the air to explain things to you."

"Greg Fischer's an old friend. He told me about some arrangement which I'm not really comfortable with. I really don't want to go back to the days of minimum wage and all the records I can eat."

"Those days are over, Glenn, at least for the most part. There are very few places anymore where radio's what it was when you started… back in '72, wasn't it?"

"Yep… worked just up the road while I was going to school."

"You came here for a short time, went to Parkersburg, then on to Fairmont, Gallipolis then Cleveland, Cincinnati and finally St. Louis before you dropped out."

"You seem to know a lot about me."

"It's because I've been to some of the same places… known some of the same people. I was there before you, Michaels. I know quite a lot about you."

"How?"

"Truman Howell, for one. I showed up at his station in Chillicothe when I was just barely out of high school myself. I was his best at the time. He nurtured me… groomed me to think a lot like he did. I worked around the area until I got bored and moved on. I never settled, never had any roots. I did have Truman's ear, though.

"You remember that night not long after you started in Parkersburg when you started the talk show under Joe Campbell's nose?"

Glenn smiled. "Yep…"

"Campbell wanted to fire you. Truman asked me to listen in on a phone line he had set up. I listened, liked what I heard and told Truman he would be making a mistake if he let you go."

"I suppose I might want to thank you, then. My career on the air was better than most… that's why I'm not very anxious to go back to the early days of lousy pay and no benefits."

"I didn't think that you would be, Michaels. Neither did Zeke. That's why your friend Fischer was hired and that's why Zeke asked me to talk with you this afternoon."

"And when did he do that?"

"A little over a week ago. The plan was that we were both going to talk with you about the gift you were offered on Sunday."

"Meaning these radio stations…"

"Yes, meaning these radio stations. First and foremost, Zeke wanted you to know that the term free and clear with everything he left behind means just that. The stations are yours, without any liens or encumbrances. You can keep them, you can sell them, you can burn them down. Do whatever the hell you want with them. They're a gift. He knew that if you came here, did the show and ran the place, he wouldn't have to worry about what happened after he was gone."

"I told Greg that I'd do the show until the end of the week… that as a personal favor to Zeke. After that, I'm outta here."

Jack Jankowski tried hard to suppress a smile. "And you certainly may do that, in which case Big Thicket Broadcasting will be here within the next week or so to try and take this place over and run things their way. While you'll still own this building, Big Thicket will have someone down here to figure out a way to gain rights to the frequencies. As I understand it, the AM will resurrect as just another outlet for the usual mélange of right-wing talk radio pundits, while the FM allocation will be moved to Huntington, West Virginia… at least that's one of the plans I've heard. But what the hell should you care, right? You'll have some real-estate, and a café which will soon fold from lack of traffic. Zeke's kept these radio stations and the café downstairs alive. For that matter, Zeke Collins kept Magnolia alive, almost single handedly by sitting in the front window nearly every weekday morning for the past forty some odd years."

"And you think that I'm able and willing to do the same."

"Zeke thought so at any rate."

"What about you? You said you've followed me… you know why I quit the business, right?"

"I've resisted Zeke's wishes, to be honest with you, Michaels. I'm not sure what you want any more myself."

Glenn got up and started pacing the room, his eyes sometimes being caught by the mementos on the walls.

"I've built a comfortable life. I don't have to worry about anything more than helping the next customer coming in through the door. No ratings, no back-biting, no having to worry about some idiot consultant coming in and wanting to hire all of his best friends. I make real money… not this minimum wage and all the records you can eat, shit."

"And all this time you've been selling appliances you've been slowly dying, Michaels. Seriously. You've worked yourself into a hole and you need to get out. Money's not everything, Glenn. You made real money in Cleveland. You made real money in Cincinnati; you made real money in Saint Louis."

"At the same time, though, I lived like a gypsy. I own my own house, now. For once in my life, I'm stable."

"You're also ten years and half a dozen girlfriends past your divorce."

"Living like a gypsy cost me my marriage."

"Settling down cost you your marriage, Michaels. The woman you married didn't care about you in the first place. You were her ticket to having children. That's all you were to her. A sperm donor. Zeke knew it from the beginning. You should have gone ahead with the plan you had with Hannah Smith and taken her with you to West Virginia. It would have been awkward at first, but you would have managed. We would have backed you up."

Glenn was surprised. "Just who is this 'we' and how did you know about Hannah Smith?"

"You were working for Truman. I had worked for Truman. I already told you that. Truman Howell was linked with Zeke and Truman liked you. He kept you out of a lot of trouble without you knowing about it. Remember when Joe Campbell left? He didn't leave on his own, Glenn; he was fired for skimming money out of station accounts for his own use. One of those accounts was money earmarked for a bonus for you. The station was pulling in a considerable amount of additional revenue when you quit spinning records and started talking. Truman set up a fund to give you a bonus, and Joe decided to steal from that fund. He still blames you for getting him fired.

"Eventually, Joe went to work for Big Thicket. Chances are that if you were to give up on this place, Joe will come in to take over and make sure that you suffer in some way. He's in a position now where he likes to even old scores."

"Wouldn't he have a score to settle with you, too?"

"Yes… that. To this day I don't think he knows who ratted him out."

"And what about Hannah? How do you know about her?"

"Truman heard something from someone who worked here on the weekdays. He said something to me at about the time you started talking over in Parkersburg. Joe wanted to hit you over the head about that relationship, her being underage and all. He made some phone calls and tied you to Hannah Smith. He tried to get Truman to bite, but he didn't. Truman knew you had done nothing… I knew that you hadn't done anything. I was in a position to know."

Glenn decided to mull things over for a few moments. He made his way to Zeke's side of the desk and sat down.

"By the way, Glenn, there's an unwritten rule here. Whatever is said in Zeke's office stays in Zeke's office. Zeke doesn't have to be here. The rule continues.

"I know about you and Hannah Smith. I know that at least once you had a plan to bail her out of what was for her an impossible situation. All I can say now is that if you had acted, you would have been backed up."

Glenn pondered for a few moments while the memory of that summer raced through his head. He was at the time poised to drive to Magnolia from Parkersburg to see Hannah, perhaps even to take her back to the efficiency apartment he had on the Ohio side of the river. There were, however, consequences, not the least of which was his financial situation at the time. By the time he finally decided to dare the odds and follow through with his plan, she had already been forced into her unholy marriage with Harlan Murphy.

It was at the moment he remembered his aborted rescue effort that he recalled the last words he heard from Hannah when they first parted… when he left Magnolia to go to work in Parkersburg.

"Be careful," she had told him.

The Stoned Guest

Tricia thought briefly about calling Glenn and asking him to dinner. There was more that she wanted to find out about him. He piqued her interest. She wasn't certain what it was about him that fascinated her. What she did know was that a part of her which had lain dormant for a few years had suddenly come to life. She wanted companionship. Not just any companionship, not just anyone's companionship. She wanted <u>his</u> companionship. After all, he liked Springsteen and didn't seem to mind being seen in his birthday suit in front of her without showing an erection. She could get comfortable with him out in her garden, working side by side without inhibitions or a hidden agenda.

She put on the outfit she had worn that morning and drove down to Magnolia, hoping to gather the courage to knock on his door if he didn't appear at Ed's Church and Grill.

There was no crowd at the grill; there was no Glenn. There were just a few scattered locals, more interested in shooting pool and swapping lies despite Zeke's demise and the consequences which would possibly come with it.

"Miss Knox… how good to see you!" John Jankowski approached her as she sat in a booth waiting for the dinner she had ordered.

"Jack Jay… You're here because of the news?"

"Oh, yeah," he said as he sat opposite her. "Zeke asked me to come here the last time I saw him. He wanted me to sit down with his 'chosen one'."

"Glenn?"

"Yes. Glenn Michaels."

Tricia felt a slight flutter at the mention of the name.

"What do you know about him?"

"Not a lot. He just turned fifty-six back in February, divorced, two grown kids, runs an appliance store in suburban Dallas, and for twenty years he was one of the best people anyone's ever heard on the radio."

"Does he have a girlfriend or a significant other?"

"Zeke and I've been tracking that. Since his divorce ten years ago, he seems to have had a few relationships, none of them lasting more than six months.

"It's because of the girl he was hung up on the better part of forty years ago. Hannah Smith."

"She's the girl… we went there this afternoon… up where she's buried."

"That doesn't surprise me. Zeke told me that he made a point of visiting her grave every time Glenn came here to visit him. He said that there was some sort of special connection between them."

"He severed that connection earlier today."

The server came with Tricia's meal, interrupting her. Jack ordered a beer.

"So he severed the connection? How?"

Tricia described Glenn's ritual with the whiskey. Jack laughed.

"She never drank. Neither did her mother… at least when I knew her."

"You knew her mother?"

"At one time, yes. I met her when I was doing a gig in Portsmouth. Long story. Anyway, back to Glenn. From everything I can tell, Glenn's relationship with the Smith girl had a profound effect on his later relationships, especially after she was murdered."

The server came back with Jack's beer. He ignored the glass and started drinking out of the bottle.

"You said something about doing a gig in Portsmouth. I take it you once worked this area?"

"I actually started at the same radio station that Glenn did up in Chillicothe, only thirteen years earlier. I bounced from place to place, gig to gig, before deciding that what I wanted to do was some honest work, like consulting." He gave a snort of self-satisfaction, as if he had just made an inside joke. "I first heard of Glenn when he was working in Parkersburg. He didn't know it until this afternoon, but I got him out of a jam there. After that, he hit the major markets, first in Cleveland, then in Cincinnati and finally St. Louis before he quit. His wife pussy whipped him into it… if you'll pardon the term, ma'am."

"I've heard worse... so eventually he divorced?"

"His wife was seeing someone where she worked. She ran off and left him, taking the kids. He could have used the opportunity to turn his life around… but he never got around to it. He's spent the last fifteen years in storage at the appliance store. End of story. The way it looks, he'll be crawling back into his hole by this time next week."

"How do you know so much about Glenn Michaels?"

"We have a common thread – you could say that we were almost related." Jack took another pull from the bottle, held it up to see how much he had left and then signaled the server to bring him another.

"Make that two…"

She turned back to Jack.

"Do you have any idea as to what kind of relationship Glenn had with Hannah Smith?"

"It was mostly innocent. She was only twenty-four when she died… he hadn't worked in Magnolia for at least nine years which would have made her fifteen when they met."

"How do you know that they met then and not later?"

"Her mother pushed her into marrying her Pastor when she was sixteen, partly to keep her away from Glenn Michaels. Pastor kept her on a tight leash to the point where he apparently felt he had to kill her. In a way, the poor girl was lucky. There were rumors of abuse."

Tricia shuddered. Hannah Smith's marriage to an older man at a young age wasn't entirely unheard of in the area. It was a form of slavery as far as she was concerned, with death being one of few escapes. There was an idea for a future story.

Jack emptied his first beer and took a long pull from the newly arrived bottle. Tricia poured hers into a glass and started sipping.

"God, I'd have gladly killed that man myself. She didn't deserve to be treated the way she was treated. Nobody does."

Jack finished off his second bottle in no time flat and ordered a third.

"Dammit, I should have done something, anything to pull her out of there before…"

"Before what, Jack?"

"Before her mother even thought of giving her to that preacher like she was a fresh piece of meat."

Jack shook his head. "But I couldn't. Not without…"

The third beer came. The server touched Tricia's shoulder. "He had four before he came to sit with you. Are you taking him back to the hotel or should I call Harold to give him an escort?"

"Call Harold. Just a moment."

Tricia pulled a twenty dollar bill out of her purse and handed it to the server.

"For dinner and the drinks. Let me know if you need more, otherwise, keep the change."

Jack had already emptied half the third bottle of beer.

"The bitch, she hid the girl, then sold her into slavery because Glenn Michaels wasn't good enough for her daughter. Why? Because I wasn't good enough for <u>her</u>. She blamed me for fucking up her life by getting her pregnant when she was only seventeen."

Jack finished the third bottle and called for another.

"Fucking bitch had no right to do what she did. Hannah was <u>my</u> child, too. She knew it. She loathed it, and when Glenn showed <u>my</u> daughter the only respect and love she ever got from a man, her mother, goddamn her, her mother had to ruin it all by giving her to that bastard of a holy man!"

Jack put his hands in front of his face and started crying.

"My fault… all my fault… my child, my grandchildren, all dead because of a selfish act from a woman I should not have even… oh God… please help me…"

Jack was sobbing uncontrollably when Harold Richmond came in with one of the Mulligan boys to assist Jack back over to the Magnolia Inn.

Tricia stayed for half an hour after Jack was taken out trying to pull together what she had just heard. The best she could figure out was that there were some strange relationships between Glenn, Jack, Zeke and… well, she wasn't quite sure who else. Perhaps that other person was John Jankowski's alter-ego. 'Wild Jack Jay' had certainly made an appearance that evening. She wondered, too, whether or not Glenn knew about Jack's claim to being Hannah's father… for that matter, she wondered if maybe 'Wild Jack' was making up that claim.

It was only nine thirty when Tricia got home. It had been a long day with the possibility that tomorrow would be even longer. She pulled off what she was wearing and went to her patio to lie out on the hammock, watch the stars and listen to the night noises. She ended up rocking herself to sleep within half an hour of her arrival.

Guests - Welcome and Otherwise

"Be careful."

Tricia's words repeated a few times in his head.

He spent another hour going over the rhythm of the typical weekday at the radio station with Becky before she left him alone to go home for the night.

Instead of going directly upstairs and crashing, he decided to take a quick walk to Mulligan's IGA to get some frozen dinners and a six pack of beer. He had a quiet dinner, read for a while, and then went to bed.

Tired is going to bed at eight in the evening in the time zone an hour east of the one where a person lives. The swirling of the day's events had no effect on Glenn's getting to sleep.

"C'mon, we have work to do…"

The new woman faded out again just like she did the night before, leaving a gaping hole in Glenn's sub conscience which toyed with his imagination.

Hannah appeared, walking toward him wearing a careworn and faded dress. He remembered the dress from the last time that he saw her. It was her Sunday best.

"I forgive you. I love you. We love you. Go in peace. Be careful."

A weight Glenn felt building had been lifted. He watched as she departed with her children… her two boys and a nameless, faceless child neither of them would ever know.

He woke up in the dark, sweat pouring from his body, his pulse pounding.

He got up, his mind racing. "Where am I? What time is it? Was she real? Who was in the Church? What am I doing here-"

Three-eighteen. He felt as if he had just run a marathon.

He rolled out of the bed, slipped on his sandals then started walking through the apartment.

"I owe Zeke until Friday morning," his internal dialogue began.

"You owe Zeke more than that. He kept your secret. Besides, Zeke and Truman believed in you."

"I did most of it on my own."

"And you damn near got fired for it, too. Truman saved your ass."

"Zeke suckered me in."

"You owe him. He's said nothing in all those years."

"Now no one will find out."

"Not unless you tell someone yourself… you need to release the secret inside of you to be truly free…"

"I don't want to."

"It has to come out. It will come out."

The jug of tea in the refrigerator called out. The plastic cup was starting to show stains from having been used without a trip to the dishwasher since leaving Texas.

Three forty. Back to sleep for a little while, backside exposed, covers off.

Five twenty-three. The alarm on the cell phone roused him from an uneventful snooze. Thirty seven minutes remained between the bed and the table by the window on the first floor.

Shave, shower, dress, check in to let Earl at the control board on the second floor know that today would be business as usual.

He made a quick check of the briefcase. Still there; now down to four glasses and a less-than- full bottle of Jack Daniels. Perhaps just a little bracer before the show? No. "The bottle trick" had been the downfall of too many of his contemporaries. Greg <u>did</u> bring a bottle of vodka for a bracer in the basement of the Baptist Church the day he was preparing to marry Alice, but that was different. Greg had been forgiven for his role in that marriage on the day after the divorce became final.

"Good morning, Magnolia, and welcome to Day Two of my reign of terror on WZEK. Yesterday was a little rough for everyone here. Let's try to forget most of what happened and see if we can do any better this morning."

Fewer people. No problem. The anticipation of the previous morning just wasn't there. Besides, it was Wednesday. Still, it was moderately busy. The audience flowed in and out of Zeke's past his station in the window, leaving cards of condolence, perhaps saying hi and making introductions. Glenn didn't let on that he intended to be a short-timer, out the door and on the road on Friday at ten after ten if he could manage it.

WZEK would then be someone else's problem.

John Jankowski came through the door shortly before the seven o'clock news break to occupy a booth close to the front of the window. Glenn became a little nervous.

"Slow down a hair. Otherwise, you still have it… presuming that you lost it in the first place," John coached him between live sets.

Glenn had an ominous feeling about John Jankowski. Something wasn't quite right about his presence. There was something more; something not quite right about him. Tricia might know.

He had been told that the man lived in Lexington and had been hired as a consultant. "Wonder who else he's consulting with," Glenn thought to himself.

He focused his attention elsewhere. Tricia had come into the room during the news break at eight thirty. Slacks, a nice shirt, a large shoulder bag. It seemed to him that she sat at the same table for the third day in a row, taking notes as he wove the show through the ritual the people of Magnolia had been used to for at least the past forty years. Her presence had a calming influence on him; in fact, he felt better about himself in general when she was in the room.

Jack finally left at nine, but not before passing on more friendly advice. Tricia moved up to the table next to the broadcast table when Jack left.

"I ran into Jack last night at Ed's. He told me that you were a natural. Why did you give it up?"

"I didn't give it up. The business changed. This place is an anomaly. This show is an anomaly."

"It's popular around here, still."

"Around here, electricity is still considered to be a fad."

"I'm not going to debate that," she smirked.

"To answer your question, I found a job where I don't have to worry about the latest ratings, where I don't have to worry about whether or not someone will take offense at something I do or say, wondering if maybe I should buy a gun for protection."

"No one's job is entirely safe from nut jobs these days."

"I came close to being shot for firing someone nearly two weeks ago. That's part of the reason I came here."

"I had heard about that. The story made the national news… so you ran away, all the way to Magnolia, Ohio."

"Yep… This has been my refuge. I honestly didn't expect to stay here past yesterday, though."

"So what's next for you, cowboy?"

"I hate being called cowboy."

"Sorry…"

"That's okay… I was thinking of heading up north, perhaps even going to Canada for a day or two just to say I did. Sad part is I'll be stuck here at least through the weekend, what with all the paperwork with the radio stations and the funeral."

"What are you going to do with them?"

"I haven't completely decided. At first I thought about just ditching the place, but now, I'm not so sure of anything other than I want to keep this place out of Big Thicket's hands."

"Have you thought about what you <u>would</u> do?"

"Maybe I can talk this Jankowski into running the place… maybe sell the place to him."

"Just a thought, it may not be the best idea."

"Why not?"

"I can't really say. He said some things last night and I'm not really sure if it was him or the alcohol talking. I'm not sure if he wants you to stay and run this place pretty much as Zeke did or if he'd rather you take a hike."

"Now you have me worried. There used to be something we called 'the bottle trick', referring to radio people's drinking habits getting them into trouble."

"Drugs, too, I would imagine…"

"And sex… a lot of the local stations around this area literally became bordellos. Young guys… stupid… full of themselves… you know the story."

"I've heard it. I've known more than a few girls who've been just as stupid, believe me."

Glenn laughed. "Just the same, I'm still concerned about Jack when you said he might be letting the alcohol do the talking."

When ten o'clock rolled around, Glenn was ready to chart out the rest of his day. No doubt Becky would have a number of chores waiting for him which no one else could accomplish. He really didn't have the heart to break the news to her that his stay was only temporary. That he would be gone at the end of the week.

"Up to the hornet's nest, I guess," he told Tricia as he went toward the back of Zeke's.

Tricia lightly touched his shoulder.

"Glenn, before you go up, you may want to know that there's this strong possibility that you may be dealing with two Jack Jankowskis."

"Do you think he's chizophrenic?"

"Possibly, yes. He can sometimes be your best friend, but at the same time, he could just as well stab you in the back. Be careful."

She had said it again.

"Be careful," he repeated softly. It seemed to be a natural, almost automatic response. There was definitely something going on between the two of them. He could feel it.

"I'll be up in a few minutes by way of the back stair if it's okay…"

"Sure… hey, if you need to freshen up, feel free to hit the apartment." He handed her his key card when they arrived at the second floor.

Earl met him there. "You may not want to go up to the front quite yet… the place is crawling with 'suits'."

"Do you know who?"

"Zeke's new lawyer, that Jack Jay or Jankowski or whoever you call him and a couple of guys I've never seen before. My guess is that they are connected with Big Thicket."

"Remember any names?"

"Nope… No names. Zeke was the one who was good at names."

After thanking Earl for the warning, Glenn went in to see what might be going on. He arrived in the reception area in the center of the building to find Greg Fischer, John Jankowski, Randy Green and another man; one who sent a shiver up his spine.

"Joe Campbell. What's it been... twenty-five, thirty years since you tried to bounce me from KY?" Glenn maintained his composure despite being terrified of the new arrival.

"It's been twenty-nine since Truman saved your ass and fired me, my friend," he snarled. "Tell you what, though... I'm still in the business while you're smothering yourself down in Texas selling washing machines. You never could measure up, could you?"

"I take it that you two know each other," Greg interrupted.

Glenn and Joe exchanged scowls.

"Now, Glenn, before we get started, I need to tell you that our conversation yesterday and any other conversations you have had with Mr. Jankowski, Zeke, or Mr. Green are confidential," Greg interjected. "I am here as your representative as spelled out in Mr. Collins' will."

This wasn't going to be a very pleasant conversation. Glenn inferred from what Greg said that Big Thicket was probably playing cat to Zeke's mouse and had been doing so for a while. What made things worse for Glenn was Randy Green's presence. Despite what was said between them on Monday, Glenn remembered when they were actually very good friends.

"As I mentioned to you yesterday, according to the Last Will and Testament of Zeke Collins, you are now the sole owner of WZEK. This includes all rights and licenses, real property and equipment. That's what I told you, right?"

"Yep..."

"Mister Green and Mister Campbell are here as representatives of Big Thicket Broadcasting."

"I know who they are..."

"They would like to make an offer to purchase your legacy from you for a price to be determined later."

"A million dollars… cash," Glenn blurted out. Joe's jab about him not measuring up didn't sit well with him.

Randy Green and Joe Campbell smiled and nodded their heads. It was obvious that the asking price was way more than they intended to pay.

John Jankowski looked at Glenn, winked, giving tacit approval to Glenn's hasty offer.

"Mr. Michaels, this property is worth maybe three hundred thousand on the outside. We are prepared to offer you half a million dollars here on the spot for WZEK, WZEK-FM and the real property attached to those stations." Randy looked calm as he made the offer. Glenn knew Randy well enough to know that he was sweating bullets, especially with his superior watching him. Joe looked as if he was willing to put up a fight.

"That sounds reasonable, Randy… and seeing as how we had been friends once upon a time, I'll up my price to a million five, then!"

"Fuck you, Michaels," Joe Campbell blurted out, "two fifty and you can rot in hell if we offer any more!"

"Six fifty, Glenn, and that's our final offer," Randy interjected.

"A million five and a covenant not to move the frequencies out of Fuller County, Randy."

"That's preposterous, Glenn. There's no way in hell we can recover a million five without moving the –"

"Shut up, Randy," Joe snapped. "Michaels, you're fucking with the wrong people. We have other ways of getting what we want… Randy, let's go."

Joe Campbell literally stormed out of the office with Randy on his tail. Those in the office heaved a collective sigh of relief.

"You know that the Big Thicket boys have other ways to get what they want," Jack stated.

"Well, they're not going to get it from me… not if I can help it."

"So you're going to stay?" Tricia asked.

Up to this point no one had noticed that Tricia had come up the back way and had witnessed most of what had gone on.

"The way I see it, I can't possibly get out of here before introducing Zeke's replacement on Monday morning's show… if I can manage to find someone willing to do it on such short notice."

"You're not selling, then…" Greg was making sure that what he had heard was correct.

"No, I'm not selling, at least for now and definitely not to them. If Joe Campbell wasn't part of the deal, I might consider entertaining some sort of offer from Randy or from someone else with Big Thicket, but I'll be damned if I'll let that bastard tell me how to run my business."

There was silence for a few moments.

"You do realize what you just said…" Greg said.

Silence for a few more moments.

"You just took ownership. You just said that this was your business."

Glenn took a deep breath.

"I guess I did, didn't I?"

He felt Tricia's hands on his shoulders.

"Sometimes your fate chooses you," she told him.

"I'm still going to leave this place and… I… I don't know. I need some room to think."

He turned to look at Tricia before heading out the main entrance down to the street.

"Be careful," she whispered just before he turned away from her.

"Thanks…" he mouthed as he turned.

Moments later he was sitting on the bench across the street, next to the yellow rose, oblivious to his surroundings.

"It's only a temporary thing, you see…"

Hannah Smith's voice came back to Glenn from across the years as he sat alone in the late morning sunshine. He always felt her presence when he came to Magnolia to sit on that particular bench. This was the first time, though, that he heard her.

"I'm talking about life. All life is fleeting."

He sat still, wondering how he could be hearing her talking to him. It was definitely her. In just a few words, the cadence, the intonation, the slight 'catch' were the same as they were the last time they were together.

"I know that you said goodbye. I was touched. I understand. I am happy that you have decided to start a new chapter in your life."

A million and a quarter questions raced through his mind at once.

"I feel your thoughts. I feel your embrace of my being. All I came to say is thank you. You were the shining star of my existence as a living and breathing human being. You have felt sorry about and have blamed yourself for my earthly demise. There is no need. My demise was a release from the prison in which I was trapped. Don't be like my father. Don't live the rest of your life imprisoned by your memories of me. Live your life as it was intended. Know that you gave me joy."

For a minute he sat and let Hannah's words sneak into his being before tenderly picking up the rose on the side of the bench and giving it a tender kiss.

He's Poison

"Jack, I need to see you in Glenn's office. Alone."

Tricia marched back to what used to be Zeke's office. Jack Jay followed. Greg stayed put, figuring that if his input was wanted, Tricia would have asked for it.

"Close the door…"

Jack closed the door behind him but kept his hand on the knob in case he had to make a hasty exit.

"Last night… is what you told me true, or were you just letting the alcohol do the talking?"

Jack stared at her and stayed silent.

"You know that nothing leaves this room… but… if what you told me is true, Glenn has got to know that Hannah was your daughter, and he has to know from you," Tricia lectured.

Jack clicked the door shut and slumped down in one of the chairs facing Zeke's desk.

"There's a lot of stress in this business, Tricia."

"I know. I got the idea from talking with Zeke for my story. Sobriety and stable relationships take a back seat in this business. Sometimes reality takes a beating, too. Now that you're sober, were you Hannah Murphy's father?"

Jack reflected for a few moments. "Yes."

"And you are aware that Glenn Michaels at least knew Hannah Murphy?"

"He knew Hannah Smith, Miss Knox."

"She was married…"

"Forced… to keep her away."

"From Glenn?"

"From Glenn." Jack paused for a moment. "He could have saved her, you know."

"How?"

"He could have rescued her from her mother before she was forced to marry. I would have helped. I was her father and I was in a position to do something."

"What did you do?"

Jack appeared to stare into space.

"Nothing…" he mumbled. "I couldn't."

The room became deathly quiet.

"I wouldn't…" he finally said in a barely audible whisper. "Her mother was right. Glenn Michaels was no good for her. He was just like me… glib… insincere."

"Is he still?"

"He'll never change, none of us ever do. It's the nature of the business, Miss Knox."

Jack looked around the room. "I want to be here, near her. He didn't help. He needs to go back home."

"I see…" She waited for a few moments while silence once again filled every inch of the room.

"Jack," she finally continued, "do you have any idea how much Hannah meant to Glenn?"

"I know how much Glenn meant to Hannah, but I didn't want her to be disappointed later in life like her mother was with me. This character, this Wild Jack Jay I once was – he was the face for a soulless nothing that I really was. Radio people; we're all artificial," he huffed. "You think about that, young lady, before you get entangled with the likes of Glenn Michaels. He's poison, I tell you. He'll be the death of you, just like he was the death of Hannah."

Pro-Bono Advice

A MINUTE AFTER HE HAD placed the rose back in its holder, Glenn Michaels had come to the conclusion that he had put his foot into his mouth. He knew it and he stared at the building he had inherited wondering how he would be able to pull his foot out. If it was anything, it was a Freudian slip. Maybe his subconscious was trying to tell him that he really needed to stay in Ohio and not go back to Texas except to collect his belongings and sell the house.

Glenn looked down at the rose next to him again. For the better part of the past twenty-five years, he had sent a sum of money to Rita's Florists to place and maintain a rose in the holder attached to the bench for the month of July. It was a confidential arrangement. Only Zeke, Jessica and Rita knew about it. It was his tribute to the woman he would never have because of circumstances beyond his control.

Yesterday he had cut her loose; at least he thought he had cut her loose. Instead, the ceremony at the cemetery, like the ceremony he had performed the day before, had put him in touch with his own mortality.

From fifty-six, it was a short jump to sixty-five, then an even shorter jump to seventy-one. His father died at seventy-one.

He pondered for a few minutes, alone. She would have turned fifty this year, had it not been for the tragedy.

"Would she have been any better off had she not known me?" he asked himself.

"No. If it hadn't been you, it would have been someone else."

"Would it? Maybe she'd be just another face, someone else who was living out a '…life of quiet desperation'."

"Her life mattered."

"All lives matter… even those cut short."

He paused in his argument. Perhaps the meaning of life wasn't how much fortune or pleasure you obtained, but how much your own life mattered in the lives of others.

"How much does my life mean to the people I deal with back in Texas?"

He couldn't answer without the thought of Tricia Knox crossing his mind. He had known her for a little more than forty eight hours and she was stuck there. He needed advice.

Greg appeared across the street emerging from the front door of the radio station just as Glenn decided to go and seek out his old friend.

"There you are… Becky said that you might be here. A bit warm, isn't it?"

"Greg, you've never been sitting on a bench in Texas heat, have you? Let me tell you… except for the humidity an eighty-eight degree day in Dallas in July would be referring to a cool night-time temperature and you'd have people pulling out their winter coats."

"Heat's all relative, I guess," Greg chuckled.

"You've got it… So… I need some advice."

"I figured you might, that's why I came downstairs."

"What do I do?"

"Do you want to follow your head or follow your heart?"

"Funny you should say that… back when I was a kid, before the family moved down to southern Ohio, we attended a church carnival where one of the women dressed as a gypsy and read palms."

Glenn held out the palm of his right hand to show it to Greg.

"You see these two lines?" he traced a couple of lines on his palm. "One of them is my heart line; the other has to do with my intellect, sort of a mind line."

He pointed to another feature.

"You see these two "X" marks? They are supposed to represent a time in my life when I am going to have a conflict between my heart and my head. The first one had already happened."

"With Alice?"

"Alice."

"The writer?"

"Yep… Patricia Knox. I'm starting to think that she's the second 'X'."

"You know that she just pulled Jankowski into Zeke's old office…"

"No, but if you hum me a few bars, I'll fake it!" Glenn gave a short chuckle at his joke. "Seriously, I wouldn't doubt it. She mentioned something about Jack being schizophrenic. What do you think?"

"I'm not really certain, Glenn. Zeke told me that Tricia might have some insight as to what's going on with Jack. Whatever's going on with him, she probably has a good handle on the situation."

"Probably so."

"Are you starting to like the woman?"

"Oddly enough, the thought has crossed my mind… off the record, of course."

"Of course." Greg smiled at Glenn and hesitated for a few moments. "Before the divorce, you never used to be the adventurous type… when it came to women, that is."

"Nope… never was. Not like some people I know…" Glenn remembered stories about Greg's sexual exploits before he settled down and married a woman he had met in law school.

"I've heard stories about you and some of the women you've dated since your divorce from Alice."

"Stories? What stories?"

"Let me put it another way. I've known you long enough to almost read your mind, Glenn. Let me assure you that there's nothing to worry about. I won't be telling anyone."

"Attorney client privilege?"

"How about a best friend who would rather have you move a thousand miles closer?"

The two men sat without saying a word for several minutes.

"By the way, you sounded great this morning."

"You sure know how to be encouraging."

"I detect a hint of sarcasm in your voice."

"Really… what makes you think that I would be sarcastic other than the fact that now that I've proven what I came here to prove, all I want to do is to go home and live in peace."

"Maybe you're already home."

"No, Greg, I have a home in Texas."

"How often do you feel at home there? Let's be honest. How often have you called me in these past few years about the traffic and the noise and the loneliness? You lock yourself in your house as if it were a prison - coming out to work, to go to the grocery store or to go to some girl's house so that the two of you can screw. Is that what home means to you, Glenn?"

Before Glenn could reply, Greg continued:

"That fellow blowing his brains out in front of your store… you know that made national news, don't you? Is that what your life has come to? Was he after you, Glenn? Was he coming to get you just like Harlan Murphy was?"

"Brother Murphy wasn't after me…"

"Yes, he was, Glenn. I remember you telling me that you thought he was after you when he shot himself dead twenty-five years ago."

"I… yes, I suppose I did."

"Why you? Why not Zeke, or someone else? You've told me several times he was after you in particular. There had to be a reason."

"I was writing to his wife and she was writing to me in secret," Glenn confessed. "Harold… the officer on the scene told me that the investigators found an envelope with my name and my business address on it in the car. The man was insane. Everyone knew that."

"That's all? The man wanted to kill you for writing to his wife?"

"That's about the size of it."

"Sounds like he really was insane."

"That's what I've been telling people all along."

They sat for another minute or so in silence.

"That's bullshit, Glenn. Zeke told me the real reason a week ago Monday. Honestly, I didn't think that you would do such a thing. What he told me about the affair you had with Hannah made sense of the whole incident."

Glenn felt a jolt going through his body… his being. His secret had been penetrated outside of the small circle where it had remained hidden for so long.

"I'm not telling, though. You are my client… the information is privileged. I won't even tell my wife."

Glenn heaved a sigh of relief.

"So what's your plan, Glenn? I need to know something… anything. Free and clear, remember? Plans need to be made, one way or another."

"That's why I'm sitting here. I need to do something, but I don't know what."

"Let's start with a couple of basics, then. You have two businesses which employ a total of, say, twenty people. Someone needs to run the businesses. Never mind the radio show from six till ten… the businesses need to continue at least for the sake of the twenty people who rely on the businesses for basics like food and shelter."

"There are managers for that, right?"

"Yes, there are managers, but you run the show. You sign the paychecks and you have the responsibility.

"Until such time as you transfer that responsibility to a new owner, you are responsible for the lives of those people."

"That can be done here or in Dallas, right?"

"I suppose you can run the business from Dallas if you'd like."

"I'd like that."

"Consider it done. Now, about the morning show. You need to find someone willing to come in and be the next Zeke Collins… someone who would be able to run the same type of program and would appeal to a broad audience."

"Someone can be found rather easily I would think…"

"My understanding is that Zeke and Jack worked for a good six months before they settled on you."

"There's a lot of people who could pull off Zeke's act."

"Really? Name someone."

"Dave Thompson over in Vanceburg, Kentucky."

"Dead. Overweight, diabetic."

"'The O-Man'… Otis Byrd up in Wheeling."

"Terminal Cancer. I called. Six months, tops."

"Ray Jensen? He was last seen in Toledo if I recall."

"He's got his head up his ass. He's now a program director at the Big Thicket station in Muskegon, Michigan."

Glenn fired off half a dozen other names with the same results. Most of them were either dead of respiratory problems or had literally dropped out of sight.

"Okay, so why me?"

"You're still breathing and in good health. You have business experience and you're familiar with the area."

"And what about The Incident?"

"This incident as it's called is largely forgotten. That was a generation ago. It seems that the only person to whom The Incident really matters to any more is you. Zeke and I are the only people, other than you, to know why.

"If anyone needs to know more, your story about the police finding an envelope with your name and address is as good an explanation as any. If you want to know what I think you should do, I think you need to confront what happened. Tell someone in your own words. Live the pain again. Once you do that, you might find that the truth will set you free. Tell you what," Greg said as he looked at his watch, "I need to be headed up to Chillicothe.

"As counsel hired by Zeke Collins, let me suggest that you and I get together with some plans to run Zeke's enterprises here in the next couple of days so that the people working in that building in front of you have some assurance that they will continue to be paid. And while you're at it, you might want to think about how all of the other people in this community depend somehow on what goes on in that building across the street.

"And the 'whatever-it-is-we-didn't-talk-about' that's holding you back, buddy, you'd best be letting it go real soon before it drags you down," Greg said as he got up from the bench.

Within a minute, Greg was driving north on Main Street, headed back to the highway to go to Chillicothe. Glenn watched and contemplated as he stroked the yellow rose at the end of the bench. Greg had always been his best friend. Why had never been questioned.

Confession

GLENN TOOK A WALK AROUND Magnolia, eventually walking back to Zeke's to have a light lunch of a ham sandwich and a glass of iced tea before heading upstairs to "his" office to see if he could make heads or tails of what Zeke's selection process was and if there were other candidates who would be willing to take on the task of running Zeke's morning show. He arrived upstairs to find Tricia perusing some files which had been left open on Zeke's desk.

"I hope you don't mind, but if you're set on leaving, you need to be looking through these files and making some decisions."

She put a stack of manila folders on the desk and motioned for Glenn to have a seat.

"Have you had lunch yet?" he asked her.

"Becky ordered me a Caesar salad and had it brought up shortly after my conversation with Jack. She thought it would be okay."

"No, no problem."

"Maybe we can have Chinese tonight up at Ding's in Prentiss. My treat…"

"Sure, I'd like that."

Glenn had been thinking about taking a quick trip to Parkersburg after lunch to see if he could pick Mark Spencer's brains. Mark was, in Glenn's opinion, one of the best people he had ever known in radio. A personal appeal, perhaps, would convince Mark to leave his comfortable position in Parkersburg to come and sit in the window at Zeke's. The thought passed. Spending an afternoon and evening with Tricia seemed more appealing.

Becky came into Zeke's office after knocking softly on the door. "I need you to sign these logs, please."

Glenn silently summoned her in, signed then watched her leave, leaving him alone again with Tricia.

"Zeke sure collected a lot of junk, didn't he?" Glenn remarked.

"The place seems like it would be a fire trap… papers spread everywhere, willy-nilly; letters; awards; commendations… and these are just the items out on display. There are five file drawers in here which need to be combed through.

"By the way, I saw John Jankowski rifling through this drawer here yesterday afternoon. I didn't have a good feeling about it."

There was another knock on the door. Tricia opened it and let in Jessica Collins.

"Hi Jessica," Glenn greeted her. "Needing a little break?"

She smiled at him. "I just wanted to be here. I've always felt that this room was as much a part of Zeke as Zeke himself, that's all."

"If you'd like, we could leave and give you some privacy," Glenn offered.

"I've had enough privacy. You two can stay here. I just want to commune with Zeke's spirit."

Glenn understood. He had always felt close to Zeke in this room regardless of Zeke's personal presence. He looked over at Tricia. She gave a slight nod. She understood.

"The viewing will be on Friday night from seven till nine; the memorial service will be held on Saturday," Jessica informed them. "It'll give people a little time to get here. We'll have a private burial before the memorial."

"Glenn and I will be there both nights."

"Thank you. I was hoping that you would." Jessica looked around the office while Tricia and Glenn tried to make sense of the files spread out on the desk.

"Zeke wasn't this disorganized at home, was he?" Tricia asked.

"Dear, you've never been in our house. Glenn has, and Glenn could tell you that the place is as neat as a pin. This disorganization was very organized, but organized the way that Zeke wanted. Take this file here, for instance…"

Jessica seemingly took a file at random from the middle of an 'in' box on the corner of Zeke's desk.

"Let's see… ah! Clippings from July, 1985. That would have been from the Murphy murder and suicide."

The Incident. Glenn froze as he felt a mild wave of panic strike. It was bad enough that one of his best friends knew the truth about the affair. If Jessica knew and told Tricia, Tricia might not…

"The girl involved was Hannah Smith, Tricia. I believe you went out to visit her with Glenn yesterday."

"Yes, we did. I was telling Glenn about reading about the case. There never seemed to be a motive for the killings."

"Yes there was, but there are only three living people who know what it was… and that knowledge never left this room."

Jessica knew. The wave of panic intensified.

"I know the motive, and so do you, Glenn."

"I have no idea what you're talking about."

"Glenn Michaels, you know damn good and well what I'm talking about," Jessica scolded. "You came here partly to rid yourself of that demon you've kept bottled up inside of you for all those years. It's time you got rid of it."

"How… when did you know?"

"I started to put it together just after Hannah's funeral," Jessica told him. "The Incident didn't make sense. Why would a man butcher his sons and his pregnant wife, torch his church and then blow his own head off at a routine traffic stop? The only reason I could think of was that Hannah was carrying another man's child."

Dead silence. Even so, Glenn could hear his heart pounding. The circle had already grown larger than he thought. Of course, Zeke would have told Jessica. Zeke held nothing back from her. Their marriage worked in part because the two of them never held anything from each other. Greg appeared to know, now Tricia was going to know.

"It was your child, wasn't it, Glenn?"

"Yep…" he mouthed silently as tears started to fall down his cheeks. "She was my child. It was my fault."

Glenn spent a minute or so in silent contemplation before he spoke again:

"We… she called me about two weeks before she was killed to tell me that she was pregnant." Glenn spoke in a quiet monotone. "I was in a hell of a mess. The son I had with Alice was four months old. I needed to get a divorce, keep my children and get Hannah and her boys out of that hell hole she was living in so she could come and marry me.

"Hannah and I had been writing back and forth to each other for years. Zeke played the middle man. He saw that her marriage and my marriage had been bad choices from the start. She was too damn young, I was too damn stupid.

"My dad died in March of that year. My son, Christopher was less than a week old and Alice decided not to go to the funeral with me. Hannah had slipped away to a friend's house to call me at work when she found out about Dad and we planned to meet to talk afterwards.

"We were coming down the hill from the cemetery, headed to the church when I noticed a dilapidated Chevette lurking on one of the side lanes. I hung back. It was her. We stayed there, parked, after the others had gone.

"We talked for a couple of hours, walking the cemetery before deciding that we were going to do something about our mutual problems.

"When we got to the church, it was empty… the reception was over."

Glenn paused for a few moments before he continued.

"We got in and went upstairs to use the bathrooms above the Great Hall. It only took a minute for it to happen, but we found ourselves alone in the nursery, nestled in the very center of the building."

Glenn's heart continued to pound… sweat was pouring from his brow.

"We greeted each other again, first with a touch, then with a passionate kiss. We re-grouped. I recall her taking off her coat to reveal a faded dress. It was her Sunday best.

"After a few minutes of drinking each other in, she pulled back and started to take off her dress. 'Let me…' I told her."

Glenn paused in his narration as he recalled how he had guided her hands in different directions before exploring her body with his own. As they undressed each other, they came to appreciate each others' reactions to the others' touch in unexpected places.

Glenn continued, "We were experiencing pleasures with each other we had never experienced before."

Again, his mind drifted back. His hands were followed by his mouth, his tongue, tempted by the deliciousness of her neck, her shoulders and eventually her breasts. He teased her by ever so lightly nipping at her nipples as they came to attention.

Hannah's hands were exploring him at the same time; exploring his body in places he didn't expect; in ways he couldn't anticipate.

"As our bodies joined – our souls melded. It may have been minutes; it may have been an eternity. We were in communion; our bodies, our souls bound as one. The animal act each of us had experienced with the people to whom we were married seemed to be elevated to a higher art form."

The room was dead silent.

"When Harlan Murphy killed Hannah, he destroyed the only soul mate I had ever known. I came to the conclusion that my children were conceived using Alice as a body proxy. In my mind, I've loved only once. I don't think I will ever love again."

Glenn got up from his seat at Zeke's desk.

"So if you'll excuse me, I have to go and pack. I'm done. I'm out of here."

The Missing Link

"Holy Crap. Why didn't I think of that possibility? Tricia asked herself while Glenn bared his soul to recount his tryst with Hannah Smith. Most of the evidence was there, in front of her, except for one very vital fact. Tricia's eye caught a passage in the medical examiner's notes on Harlan Murphy in the dossier in front of her, a passage she had not seen in any other copy: *Victim had Vasectomy performed in-office 5/13/83.*

As Tricia continued to listen to Glenn's story, she could imagine the scene in the Murphy household as Harlan Murphy confronted his wife about the letters and the phone calls she had been making behind his back. There were probably subtle hints that the woman was preparing to leave and to take her sons with her, as well as other hints that she was pregnant.

He was seething with rage.

He had hidden his vasectomy from her, suspecting that such a young wife might be unfaithful and afraid that he might not live long enough to properly raise a third, or even a fourth child.

Yet here she was, pregnant, and here he was, bereft of seed.

Tricia winced as she imagined the blows suffered by this young wife, praying that at least one of the early blows would have been enough to knock her unconscious so that she would not have to suffer what came next.

The boys had been asleep for hours. They never knew what hit them as their father severed their heads to take to show to their mother.

He then cut her open while she was still alive. Tricia felt as if she was going to be sick to her stomach as she thought about the preacher who aborted the pregnancy by killing the mother and leaving the neonate in the middle of the floor to die.

Glenn left.

But he didn't leave before telling her that he felt he had shared a perfect love with Hannah Smith… that he and she had shared their souls and their bodies in such a way that would make any woman jealous.

It made Tricia jealous.

She had been cheated of a perfect love by an accident on a wet, slippery road.

She had been cheated of a perfect love by living with a man who deserted her so that he could live with another woman.

She was not going to be cheated out of love again, despite what Jack had told her earlier. She knew what she felt for this man, this visitor from Texas.

"Give him a few minutes before you go upstairs…" Jessica Collins lightly restrained Tricia as she was about to follow Glenn. "He's probably angry, hurt, and maybe confused. He has had that story bottled up for years now. He needs time before you tell him what you want desperately to tell him."

"What will I say… what can I say?"

"Say as little as possible. Remind him of the rule, that what is said here stays here. Reassure him that you won't say or write a thing about what you just heard. He will understand."

"You know this?"

"I know this."

Tricia looked into Jessica's eyes. Despite the sudden burden of being widowed, there was still a twinkle which spoke of a deep wisdom.

"I'll be giving up one hell of a story, you know."

"You will gain so much more. The seed has already been planted. Nurture it. Let it grow."

Tricia closed her eyes and the image of someone she once knew came to her, before he just as suddenly disappeared, giving her permission to move on to the next chapter of her life.

"I'll be at home if you need me, Patricia," Jessica said as she left the office.

"Love you…"

"I know," Jessica winked.

"Him too," Tricia admitted.

She paused for a minute or so after Jessica left to gather her thoughts before going upstairs. There was hope that maybe he hadn't left, that hope buoyed when she arrived at his door and heard him puttering around on the other side.

Patricia Knox steeled herself for an onslaught as she knocked on his door.

Knowing Without Saying

Violated. Betrayed. Glenn Michaels had kept his secret for a quarter of a century and it had been betrayed in front of someone who had the power to take it and reveal it to the public at large.

The secret could possibly follow him back to Texas, to shame, to retirement in disgrace. He stomped up the stairs straight into the apartment determined not to see these people again. His thoughts returned to what had gone wrong in the plans he was making to make things right for Hannah, for his children, for the child who would never be.

Thoughts of gloom and despair were interrupted a few minutes later by a knock at the door. He hesitated momentarily before returning to his inner hell.

There was another knock at the door.

"I sort of got the impression that I'd be the last person you'd want to see right now." Tricia stood back from the door when he opened it.

"I sort of think you're right. Good day."

He had a fleeting thought of slamming the door in the face of the woman outside. Instead, he chose to close it quietly.

"Glenn…"

He stopped the closing movement.

"Zeke had a hard and fast rule. Nothing said in his office leaves his office. I am bound by that rule until or unless you release me."

Tricia managed to look directly into Glenn's eyes.

"Even if that rule didn't exist, I would not say or write a thing about what you just revealed."

He opened the door just a little wider.

"What happened wasn't your fault. It became obvious to me yesterday when we went out to Hannah's grave – you loved her. I can respect that."

"Thank you."

"You had said that you would be doing the show until Friday."

"I did… and I will," he sighed. "I'll keep my promise."

"I can respect that," Tricia told him.

They stood, facing each other, uncertain as to what to do or to say next.

Without saying a word, they were speaking volumes. A sense foreign to Glenn enveloped him as he stood there… mesmerized. "Be careful" he thought he heard her say again… or did he imagine it this time?

"Our time will come, and it will be beautiful." He attempted to open his mouth to say the thought out loud.

"I can almost read your mind," she whispered. "Not yet… be careful."

She kissed him lightly on the cheek before turning to go downstairs.

He stood and watched her. "Tricia, dinner tonight at that Chinese restaurant as you suggested earlier?"

"I sort of thought you might ask…"

"You're sort of right. Meet you there at 5:30. Be careful…"

Trojan Horse

Glenn cast himself on his bed soon after Tricia left, meaning to lie down for "just a minute". When he got up, he noted that his "just a minute" had turned into two hours. He shook off the effects of his nap to go downstairs and talk with Becky at the reception desk. He noticed that John Jankowski was in one of the radio studios talking with the afternoon guy, a Gary something-or-other, on the air. Jack noticed Glenn, and excused himself to come out to the reception area.

"Zeke's office… we need to talk," Jack told Glenn as he headed to the back of the building.

Glenn followed and was ushered in by Jack who closed the door behind him. Glenn sat down on Zeke's side of the desk. Jack stood opposite him.

"You realize that there is a privacy rule involving this office in particular, right?"

Glenn nodded.

"Good. First of all let me tell you that I had nothing to do with it, but the Town Council met earlier this afternoon and voted you in as the next 'Zeke Collins'".

"Oh, great…" Glenn groaned. "So what happens Monday morning when I don't show up?"

"That's why we're in here with the door closed. I need to tell you a couple of things.

"First of all, you were Zeke's first choice to be in charge once he was gone. He and I went back and forth over a six month period reviewing a number of other candidates. We ranked them in any number of ways and, for some reason; your name always came to the top of the list. I told him to name at least two other possible candidates before putting the whole deal in stone in his will.

"I'm sorry… he didn't listen."

"I'm sure he meant well, Jack…"

"I knew he meant well, and I also knew that you might not want to come. I suspected that it might have something to do with Hannah Smith."

"Why would you think that, Jack?"

Jack went over to the door peeked out, then reclosed it. He came close to Glenn and spoke softly. "Hannah told me herself about your relationship with her. I am her father."

Glenn was stunned.

"I know that it took a lot for you to come up here, especially at this time. It's no less painful to me, believe me. You're young; you can go on without the burden you carry. Let me say that I am here to help you move on – to help you put Magnolia behind you."

The men sat staring at each other, their thoughts racing.

"I look back at what happened and I could find it very easy to stand in front of you and blame you for her murder. But at the same time, I know that you loved her and you were devastated by her death. If there was blame to be assigned, I share in that blame and I forgive you for your part in it. She would forgive you too, if she were able."

Glenn put his face in his hands as he collected his thoughts.

"I still need time."

"I understand… but we need to be prepared for Monday. We need to be prepared so that you can move on. I took the liberty of pulling

Zeke's files on the other candidates so that you can make a choice. Their folders are in the front of the top drawer of the wooden filing cabinet to your left. I'll trust you to make the decision and to contact your choice. You'll still retain ownership according to Zeke's wishes, but you can do that easily enough from Dallas."

"Thanks…"

Jack paused for a moment. "There is another alternative…"

"What's that?"

"You could sell it to me… the stations, the restaurant, the whole kit and caboodle. I'm willing to pay a fair price."

"Less than a million five, I suppose…"

"Yes, less than a million five. I have three hundred and fifty thousand I could invest. I have more which I would keep in reserve. Honestly, I would like to be back here in southern Ohio to retire and be close to Hannah. WZEK would make a great hobby."

"That's another way of looking at it, I guess."

"At least give my offer some thought, will you?"

"I'll give it some consideration."

Jack started to leave the room.

"Another minute, Jack?"

Jack paused.

"Just a thought… would Hannah want me to continue here… in her memory, so to speak?"

"I really think that's up to you. She loved you, Glenn."

"I loved her, too, Jack."

"She wrote and told me so. You know that you set her free?"

"I caused her death."

"She was in a place worse than death, Glenn. My inaction condemned her to that place. You set her free."

Jack left Glenn alone to ponder what to do next.

Glenn went over to peek in the file drawer to see who Zeke's other choices might be. Of the six people in the front of the file cabinet, he knew only one; Mark Eveland. The last he had seen Mark he was working in Fairmont, West Virginia at a radio station based in a barely renovated former motel. Glenn pulled the file and dialed the most recent number listed.

"Mark… Glenn Michaels here… how the hell are you?"

"I just shot a seventy-two at the club just now. How the hell are things going in the Big D?"

"Not shabby… I'm up in your general direction for a few days, though, and thought I'd give you a shout."

"You're in Magnolia pitch-hitting for Zeke, aren't you?"

Glenn laughed. "Hell, you can't keep any secrets around here, can you?"

"I tuned in yesterday at about the time the news broke. You did one hell of a job for someone out of practice… at least I assume you're still pushing washing machines on unwary housewives…"

"Yep… it's been a few years… and that's why I'm calling. This is only a temporary gig for me."

"I take it that you came up for a visit and Zeke just died on you."

"That's it in a nutshell…"

"Has 'Wild Jack Jay' shown up yet? He and Zeke had been real close, off and on, for at least forty years…"

"Who?"

"'Wild Jack Jay'… Jack Jankowski."

"Oh, him… I was just talking with him."

"No shit… hey, if you get a chance, tell him I said hey."

"How did you know Jack Jankowski?"

"He's part of Thicket… or at least he was. He retired, maybe, five years ago."

"Could he have come out of retirement?"

"There's too much of a wheeler-dealer left in him to fully retire. He's been all over this neck of the woods brokering broadcast properties, trading equipment and finding people who can fill in on the air."

"You said all over this neck of the woods. Joe Campbell was in here earlier this afternoon. Does Jack have anything to do with Joe?"

"Joe's off limits as far as Jack's concerned. Joe does a lot of the same thing that Jack does… he brokers for Big Thicket. Joe's probably looking for a perk. Most likely both of them are after the stations in Magnolia. Brian Thompson, Thicket's owner, wants that property and is supposedly promising a big fat bonus to whoever gets it."

"Jack told me he has money available to buy and run this place. You're saying that he's most likely using Thicket's money?"

"That would be my guess. From what I hear, Jack's broke, or nearly so. Zeke's paid him pretty good, but Zeke's retainer is nothing more than chump change. The rumor is that Thompson is offering half a million dollars bonus to whoever is able to get the property."

Mark chuckled. "So, to what do I owe this call on the rap rod?"

"Well, I called to get your reaction to coming over here to Magnolia to be the next Zeke Collins. Apparently the Town Council here has decided to make Zeke into a franchise."

"You know, I'd love to, but since I started to work for Big Thicket, I have something I've never had in the radio business… security. It's nice to have a pension, major medical and I had membership in the country club thrown into the deal to boot. I hope you understand…"

"I know, Mark. I also know that all Big Thicket has to offer is cookie cutter radio. That's part of why I left when I did, remember?"

"Well, that and Alice telling you over and over again what a schmuck you were on the air. Let me tell you, you haven't lost it, buddy. You sound as good as you did when you were in Cincinnati. If you're looking to get back into the business, I'll do what I can to get you in on the gravy train with Big Thicket. What you call 'cookie cutter radio' ain't as bad as you think it might be."

"Thanks for the offer, but I have the feeling that I'm going to be fighting Big Thicket tooth and nail here in the next few days if what you said about a bonus was correct. For the record, I now own the radio stations in Magnolia."

"What?"

"I own the place - according to Zeke's will."

"Are you going to hang on to it?"

"Not for long, I hope. I'm looking for a buyer."

"That would explain your visit from Joe Campbell."

"I already told Campbell that he could to go to hell."

"I take it that you're still on Joe's shit list?"

"Afraid so…"

"Hate to tell you, but you might be in for a hell of a ride if you decide to keep the place. Joe has ways of getting what he wants. Not all of them are nice. He made a power grab for a station over in Davis a couple of weeks ago. The owner died; Campbell was in town contesting the will within three days. Hell, Willy Parker wasn't even cold in the ground when Campbell took over."

"Let me ask you… are you really okay with those sorts of shenanigans?"

"I'm a company man, Glenn. They pay my bills. They take care of me."

"And you look the other way, as if it never happened."

"I suppose I do," Mark said after contemplating for a few moments. "After years of living hand to mouth in this business, working for Big Thicket has been like hitting the big time. They're not perfect, but the bennies sure beat what Truman ever offered. Sure beats minimum wage and all the records you can eat. Everyone has a price, Glenn. I gave up a part of my soul, but good intentions don't pay the rent."

"So I hear…"

"Sorry to disappoint you, Glenn. Hope everything works out for you."

"Thanks Mark. If you're over in this direction in the next couple of days, call me and we can have a drink."

"I might have to come and take you up on that offer. In the meantime, watch your back. If Campbell is there and Jankowski is there, I can almost bet that one or both of them are ready to jump right in and take the stations out from under you."

"Thanks for the heads up, Mark."

After finishing the phone call, Glenn hung up and called Bill Preston.

"What do you know about Joe Campbell?"

"He's in charge of Big Thicket's northeast division based in Pittsburgh. Why?"

"He was here right after I did the show this morning and I'm concerned that he might be planning on pulling an unfortunate stunt here in the next couple of days."

"You might be right. I've heard that there'll be a meeting here in Chillicothe with Joe tonight at eight."

"I take it you're not invited…"

"I'm contract, remember? They don't like me. They think I'm colored. I do know someone who will be there, though."

"Bill, can you watch my back for me?"

"I'll see what I can do."

"I owe you one."

"I take it you're staying?"

"The way it looks, I'll be here just long enough to keep Big Thicket's hands off the place."

"Better watch yourself, Glenn, next thing you know, you'll be stuck here… enjoying every minute of it."

On the Warpath

Jack Jankowski settled into his hotel room and made a phone call.

"Brian… Jack Jankowski. How's it going?"

"Doing well, Jack, how about yourself?"

"I'll be doing better once I get some definition. Why was Joe Campbell here today? I thought Magnolia was going to be mine."

"It will be, but Joe's in charge of the region. Besides, I'm thinking about having this Glenn Michaels working for me. Green in Chillicothe piped-in a feed of Tuesday's show. Pretty impressive for someone who's been out of circulation for a while, don't you think?"

"Well… yes… but Michaels is the problem. The old man's will stipulates that Michaels gets the stations and the property free and clear."

"They're his to sell, too, right?"

"I thought he wanted to sell and get out of town, but now I'm not so sure."

"That's part of the reason I sent Joe Campbell."

"Did you know that Glenn Michaels once worked for Joe Campbell and that Joe was fired because of Glenn?"

"When was this?"

"Over thirty years ago. Campbell's held a grudge against Michaels ever since."

"How does Michaels feel about Joe Campbell?"

"The feeling's mutual. Glenn all but told Joe to go to hell, when Joe made an offer to buy this afternoon."

"Hmmmm… that won't do. Perhaps I should send Randy. I believe he and Michaels are friendly."

"Randy came in with Joe. If Randy and Michaels are friendly, you couldn't tell it by me."

"It might just be Joe. I wonder if he was out of the equation if Michaels might be more amenable to an offer."

"In my opinion, he would be much more amenable to an offer if Big Thicket were out of the equation. I get the impression that part of the reason he quit the business was because of Big Thicket."

"I'm getting a lot of that lately," Brian stated. "I presume that Mr. Michaels is unaware that you're connected with us?"

"If he knows, he hasn't said anything. If he finds out, I may have a problem."

"What do you need to move this project along, Jack?"

"I need a morning guy who can relate to this bunch of farmers and yokels."

"I'll see what I can dig up. In the meantime, I'll do what I can to keep Campbell out of your hair."

"Thanks…"

"Don't mention it."

The conversation ended. Jack brooded for a few minutes, finally deciding that he might have to take another direction to keep Glenn Michaels out of Magnolia.

Joe Campbell spent an hour in the employee lounge at the Chillicothe radio stations fuming. He wanted revenge. Of all the people he had been associated with in his long career in radio, Glenn Michaels was his least favorite. In second place was Jack Jankowski, even though Joe had no idea that it was Jack who provided the means which led to his firing from the radio station in Parkersburg.

It was mostly Glenn Michaels, though. It was Glenn Michaels who saw no point in his practical joke of having Mitchell – drunken, hare-lipped Mitchell – read a series of made-up ads to play when Joe held one his many "parties".

"Hell, it was Glenn Michaels who questioned the parties in the first place," Joe told himself. "We only did it for a bit of fun. The people I was making fun of were going to jail anyway… why not have a yuk or two or three at their expense? The catcalls under his breath in the courtroom… well, perhaps I shouldn't have, but then again, it was payback."

"I thought you went back to your hotel room," Randy Green said, interrupting Joe's train of thought. "Is everything okay?"

"I'm still pissed off about Michaels throwing our offer right back in our faces."

"What's the big deal? I tried to tell you that Glenn wouldn't bite before we walked in the door. You didn't listen."

"That fucker's been a pain in my ass since he first went to work for me in '76. Got me fired."

"Was it he who got you fired or you who got you fired? I've heard some stories about you."

Joe was starting to develop a dislike of Randy Green.

"Glenn and I were friends at one time, Joe. I've never known him to demean anyone. I'm not surprised that he doesn't really care for Big Thicket. He's suspicious. Sorry, but all you did this afternoon was to yank his chain… and he really doesn't like that. Tell you what… go back to Pittsburgh tomorrow morning and let me talk with him. I might be able to get something arranged."

"I don't want an 'arrangement', I want his ass," Joe said to himself.

"You're probably right, Randy. I'll touch base with you before I head back to Pittsburgh in the morning."

Joe behaved himself as he walked out the back door and drove away in his Big Thicket issue Chevy Impala. By the time he was out of sight of the radio station, though, he was already back on the warpath. His mind was developing a plan and he knew just who to call to help him carry it out.

Starting Over Again

She appeared to be the Earth Mother. Tricia was waiting on a bench in front of Ding's dressed in a simple blouse over a long, lightweight skirt which seemed to flow when she got up to meet Glenn.

"Doing better?"

"Yes. Actually I feel as if a weight has been lifted from me."

"You had it bottled up for way too long, you know. I sort of get the impression that the whole affair had affected your social life."

"Truth be known, you're sort of right. Hannah is the only woman I have ever genuinely made love with." "Better than any of your 'wham, bam, thank you ma'am' encounters, at least that's the impression I'm getting."

"Yep…" he agreed as he accompanied her inside.

She seemed to glide in, brushing past him ever so slightly as if she was teasing him. All through dinner, he observed her body language as they conversed about a number of subjects.

He found her to be fascinating. She exuded confidence which he found to be particularly appealing.

"What does your fortune say, Glenn?"

They had just finished their meal and paid the check. They decided to linger a short while over the remainder of their tea and the fortune cookies.

"'Hard work and perseverance pay off in the long run'. What does yours say?"

"'You will find love in an unlikely situation'."

"That's almost as lame as mine."

"Is it really? She smiled and winked at him.

"I hope you're not getting attached to me, after all-"

"You're headed back to Dallas immediately after the memorial service. You know, Magnolia Town Council voted you in as the New Zeke Collins."

"So I've been told. Jack Jankowski came by for a visit in the office a few hours ago and gave me the news."

"I could try to seduce you into staying…" She pulled on the collar of her blouse to look down at her breasts. "What do you think, girls… should we give it a try?"

"Stop that…" Glenn said in a sotto voice, barely able to contain a laugh.

"So much for 'Plan B'," she shrugged. "So my next question is what if I am finding myself becoming attached to you?"

"You might have found the wrong person to become attached to."

"I sort of don't think so," she said softly.

"You sort of could be wrong. My last girlfriend left me after three weeks. She left pissed because I couldn't service her… or didn't service her the way she wanted to be serviced."

"Demanding bitch?"

"More like I couldn't relate to her. Like with my ex in the last five years we were married. We went through the motions and that was about it. For her, foreplay was telling me to put a rubber on."

"My ex would warm up the KY before diving right in, whether I was ready or not. It wasn't my idea of romance, let me tell you. Toward the end, I finally got the idea that I wasn't the only woman he had been porking."

Glenn looked around to see who else was in the immediate area. "Ummm… maybe we should continue this conversation somewhere else?"

"That's a good idea. My place is just a couple of miles away…"

"How about we head up to Steadman Park instead?"

"I haven't been there for a while. Sure."

As they left the restaurant they were hit with humidity so thick it could almost be cut with a knife. The park wasn't much better; the only respite being the relatively cooler breezes moving up the hollows. Glenn stopped first at the fire observation tower at the top of the hill.

"Ever been up to the top?"

"Never. This is my first time here at the tower."

"You live outside of Prentiss, at least that's what I thought you said."

"I live out the state highway a ways, north and a little east… on the east side of this hill."

"And you've never been here?" Glenn shook his head. "I swear you don't know what you've missed. C'mon. Let's go up and have a look into the valley."

They went as far up the ladder as they could to look out over the valley, stretched below them. Glenn enthusiastically pointed out various landmarks as Tricia clung to him.

He wasn't certain whether she was clinging out of fear or if she just wanted to get closer to him. He was sure, though, that it was good to feel her body next to his.

When they got back down, Glenn drove down the hollow, ending up at a picnic area situated on a small islet on a small lake. They took a slow, lazy walk around the lake, pausing here and there while Glenn relived memories of his childhood and young adult forays into the park.

"I sort of get the idea that you have a lot of good memories, here."

"Yep…"

"Enough to offset the bad memories?"

Glenn stayed silent as they walked the shoreline near the creek feeding the lake. He picked up several flat stones and skipped them.

"I don't want to go on a nostalgia trip. I want to move forward with my life," he said, watching a stone make four hops before disappearing in the lake.

"We all want to look forward, Glenn. No one wants to live in the past, but at the same time, what we did in the past helps to define who we are today. We can either build on our experiences, or we can allow them to destroy us."

They continued to walk in silence on the south side of the lake. Glenn began to feel the emptiness caused by Hannah's murder which started to wash over him again. He tried not to show his feelings, but he eventually stopped and broke down in tears.

"Dammit… it… still… hurts…"

He felt her enveloping arms, wrapping around him to staunch the wound which was tearing apart his soul. "I know," Tricia whispered, "it will always hurt. We just try to remember the good times."

After comforting him for a minute or so, she continued: "The boy I was going to marry… my high school sweetheart… was killed in a car crash when he was returning home from college on Christmas vacation. It was outside of Jamestown on a piece of road nicknamed 'Death Strip'.

"He had bought a ring…"

Tricia started to cry, so he enveloped her with his arms. They held each other until the gathering darkness dictated their return.

Glenn and Tricia rolled into the parking area of the strip mall a little after nine. They were both emotionally spent. He walked her over to her car. They exchanged another hug and a polite kiss then paused to look at each other, waiting for some sort of sign.

"Not…" they tentatively spoke together. They stopped.

"I sort of know what you're thinking."

"I believe I know what you're thinking, too."

"Not yet…"

"Not yet. We need to sort some things out."

"I…"

Glenn took his index finger and placed it on her lips.

"I know. You've been saying it all along. We've been saying it all along. It seems as if I have another decision to make."

"I sort of think I do, too."

They exchanged another kiss, this time longer and slower.

"Be careful."

"Be careful."

Simmering Frustrations

Joe didn't hesitate to pull out his cell phone the moment he returned to his hotel room.

"Do you know about Thicket trying to buy the stations in Magnolia?"

"Hell yes, I know. I was there Monday, trying to talk to the old man."

"Well, the old man left the property to some punk named Michaels. I was just talking to Thompson. He's coming over on Friday to try to sort this whole thing out. I need your help. I need there to be some reason why Glenn Michaels won't be on the air on Friday morning."

"Where are you? In the 'Burgh'?"

"I'm just up the road from you in Chillicothe, cooling my jets."

"I'll come up with some muscle in the morning. Meet me in Jackson… the usual place at nine."

"I'm looking forward to seeing you, Jerry."

"Likewise, Joe."

Unrealized Consequences

Glenn slept soundly, waking up in time to be at the desk in the window of the restaurant at five fifty five.

Thursday morning's crowd was a little thicker than it was on Wednesday. Glenn noticed that people were coming into Zeke's wearing black armbands. The armbands were not only appearing on the regulars, as Glenn started to recognize them, but they were appearing on the tourists who seemed to be coming in earlier than they had previously in the week. Certainly the servers were busier and seemed to be getting bigger tips than usual.

"I hear tomorrow's gonna be our last day," a server with a substantial baby bump commented to Glenn. "Can you see if we can get work at Father Linguini's or over at Ed's?"

"Nothing's for certain, yet. I'll see what can be done, okay?"

The girl smiled and went back to work.

"Closing down Zeke's?" Glenn asked himself. He made a point of trying to follow the servers as they wound among the customers at this early hour of the morning.

There were three servers, Glenn observed, two on the floor, one behind the counter. The server who had approached him was young - early twenties - with a cute face and obviously about five months pregnant. The other floor server was a middle-aged woman who appeared to have been with the restaurant for a long time. She was quick to laugh and for the most part spent her time in a section which appeared to be frequented by the regulars. Behind the counter was Rita. She was a larger woman and was definitely in control of what went on in the establishment.

Glenn also barely caught sight of at least three people assigned to the kitchen, two cooks and a dishwasher who also served as the busboy. Then there was Sonia, the dining room manager who took care of the till and filled in wherever needed. He counted seven people who were now his responsibility.

During a commercial break Glenn summoned Sonia over to the broadcast table.

"What do these people make?"

"Ellie and Sam make a dollar above minimum plus tips," she said, indicating the girls on the floor. "Betty, behind the counter, makes three above plus tips.

"The cooks make four above, no tips and Jimmy does two above, no tips… although he is due for a raise. My salary is none of your business unless you open the books… which I guess is your privilege since you own this place now."

Glenn nodded in understanding as he mentally calculated what the payroll was costing.

"I hear you manage a store down near Dallas and that you're more than likely to run back down there at the end of the week."

"There's nothing definite, yet. I'm working with people on a way to keep this place running like Zeke did."

"You're not gonna accept Town Council's voting you in as the new Zeke?"

"I never said that and I only heard about the Council vote yesterday afternoon."

"Well, Council's here…" she indicated a table of people back in Ellie's section, "and they're likely to have a word with you after breakfast."

Glenn looked back and smiled at the people at the table. They smiled back, giving him a thumbs-up before he had to be back on the air.

He had another twenty four hours, at least, to come to a decision. He wondered how much the Council knew about his original plans. He also wondered if the Council was trying to force him into a decision to stay.

As the seven o'clock news went on, Glenn started to look to see if Tricia had made it in, yet. Her absence was conspicuous. His apprehension about Tricia was at a peak when he was approached by the Town Council.

There were just four of them. He met Steve Mulligan earlier in the week and Steve was acting as Council's spokesman.

"I suppose you've heard what we did here yesterday, Mister Michaels…"

"Yep… by the way, you can just call me Glenn."

"And you know that there's a lot riding on you, too…"

"How much… Steve, isn't it?"

"You can call me Steve…"

"How much is riding on me being the new Zeke Collins?"

Steve smiled. "We need to have a talk, just you and me, about that." He turned to the other three to dismiss them. "I'll handle it from here."

The others left, leaving Steve alone with Zeke.

"I think I can talk during breaks… you're back on in thirty seconds."

"You know the ropes pretty well, don't you?"

"I've been here with Zeke a few times and watched him. Twenty seconds."

"Do you want the job? I mean, you live here – you know everyone in town."

"Not with what I have on my plate these days, besides, I'm juggling four businesses already. Five seconds. We'll get back to this in a few minutes."

Glenn put on his headphones and was back on the air in top form in a matter of moments. Steve waited patiently until the next break.

"I'm just a business guy. My first wife… I guess you could call her that… has a degree in business management at some University in Pittsburgh. She teaches. She's also been helping me and Millie out… giving us advice on what to invest in and how to run a business once we take it over."

"And your wife is okay with that?"

"Oh, sure. Miss Katie and I had the whole thing annulled almost as soon as we hitched. We had…" Steve looked around. "Relations, and thought we had to do the right thing. We ended up in court; made the marriage go away. Katie comes by every few years to check up on us and usually steals Millie away for a day or two… I think that they're talking about me."

Steve looked over at Glenn, nodded his head and Glenn got back to his show to read a live commercial for Mulligan's IGA.

"I don't rightly know what I paid for that particular ad you just read," Steve resumed, "but I do know that if I didn't run it, I might be losing customers and that would cost me more. There are items I carry which no other market in this county or any of the surrounding counties even think about offering. I get people from as far away as Parkersburg and Cincinnati coming in on a regular basis because of Zeke's being on the radio."

"And you think I can do the same thing?"

"Zeke thought so, we think so…"

"When you say 'we', are 'we' just you and your wife?"

"We are me, Hank the Banker – that is Henry James at the Bank of

Pomeroy, Ray Thomas over at the downtown garage, Harold the police chief and Floyd over at the barbershop."

"You don't have a Floyd the Barber…"

"Nah, I just threw that in just to see if you were paying attention." Steve threw Glenn a broad grin.

Glenn smiled and shook his head and chuckled as he continued his next segment.

"Now, I just said a little bit about how Zeke helped out my IGA," Steve resumed at the next break. "The hardware store, Ed's Church and Grill and Father Linguini's all get business from outside the county because of Zeke. The antique shops over on Cherry Street, the bank… everyone in town benefits when money comes into Magnolia from outside. I have something like a hundred people who work for me. Zeke has twenty if you count the restaurant. The other businesses in town have another few hundred people who all depend on what goes on here, at this table, at this restaurant, five days a week."

Steve stayed until the seven-thirty news break.

"What I'm saying, Glenn, is that Zeke's death could leave a big hole in our economy, unless Zeke is replaced with someone as compelling as he was. Zeke knew this. That's why he searched you out. You may not think so, but Zeke put faith in your ability to continue to draw people into our little burg so that we can continue a way of life we have had for the past forty years or more."

"I understand…"

"So, you're going to be the new Zeke…"

"The jury is still out. I don't want to disappoint you by saying 'yes', then pulling out but, at the same time, I don't want to flat-out reject you. I'm flattered by the offer, but I need to look at my alternatives. The soonest I can make a firm decision will be after I do the show tomorrow."

"I see…" Steve sounded as if he was disappointed. "I'll… tell the others."

"Shit…" Glenn thought. "There's something I never really thought of – the people involved. "

"Michaels! You're on!" Earl was practically screaming at him through his headphones.

Glenn finished out the seven-thirty to eight portion of the show with the weight of the well-being of Magnolia weighing heavily on his mind.

Meeting a Deadline

"A woman needs a man like a fish needs a bicycle."

For some reason, that line seemed to get stuck in Tricia's head at around four-thirty in the morning before resonating again fifteen minutes later when she rolled out of her hammock. Perhaps it had something to do with the events of the past week, the past month, or for that matter, the past twenty years.

Her cohabitation with, marriage to and subsequent divorce from Steven was followed by a parade of men primarily interested in bedding her. Her thinking had become jaded. She had gotten to the point where she would consent to a date maybe twice a year and would usually resent having done so.

After turning on her computer, Tricia fired up the coffeemaker to fix a cup or two of decaf. The microwave told her it was four-fifty seven.

She hopped on the internet while Mr. Coffee was making his brewing noises to find that her in - box had accumulated twenty-seven items… most of them dispatched with a push of the delete key.

She cruised over to Facebook - staying there far too long - eventually reading Glenn Michaels's profile. Every detail was devoured, every piece of information sharpened her interest.

His most recent comment, made after he had gotten back to the apartment (presumably) was: "I met someone with whom I can now share my innermost secrets – finally…" There were a few snide remarks in the comments section, but one comment stood out: "If you mean you have found love, follow your heart, not your head. You deserve to be happy, Dad." The message came from Corey Michaels.

"A woman needs a man like a fish needs a bicycle."

The line started running through her head again. "What a soulless piece of advice," she thought, going after her second cup of coffee.

Sitting back down, the message from and the profile picture of Glenn's daughter greeted Tricia again, prompting her to put in a friend request before shutting down Facebook so that she could get down to the business of the day.

For the next hour, Tricia worked feverishly to complete the story she had been working on about Zeke Collins.

Zeke's viewing was scheduled for Friday night prior to the memorial service on Saturday; her story would probably be published on Friday morning as a timely tribute to the local legend.

Her story was in by eight-thirty. She hurriedly showered and dressed, not wanting to miss being with Glenn for at least the last hour of the day's show.

Evolving Revenge

Joe Campbell sat in the restaurant parking lot in Jackson. It was one of those family owned businesses which found itself well-situated when the main highways skirted Jackson a few decades previously. Just after he arrived, another Big Thicket issue Chevy Impala pulled into the parking lot and stopped in the space next to where Joe was parked.

"Joe… good to see you," the driver of the other car stated as he greeted the man from Pittsburgh, "I have here a couple of friends who may help us in our endeavors today. Let's just call them Frank One and Frank Two so that we don't get too personal."

Joe shook the men's hands, trying to look to see if there were actually eyes on the other side of their sunglasses.

"What do you have in mind doing?"

"With Frank and Frank, you might be better off not knowing."

"I don't want any rough stuff, Jerry. Just enough to scare this fellow Michaels away from Magnolia long enough for us to move in."

"We intimidate, Joe. Most of the time it works like a charm."

A short time later, both cars headed west on the Cross-State Highway toward Magnolia. They pulled into town, parking about a block away from Zeke's. Joe sat in his car to wait until the show was over.

Within seven minutes, Jerry Temples and the two Franks came walking briskly from the restaurant soon after the town cop went in. Jerry had a word with the hoodlums before going over to and getting in Joe's car.

"We're going to Chillicothe," Jerry announced, "something's come up."

Joe started the car and drove north out of town, over the causeway before he dared ask why.

"Just after we went in, did you notice a middle-aged broad come out of the restaurant headed to the radio station?"

"No, not particularly, why?"

"I know her. I met her in Jackson on Saturday night. The bitch told me to fuck off."

"What?"

"I just told you. Her name is Tish or Trish or Tricia… Tricia. That's it. Her name is Tricia Knox. She's a free-lance writer. We had a date last Saturday night in Jackson and she dissed me - told me to fuck off. Anyway, she left just after we went in and seemed to signal that Michaels fellow in the window. She's probably fucking that prick."

"You're telling me that it's personal?"

"Yeah, it's personal, all right. Bitch tells me to go fuck myself, I'll fuck with her right back."

Joe smiled in satisfaction. Both of them had personal scores to settle now.

Revenge would be sweet.

Alternate Plans

Tricia didn't show up at Zeke's until nearly nine.

"Work…" she explained when she came up to give him a polite peck on the cheek. There was a slight ripple of recognition in the room from the regulars.

She flashed him a sign, folding down her middle and ring fingers, indicating 'I love you' in sign language.

He returned her gesture before finishing out the hour on an upbeat note.

They looked each other in the eye. For the first time in a long time, Glenn felt no threat when faced with an attractive woman. She was his equal. Both of them knew it.

That part of them had to be put on hold for a while, though. Glenn still had the rest of his show to run. Tricia's usual booth was occupied, so she took a seat at the counter and ordered breakfast.

At about 9:20 Glenn noticed Tricia deliberately avoiding being seen by three men who came in the front door. Once they passed her, she went to the till, paid her check and scurried out the door as quickly as she was able.

Less than a minute later, a message appeared on Glenn's cell phone: ***Goons from Big Thicket. Will explain later.***

Glenn texted back: ***Should I be worried?***

Yes

Wait for me in the apartment he texted back.

Glenn kept a poker face while he was getting ready for the last half hour of the show. He looked over at the new arrivals. They appeared to be conspicuous given their dress, their sunglasses and the lack of the black armbands. One of them seemed to give him a cold, hard stare back.

Just as he wrapped the segment, the three men approached the broadcast table.

"You've done your last show, Michaels. We're taking over from here."

"Excuse me?"

"You heard me, Michaels. You're done. Go. Pack your bags and disappear. WZEK is now being programmed by Big Thicket Broadcasting."

"Since when?"

"Since whenever it was when Zeke died. There was an agreement in place giving rights to this station over to Big Thicket effective the Monday after the old man's funeral. The sooner you head back to Dallas, the sooner the transition is going to take place."

"I believe that my lawyer… Zeke's lawyer; will have something to say about this. In the meantime, I'll thank you to get the hell out of here and out of my face before I call the law."

"Harold's already on his way, Mister Michaels," Betty called out from behind the counter, "along with Roy and some of his deputies from the county seat."

"Have it your way, Michaels… but mark my words: You will not be on the air tomorrow. Joe Campbell told me that he would personally guarantee it."

The trio started to leave as Harold walked in.

"Gentlemen…" he said as he stopped them. "I hope you had a good meal… Betty, have they paid their checks?"

"We were just about to," the spokesman grumbled. He pulled a fifty dollar bill out of his wallet and slapped it down next to the till. "Keep the fucking change, bitch…" The three shoved their way past Harold and out the door.

"Damn, Harold. You couldn't have come at a better time."

"Good to be of service. Betty and that writer friend of yours called and said that there might be trouble when you got off the air."

Betty was grinning ear to ear. Sam was in the process of cleaning the table and had found another fifty dollar bill along with the unpaid check.

"You keep that, hon…" Betty called out. "You might need it before this is all over."

"I wasn't mentioned, was I?"

Tricia was visibly shaken by the close encounter which she had escaped.

"Why would you be mentioned?"

"The one guy, Jerry Temples. He was in here the other day up in the lobby demanding to see Zeke."

"When was this?"

"Monday, just after you and I met. I had a date with him last Saturday night which… broke up just after he announced that he intended to screw my brains out. I suggested that he go fuck himself. The bastard left me with the check."

"How in the hell did you get involved with someone from Big Thicket?"

"I had no idea who he was at the time we made the date. It was one of those computer match-up things, you see. It's complicated."

"Some of those sites encourage dishonesty."

"I sort of figured that out."

Both of them laughed. "You've done it too, haven't you?"

"Gone to a dating site? Yep… Out-and-out told a woman that I was going to screw her brains out while I was on a first date?" Glenn chuckled. "I'm not quite that crude. Not to say that I haven't been propositioned by a woman on the first date…"

"Did you take advantage of such a proposition?"

"Once… but I figured out that I probably wouldn't be able to satisfy her needs in the long run."

"You're only human…"

"So are you."

Glenn took her in his arms and they held on to each other for several minutes.

"When we met, I instinctively knew that I could trust you, Glenn. Richard told me."

"No… you told you. Just like with Hannah and me. It was all me. I was the only person who gave me permission to trust you. Be careful."

"Yes, be careful."

Are you coming downstairs now or after you've fucked? Glenn looked at his cell phone. It was a message from Jack.

We're on our way & none of your business. Glenn hit the Send button just as he opened the back door to the second floor studios. Jack, Earl, Harold and Greg were in Zeke's office waiting when Glenn and Tricia arrived.

"Jack… Greg… she's in on the deal… whatever that deal ends up being."

"You still haven't decided, then?" Greg had a look of concern on his face.

"I have another week."

"No you don't, Glenn. Zeke's former lawyer was in Probate Court the first thing this morning arguing that Zeke's will was invalid. The judge has set a hearing for tomorrow. You need to make a commitment in the next twenty-four hours."

"I need more time…"

"You don't have more time. I can go and ask the judge to delay until Saturday morning, but I don't think I can get that extension unless you go on the air tomorrow and do your full show."

"Big Thicket's goons were in just a short while ago. They made it clear that they don't want me on the air tomorrow. I think they'll do something to try to keep me off."

"Who were 'they', Glenn?"

"There were three of them who came up to the broadcast table when I was wrapping up this morning. Tricia told me that one of them was someone named Jerry Temples."

"He's the site manager at Gallipolis. He has a reputation as a troublemaker," Jack told them.

Glenn looked over at Tricia. She was rolling her eyes.

"Knowing Temples, if he said he would keep you off the air tomorrow, he will find a way to keep you off the air tomorrow by hook or by crook," Jack told them.

"An old buddy of mine told me that he has reason to believe that they might try to shut down the transmitter at the site," Glenn offered.

"Won't do us much good if they cut power to the building," Earl pitched in.

"That's why there's a Plan B, Earl." Jack wore a smug smile on his face. "Zeke and I thought that Big Thicket might try something desperate at some point, so we made some provisions. First and foremost, we have a duplicate remote studio set up here in town at Father Linguini's."

"Steve's place, right?" Glenn asked.

"Exactly. All we need to do is to have a duplicate download of station records, ad copy, commercials and music, hook into the set-up at Linguini's and we're on the air… provided we can get a carrier."

"What if we can't or what if we get delayed, Jack? When does the judge decide that the Big Thicket people are right?"

"Knowing Big Thicket, they probably have someone in their pocket, a bailiff or the sheriff, who will sign the proper documents no later than five after six, Glenn… although Greg might be able to buy us some time."

"I'm headed to Federal Court in Columbus to file a letter of intent, challenging Big Thicket's intended takeover if or when the Probate Court decides to go against us. It's a long shot, though. It may buy us time, it may not. We'll just have to see."

Everyone looked around at everyone else in the room, expecting somebody to say something.

"I'll be ready to go on the air tomorrow morning," Glenn declared.

"I'll get him there," Tricia promised

"I'll be ready to run the boards at Father Linguini's if necessary," said Earl.

"Harold and I will stand by with the paperwork if it becomes necessary," Greg told everyone.

"Glenn… I'll do whatever needs to be done to have the show ready for you to run in the morning." Jack looked directly at Glenn. "If we can get through the next twenty-four hours in one piece, I'll find the next Zeke Collins myself and release you to go back to Texas."

There was a collective sigh of relief as the meeting broke up, leaving Glenn, Greg and Tricia alone in the office.

"Glenn…"

"What, Greg?"

"There's something here you need to see."

Greg produced a manila folder from inside his briefcase.

"I had Norm Shor at the bank in Chillicothe take a look at Zeke's books for me. Zeke loaned them to me to study."

"Zeke didn't miss a trick, did he?"

"Apparently not. You know how to read a financial report?"

"Yep… that's why Beasley pays me the big bucks back in Texas."

Greg opened up the folder to point out the bottom line of the report. Glenn looked, did a double take and mouthed "wow!"

"There's a lot more at stake here than I first thought. Take a second or third look before you definitely decide to leave."

Greg left the report with Glenn before heading up to see the judge in Federal Court.

"Glenn…"

"Yes, Tricia…"

"I'm still concerned about Jack. He wants this place and he wants you to go to Texas."

"I'm concerned, too. I had a conversation the other day with an old friend who seems to think that Jack's working for Big Thicket. I don't completely trust him."

"Your mistrust may be well placed. Zeke told me that he only believed half of everything Jack said, and even took what he believed with a grain of salt. For instance, Jack tells everyone he raises horses outside of Lexington. I have sources that he lives in subsidized senior housing, living on Social Security.

"He came here to run the morning show when Zeke was recovering from his heart attack last year and has been coming back on an almost regular basis ever since. Zeke felt sorry for him and paid him as a consultant out of his own pocket. He might feel that his back is against a wall, now that Zeke's gone. Maybe he thinks that you'll continue to pay him like Zeke did."

"I intended to give him something for his troubles once all this is over," Glenn stated.

"I thought you might. Now the only question is whether you'll stay or leave. You seem to be wavering between your choices."

"The reason I'm wavering is that I'm not really sure any more what I should do. From the looks of the books here, there's too much at stake to make any definite plans on going back just yet, if I decide to go back at all."

Glenn looked at Tricia and smiled. Both of them knew that Glenn was unlikely to go back to Texas.

Covering Bets

"Earl…"

Jack cornered the board operator as they went down the back stairs together.

"I need your help this evening."

"What is it, Jack?"

"I need you to come with me to get the equipment from Linguini's. I think that there's a joker in the deck who might try to sabotage tomorrow's show… even if power *is* cut to the building."

"Who would it be?"

"I'm suspecting the Lawyer."

"Well, Zeke hired him…"

"After years of having Alvin Bates handle his legal affairs? Think about it. This fellow Fischer *has* to have some sort of angle to become Zeke's legal advisor less than ten days before he died. Why… that's the question, Earl… why?"

Earl wore the expression of a deer caught in a pair of headlights when Jack asked the question. Doubt crept into him while they were making their way to the bottom of the stairs.

"I need your help, Earl. I already have Steve Carver helping me, but I need you, too."

"Okay," Earl nodded in agreement.

"What I need you to do is to meet me tonight so that we can take the equipment out of Father Linguini's and into the back of my station wagon so we can set it up elsewhere at a moment's notice. Think we can handle that?"

"No problem, except…"

"Except what, Earl?"

"Except I usually go bowling on Thursday nights."

"The perfect cover, don't you see? I'll pick you up at the alley, say, eight-thirty?"

"Okay, Jack…"

"Remember… don't tell anybody. If anyone else finds out about the plan, the lawyer will find a way to fuck up everything and the next thing you know, everyone in this building will be without a job… including you. Understand?"

"I understand, Jack. You can count on me!"

Jack had followed Earl to his car. They shook hands on the deal and then Earl headed home to get ready for his rendezvous.

After Earl left, Jack casually strolled to the bank building and headed upstairs to an office on the second floor.

He was expected.

Jack was greeted by a thin, angular man in his late seventies wearing a crew cut which dated back to the 1950s.

"I take it that it was you in Probate Court this morning, Alvin."

"All you have to do, Jack, is to keep him off the air."

"I've made arrangements to see that Michaels is detained, or at least delayed in the morning."

"Nothing illegal, I would hope…"

"Well, if it comes down to it, I'm sure you can come up with a solid defense, counselor."

"Just don't play rough with anyone, okay, Jack?"

"You have my word…" Jack shook hands with Alvin Bates to seal the deal.

"It should all be over soon after we go in front of the judge, Jack. Congratulations. I'm sure that Magnolia will continue to prosper under your leadership."

"I'm sure it will, my friend, I'm sure it will…"

Coming to a Decision

"Are you going to take Jack up on his offer?" Tricia asked just to make sure that what she felt just moments earlier was accurate.

He silently took inventory. He had said goodbye to Hannah and he had fulfilled an egotistical desire which he should not have put on his list of ten in the first place. He was satisfied, but at the same time, he was placed in several quandaries.

Besides, something didn't seem quite right.

His first riddle was sitting across the desk from him. Tricia Knox was the unexpected find. Before he came to Magnolia, he was positive that once he had purged himself of Hannah Smith, he would be able to return to Dallas to find someone decent who would put up with him. His plan was for the two of them to settle down and enjoy the remainder of their lives together in relative bliss.

Tricia came along to abbreviate the process. She just had to be a witch. Almost from the first moment he saw her sitting at the back of Zeke's, he knew that she was someone special. Besides, they were both bruised and battered from previous relationships. It had to count for something.

So, what to do about Tricia Knox? The only time he had felt such a connection to a woman, any woman, was in a second floor nursery above a church meeting hall… and that was after years of knowing her. He had known Tricia Knox only since Monday.

Glenn recalled a sermon he had heard several years prior about the Apostles meeting with Jesus after his death. The priest related the Biblical experience to that of meeting his own wife for the first time… he, as the Apostles, "knew without knowing" that this was the one person meant for him to spend his life with.

Glenn knew without knowing that Tricia Knox was that one someone he was searching for. "So much for an extended period of loneliness," he thought.

Tricia wasn't his only concern. He was starting to fall in love with Magnolia again. The people coming into Zeke's the past couple of mornings seemed aware of the conflict roiling around in his mind. There were little gestures of support for what he was doing. It was genuine support, not something orchestrated from the outside.

Steve Mulligan's reminder of what having WZEK meant to him, his family and to the people who worked for him weighed heavily on his mind. There wasn't nearly the sense of community back in Dallas that there was here. Bob Beasley's generous compensation for the events which propelled Glenn to Magnolia was about the highest point in the entire time he had worked for the Beasley brothers. Glenn didn't dislike Bob Beasley or his co-workers at the store… he just didn't feel as attached to them as he felt he was becoming attached to the people he was meeting in Magnolia.

There was also the matter of trust. The thought occurred to Glenn that everyone in Magnolia trusted him. That sense of trust was mutual. He was particularly mindful of the trust placed in him by Zeke and Jessica Collins. He looked down at the folder on the desk in front of him – a report from Greg's accountant regarding the worth of Zeke's legacy.

The worth of Zeke's holdings was substantial. In fact those holdings were almost more than Glenn could believe for a town as small as Magnolia.

Glenn started to understand why he had been chosen to fill Zeke Collins' shoes.

He looked up at Tricia.

"What's said here stays here," he reminded her.

She nodded.

Her hunch that Glenn Michaels was going to stay in Magnolia had finally been confirmed.

Running Away

"We need to leave here. You need the space and I need to be with you."

Tricia took Glenn's arm and led him toward the back stairway.

"Where are you taking me?"

"Away from here. Somewhere. Anywhere."

They went downstairs and got in her Mustang. She put down the top and made a beeline out of town headed north, Springsteen blaring from the sound system. She looked over to see him smiling as they squirted up toward Prentiss.

"You like The Boss, don't you?"

"How could you tell?"

"You were playing him the other day when we went up to the cemetery."

"Yep... you're right."

"I still get goosebumps every time I hear 'Born to Run'."

"Me too. I met him when he was in Athens in '75."

"Really..."

"He was hanging out in a bar the day before a concert. 'Born to Run' was a mega hit at the time."

"Ever get an autograph?"

"I should have. I still have a promotional 45 of his first release.

"Is it worth anything?"

"Maybe, but I ain't letting it go. I've never willingly let go of anything I've really cared for."

They drove through Prentiss, top down, Springsteen on the CD player and all smiles.

"Where are we going?" he asked as they drove north out of Prentiss on the state highway.

"My place. We're going to get naked this afternoon."

"What?"

"We need to get naked and connect with each other."

"You're joking, right?"

"I'm serious."

"We hardly know each other."

"I know. I can't think of a way to know you better in a short time, so…"

"So you've gone insane. Take me back."

"No," she laughed.

"Take – me – back."

Tricia sensed that Glenn was getting frustrated.

"But Glenn, I love you and I want to have my way with you," she crooned.

"I'm not going to ruin a perfectly good relationship by having to perform like a monkey at your command."

She drove in silence, casting a glance in Glenn's direction. She gave him a mischievous smile every few minutes, until she reached the driveway of the house she was renting. She turned in, stopped the car and shut off the ignition.

"Just last Saturday I had the Date from Hell. That sleazy Temples guy who seemed okay on the internet made it clear that he wanted to get in my pants even before dinner started. If he'd have been the first guy to try to take advantage of me in the fifteen years since I've been divorced… well, he wasn't."

"I have no intention of taking advantage of you like I've…"

"I know what you're saying. Your actions speak louder than words. I wouldn't have come this far with you if I didn't somehow trust you. Good relationships are based on trust."

She unbuckled her seat belt to lean in his direction.

"Now, that doesn't mean that I don't have intentions of taking advantage of you… I have needs, too. It's just that I don't see you as being a cheap, tawdry affair, Glenn Michaels…"

"I'm good with that," he smiled. "I've been involved in more cheap, tawdry affairs than I care to recount. Part of why I came up here was to break with my past so that I could find something, someone more substantial than just a plain old fuck."

"I love it when you talk dirty to me," she laughed. "We're here, by the way. You may as well come in for a little bit before we head up to Chillicothe to get you the suit you'll need for the viewing and the funeral."

She kissed her finger then placed that kiss on his forehead.

"Can we say it now?"

Glenn had unfastened his seat belt to face Tricia.

"We've been saying it already."

"I know… and that's why you're staying."

A warm feeling coursed through Tricia as she reached over the console of her Mustang to give him a light kiss on the lips.

"First base," she whispered.

Randy's Problem

"Randy, this is personal. This thing ends here, no later than tomorrow. I ain't going back to Pittsburgh without owning WZEK and putting Glenn Michaels' head on a pike."

Randy Green was literally pinned inside his office by Joe Campbell. Joe had been making Randy's life miserable for most of the morning into the afternoon.

"That son of a bitch went over my head and had me fired from one of the best gigs I've ever had before Big Thicket came along. This is payback."

Joe was pacing back and forth attempting to burn off energy.

"I'm telling you. I had a perfectly good thing going until Truman told me to hire Glenn Michaels. I did it as a favor so that Truman's buddy, Zeke, would stay out of some sort of trouble by having Michaels around. I found out later that Michaels was involved with an under-aged girl."

"This would have been just after he got out of college, right?"

"Just a kid fresh out of college… wet behind the ears… wouldn't listen to instruction. That kid would go off half-cocked with his ideas with no notion of what it might cost the people involved."

The intercom came to life. "There's a call for Mr. Campbell on line five…"

"Thanks, Trudy… Joe, you can take it here," Randy told him.

Joe Campbell reached for the telephone and quietly held a conversation for a minute or so while Randy waited, uncomfortable with Joe's tirade against Glenn. Despite the animosity which had crept up between them over the years, Randy felt that deep down; Glenn Michaels was still his friend.

There was a smile on Joe's face when he finished with his phone call.

"That was Mr. Carver, my eyes and ears down in Magnolia. It seems as if my planned interruption of the last Zeke Collins radio show may not be necessary. For one, Mr. Michaels and Mr. 'Jack Jay' know about our plan to keep Michaels off the air tomorrow morning and are taking counter measures. To top that off, Mr. Michaels still hasn't made up his mind about whether or not he's going to stay."

"So he still might…"

"I've taken up a little insurance policy, Randy… Michaels has been seen with a reporter who was working on a story about Zeke. We're planning to throw a little scare into her tonight, hoping we can convince her to convince Mr. Michaels to quit and go home.

"I would think that is a little underhanded."

"This is war, Mr. Green. Anything goes."

Joe Campbell picked up a folio he had left on Randy Green's desk and turned to leave. "I hope you have the stomach for what we're about to do. If you don't, I have your replacement in mind."

With that, he left. Randy collapsed in his chair, relieved that his unwanted visitor had finally gone. After waiting ten minutes, he left his office, going out of the building by the back door and walking the two and a half blocks to the city park. He pulled out his cell phone after finding a place to sit down.

"Bill, this is Randy."

"Yeah, what's up?"

"This whole Big Thicket thing's gone out of control."

"I tried to tell you that it would eventually happen when they came and took over."

Randy let out a sigh. He knew that Bill was right. "Yes you did. I didn't listen and I owe you an apology. I owe one to Glenn, too. Joe Campbell just left my office a few minutes ago fussing and fuming. This whole Zeke thing in Magnolia isn't about another acquisition; it's about revenge against Glenn."

"Revenge?"

"Yes… apparently Glenn had Joe Campbell fired, or did something that Campbell didn't like which resulted in his getting fired. What do you know about it?"

"You're on your cell phone, right?"

"I'm in the park."

"I'll be there in ten minutes."

It was a long ten minutes until Bill Preston came by in an ancient green Jeep pickup truck and motioned for Randy to get in. A few minutes later they were on the bypass headed west toward Frankfort.

"Short and sweet, Glenn Michaels started a talk show in Parkersburg almost by accident. You've heard him tell the story, haven't you?"

Randy shook his head. "I don't remember Glenn ever telling that story."

"Joe was fired for taking bonus money that Truman Howell sent to Joe to give to Glenn," Bill told his passenger. "You and I both know that Glenn's network material and that Big Thicket would stand to make a fortune in advertising if he were to join the network.

"You know, we've gone over this before and I've tried to get Glenn back on the air, maybe on a network of his own. Joe knows that Glenn is network material, too, but this damn grudge of his has kept him from ever bringing Glenn to the attention of the Big Thicket higher ups. He's actually deliberately worked to get Glenn off and keep him off the air, all because he started his talk show career by accident.

"If Joe Campbell's bosses or if Brian Thompson himself came here, listened, and found Glenn Michaels working a morning show and if it's learned that Joe Campbell has sandbagged Glenn for all these years, there's gonna be hell to pay. If Glenn is on the air tomorrow morning and if Thompson from Texas hears him, most likely Joe will lose his job, his pension and any chance of working in radio ever again."

"He started his talk show career by accident?" Randy asked, raising his voice to be heard above the noise of the Jeep. "Glenn told me about it. Some smart ass called him at four-something in the morning when he was working overnights at Truman Howell's radio station in Parkersburg, wanting to mouth off on the air. Glenn let him on and the conversation snowballed. Within a week, Glenn had the hottest show in Parkersburg between midnight and six in the morning. Joe was the manager of the station… he was pissed."

"Imagine that… he's always had a temper…"

"Anyhow, Joe didn't find out until the show was in its third week… and double pissed because some guy that Truman knew out of Florida heard some tape and was impressed. Joe's fucked with Glenn now and then ever since."

Randy was quiet as the truck approached the Frankfort exit.

"Something else you may want to know is that the someone in Florida was most likely Wild Jack Jankowski."

"Jankowski was down there yesterday when we went to the station to make an offer. Joe mentioned that he and Glenn had made plans to move the show in case power was cut to the building in Magnolia."

"I know Jack. He probably has some angle which will benefit him…"

"Do you still think that Glenn Michaels has the potential for syndication?"

Bill nodded his head while rolling up the exit ramp. "You've heard him on the air the past couple of days… he's a natural. Glenn and I talked about it a few years back when he was in Cincinnati and more recently at about the time his divorce from Alice became final.

"I've had conversations with other people about it, too… mostly Zeke. I got the distinct impression that Zeke tried to soft-sell Glenn on the idea of living in Magnolia and doing a syndicated talk show from there within the past two to three years. Other than to try to lure Glenn Michaels to Magnolia to do a talk show, there was no reason for Zeke to maintain that third floor apartment above the radio station. He did it specifically for Glenn."

Randy thought for a few moments while Bill negotiated the intersection. "I'm putting in my two week's notice with Big Thicket effective Monday. I've had it with the bullshit," he finally declared.

"Good for you." Bill had essentially made a U-turn at the Frankfort exit and was headed back toward Chillicothe. "Can you hold off long enough on your resignation to run some interference tomorrow and possibly on Monday, too?"

"Joe's said he's not going to do anything tomorrow… most likely he'll try something tonight. He's most likely going to target the reporter… Knox. Joe has a mole in the station who's told him that it looks like Glenn will be flying the coop after the funeral on Saturday. The plan is to throw a scare into the Knox woman in hopes that she will make certain that Glenn goes south and she goes with him."

"There's the possibility that Joe Campbell could be fucking with you, too. He probably knows that you know Glenn and he could find it very easy to keep you enough off balance to stop you from tipping him off."

"There is that. I guess the best thing for me to do at this point is to talk with Glenn."

"He doesn't trust you since you signed on with Big Thicket, you know."

"I don't blame him. Can you talk with him; maybe get the door open a little for me?"

"I suppose… meet me tonight at the Cross Keys just after the band starts at eight. Glenn will be there. I know him. He's predictable."

A little over ten minutes later, Randy was deposited back in Chillicothe City Park. He quietly returned to his office. He had had a good ten years with Big Thicket. It was a secure job, a job he could count on, a job with a retirement plan. At the same time, there was opportunity about twenty miles down the road.

He opened his laptop to start to compose a letter of resignation. He held out hope that he could meet with Glenn Michaels and convince him to give him the job he would need once he left Joe Campbell and company.

Proposal

It was a modest house, set back from the road and private. There was a broad screened-in front porch which afforded a view of the road below without passersby being able to see who was there.

"Nice place. You said you rented this?"

"I've rented this place for about five years now. There's a new landlord, though… I hope he's nice enough to let me keep this place… it's nice and private. Allows me to indulge in… well, it allows me to indulge."

"I take it that this is one of Zeke's properties…"

Tricia smiled and nodded.

Glenn walked in the door he noted a purple bathrobe placed on a hook near the door. He almost asked why but didn't.

"I need to dress in something a little more… dressy if we're going shopping. Come and talk with me while I change if you'd like…" Tricia disappeared into a room to the side of the hall which seemed to run the length of the house.

"I'm okay… I might just putter my way into the kitchen."

"You go right ahead. You won't find much in the way to eat; besides, it will only take me a minute."

He glanced in the open doorway of the room where she had disappeared as he walked toward the back of the house. She was naked, about to pull a dress over her head.

"I'm sorry," Glenn apologized when she caught him looking at her.

"No big deal, I caught your backside the other day, and your front side, too, for that matter. I guess we're even now. I usually run around here naked most of the time. It's the indulgence I talked about earlier."

"Why dirty clothes if you don't have to, right?"

Tricia laughed as she came into the kitchen right behind Glenn. "You, too?"

"When I hit fifty, I started indulging myself, too. It seemed only practical; especially since I was living alone. I also hate doing laundry."

"Same here. I have a pretty good sized-back yard and lots of privacy. I take advantage of it."

He looked in the back yard to see a large deck with a hammock and a hot tub. The yard itself was well manicured with a large garden area off to one corner.

"Impressive…"

He felt her come up from behind, putting her arm around his waist as she drew up next to him. He wrapped his arm around her. Both of them squeezed automatically.

"I want to keep my garden," she whispered.

"I want to keep you, too," she added after pausing a few seconds.

"I know. I wanted to take you with me, but you're already planted here."

They squeezed each other again. Time didn't seem important to them at the moment.

Tricia's cell phone rang.

"Damn…" she muttered. She let go of Glenn to go and answer her phone.

He went out on the deck to better survey the landscape.

A few minutes later, she came out with a look of concern on her face.

"My editor wants the scoop on Zeke's replacement to go along with the story I've already submitted. She thinks I may be getting involved with him."

"Well… are you?"

"I think you know the answer."

Glenn and Tricia turned to face each other. Suddenly Glenn's world had shrunk to just the two of them. Even the sounds of a southern Ohio summer afternoon faded in to the background. He knew the answer. He couldn't avoid the inevitability any longer.

"I know… and it had me torn in two. I wanted to go home and I wanted to stay with you."

"I will stay with you, Glenn Michaels. Wherever you go, whatever you decide, I want to stay with…"

Before she could say another word, Glenn had swept her up, held her tight and engaged her in a deep, soulful kiss.

"I never want to let you go," he told her when the kiss was over. "Marry me."

"I was going to ask you the same thing, you jerk. Yes."

"You've just asked someone to marry you who you've known for less than a week," he heard a voice telling him amid their celebration. "It may be the stupidest thing you've ever done, but on the other hand, it may be the best thing you've ever done."

Glenn Michaels wasn't sure who was doing the talking.

Evading and Abetting

"Are you planning on being at the Keys this evening?"

"Bill, you know me… I'm in town, the Astonishers are playing… of course I'm going to be there. I'm predictable, remember?"

Glenn looked over at Tricia as she was driving him on the back roads toward Chillicothe.

"I just wanted to make sure. There are a couple of things going on which you might want to know about. For one, Randy Green says he's jumping ship."

"Why?"

"He told me that he's tired of Big Thicket's bullshit."

"Bill, he's been saying that for years."

"This time I don't think he's kidding. Joe Campbell's been giving him grief all morning then told him that the main reason he's going after you is for revenge. That's when Randy decided he'd had enough."

"What else?"

"Randy wants to meet with you… at the Keys, tonight."

"We'll see if we can swing something. So, is the commando raid still on for tonight?"

"Randy thinks it's off, or at least he says that Joe told him it was off. Hard to tell. Something was said about trying to put a scare into that reporter friend of yours, Tricia Knox."

"That's not surprising. Goons from Big Thicket were in Magnolia earlier this morning making threats. You know of a guy named Jerry Temples?"

"I've seen him a few times in and out of here. Gives me the creeps. Runs Big Thicket's operation in Gallipolis, I believe."

"Temples was at Zeke's this morning with a couple of other guys. Tricia told me that she and Temples had a date the other night – a date which didn't go down so well. Maybe Campbell is working with Temples on some sort of twisted revenge dealie. I want to be prepared."

"I can camp out at the transmitter tonight, just in case."

"Thanks, Bill. Can you meet me at my parent's place in a couple of hours? We can have dinner then head over to the Keys before you head to the transmitter."

"It sounds reasonable, especially when you're buying. This sounds like the kind of crazy scheme I told you you'd be involved with on Monday, remember?"

"And I've already paid the bet, remember? By the way, the crazy scheme just got crazier. I just got engaged."

"You've gotta be shittin' me!"

"Sorry, pal, but this time it's for real."

"The reporter?"

"I guess I'm transparent, too. I'll give you a call when I'm on my way up. See you later, Bill."

The familiar red and white smokestack from the paper mill was coming into view as Glenn and Bill were finishing their phone call. Tricia plowed straight through on the business route instead of taking the bypass to get to the mall on the north edge of town. He found a suit he liked at a department store almost immediately. Tricia was a little harder to please, finally settling on a conservative dark blue dress.

They went back into town where Glenn shared some of his favorite haunts and views. Eventually they headed up to Grandview Cemetery to see where Glenn's parents were buried.

"The shot glasses. You came here the other day, didn't you?" Tricia remarked.

"Yes, I did. I came up here Monday afternoon."

"Did they ever know about Hannah?"

"Dad knew before he died that there was friction between Alice and me. He may have known that I had been in contact with someone else, but if he did, he never let on.

"If mom knew, she never said anything. My trips to Magnolia to see Zeke were just that to her… trips to Magnolia to see Zeke."

They stood for a long while soaking up the view of the Paint Creek Valley below them, their hands clasped, each lost in their own thoughts until they were interrupted by the sound of a car coming up the cemetery road. Glenn looked back to see a hulking old red Matador coming up and parking right behind Tricia's Mustang.

"If you two would get your heads out of the clouds, maybe you could come and talk for a while."

Glenn and Tricia walked to the car.

"Bill! Brenda! How the hell are you?"

"Damn good, Glenn… you knew that… so what's the plan for tonight?"

"Cool it here a moment. I haven't had a chance to introduce you to Tricia, yet, have I?"

"Well, I figure you might have done it at one point or another. Hey, Tricia…" Bill reached out to shake her hand. "I've met you before… at the Keys… you write features for whoever'll buy them, right?"

"Yes; if I recall, your wife was anxious to get you away from me. Hi Brenda. Good to see you, too. I'm Tricia Knox."

The Prestons were out of their car just moments later. Tricia and Brenda took off down the lane while Glenn and Bill talked.

"So, is the plan the same as it was earlier this afternoon?"

"Yep… If Brenda can spare you, you'll spend the night at the transmitter to help prevent any monkey business. Is that okay?"

"I'm pretty sure, yeah. I haven't heard back from Randy, though, and I'm a little worried. Joe's Impala was back in front of the station when I drove by just now, along with another Big Thicket issued Impala with a Lawrence County tag."

"Jerry Temples, most likely."

"He's been known to provide muscle for Big Thicket."

"According to Tricia, he's an asshole, too. She ditched him on a blind date last Saturday."

"We could be in for more trouble than we asked for. Word around Thicket is that Temples holds on to grudges."

"I'll keep that in mind."

Glenn looked to see Brenda and Tricia laughing at some inside joke.

"Bill, have you ever hear of someone called Jack Jay or Wild Jack Jay?"

"Yeah. He was a point man for Thicket down in Kentucky for a while. Retired, supposedly… got his start here in Chillicothe back after the flood of '59… came over from Vinton County. I've heard that he's been hobnobbing in the area, lately."

"Jack was consulting with Zeke just before he died on Tuesday. One or the other decided that I would be Zeke's replacement."

"Really?"

"Yep… it was most likely Zeke, though. Jack made an offer to buy the stations from me the other day, probably as a proxy for Thicket."

"You own Zeke's stations, now?"

"Yep… according to Zeke's will, I own half of Fuller County."

"I'll be damned."

"Anyway, Jack made an offer to buy the place. I'm wondering if he might have had plans of his own."

"From what I hear, Jack has a hard time rubbing two nickels together," Bill told Glenn. "If he offered more than a couple of thousand, he has to have someone backing him up… besides, he's a borderline alcoholic… at least that's what I've heard."

"So he probably has been working as a proxy for Thicket."

"It's possible. Jack has lots of contacts in the business… contacts with money. He could be fronting any number of interests. If it is Thicket, there might be a war a brewing. Thicket's owner has reportedly wanted the property in Magnolia for years. My understanding is that he worked there at one time and wants the place as a nostalgia piece. There's most likely a lot of money at stake, too. Brian Thompson has been known to provide incentives if he wants something done, and people literally fight for those incentives when they become available. That would explain Joe and Jerry. Tell me… has the site manager from Portsmouth been up yet?"

"I seem to recall something about someone from Portsmouth being up, yes."

"Hmmmm… wouldn't surprise me to find someone from the head office in Texas up here tomorrow, maybe even Brian Thompson himself."

"Sounds like there's a mess going on."

"Sure is…" Bill paused a beat. "Are you sure she's not working for Thicket?"

"Tricia? The thought never crossed my mind."

"How long have you known her?"

"I met Tricia on Monday. It's Thursday. I've all but popped the question… scratch that, I did pop the question a couple of hours ago.

I wouldn't have done it if I thought there was any funny business going on."

Bill chuckled. "You already told me. You know I thought ever since you broke up with Alice that you were going to be a charter member of the 'He-Man Woman Hater's Club'!"

Glenn nodded his head. "Sometimes you never know…"

"So I suppose with all this schemin' and talk of marryin' you intend on staying here."

"Yep… going to mean a big adjustment, but I'm staying put."

Bill gave his long-time friend a bear hug.

"Good to have you back here, buddy. It's been way too long!"

Brenda and Tricia had made it back from their private chat in time to overhear the last part of Bill and Glenn's conversation. After a quick round of congratulations, Bill started up again:

"You know, we've talked about getting you syndicated with a talk show…"

"Yep… and you and I both know that the competition is fierce. If we were to decide to do it and if it were even feasible, it'll take time to build a network… build a sponsor base… get the equipment and the people together…"

"The people you'll need are already here, working as robots for Truman Howell's old stations… the ones taken over by Big Thicket. Most of them would jump at a chance to bail out of Thicket and be a part of something better."

"Where would I get the money?"

"You saw what the properties are worth, Glenn," Tricia piped in, "if you needed more money, there are always the banks."

"Norm Shor down at Citizens and Hank the Banker in Magnolia are both eager to be a part of any crazy scheme you may come up with," Bill assured him.

"Bill, the idea of putting together my own talk show would be far-fetched at best. I'm not far enough to the right or the left to draw an audience."

"You're underestimating yourself, Glenn," Brenda noted. "Bill and I have been listening to your morning show for the past couple of days. You still have what it takes. It could work."

Tricia sidled next to Glenn in a show of support.

"Magnolia Town Council voted him in as the new Zeke Collins, if that counts for anything."

"What if I fall flat on my face?"

"There are no debtors prisons any more, Glenn. Besides, if you try and fail, you'll still be better off than if you had never tried."

"You'll still have your friends and you'll still have your family. I've already told you that I would be with you for the rest of your life, Glenn Michaels. Whatever it is you decide, I'm in."

"We are, too…" Brenda chimed in.

"I'll need legal advice…"

"Greg Fischer and I have already prepared some preliminary paperwork. We thought you might show an interest."

"I'll need a facility…"

"You have one; Zeke gave it to you."

Glenn looked at the other three and shook his head in resignation to his fate. "I guess I'm in too, then. I'll announce my decision tomorrow morning on the air."

The Prisoner

Randy Green had just barely finished entering his resignation letter into his laptop when Joe Campbell came barging into his office uninvited and unannounced.

"You had a nice ride with the guy in the green pickup truck?"

"What do you mean?

"I mean, just after our conversation a while ago, you left the place and went down to the park where you were picked up by this guy in an old, green pickup truck."

"Oh, that…" Randy tried to think quickly about how to cover his tracks. "Old buddy of mine. We meet every once in a while just to exchange jokes…"

"Information?"

"No, just jokes."

"What kind of jokes, Mr. Green?"

"Usually bad ones, Mr. Campbell."

"I like bad jokes, Mr. Green. Hit me with one of them."

Randy was under pressure. He had no idea what Joe Campbell was up to other than to try to trip him up: "There were these two polar bears in a bathtub."

"Okay"

"One says to the other, 'Pass the soap'. The other polar bear says, 'No soap, radio.'"

"I don't get it."

"That's the point. It's a bad joke."

"Lame, Mr. Green. I don't like being fucked with. Have a seat." Joe Campbell indicated one of the seats opposite Randy's desk. There was a hard, cold look in Joe's eyes. Randy stood up, closed his laptop and went to the other side of the desk while Joe went to the other side of the desk and sat in Randy's usual seat.

"I have this delicate operation I need to get done here in the next few hours, Mr. Green, and it seems that you and I don't particularly see eye to eye about how this operation is being run or even the importance of this operation to Big Thicket or to me."

Randy was feeling increasingly uncomfortable. He had a good idea of what was going to happen next.

"I know that the driver of that green pickup truck was Bill Preston; he was once a contract engineer who used to work here. I know that Preston and Michaels have been close in the past and I have no doubt that they are still closer than they should be… at least in my opinion. Mr. Preston has been sent a notice that his services are no longer required here at this or any other Big Thicket Station."

Randy's heart sank. He sensed his own demise would be coming sooner rather than later.

Joe opened Randy's laptop. "What were we working on, Mr. Green? Put in your password and let's take a look." Joe thrust the computer in Randy's direction, watching carefully as Randy put in his password. Joe yanked the computer back and read the letter Randy was composing.

"There's a mistake in here. Says '…effective Monday'. Let me correct that, Mr. Green, to '…effective immediately'."

Joe Campbell adroitly input several keystrokes, smiled a malicious smile, and then punched "Enter" with a flourish.

"Miss Meyers, would you make several copies of the letter I just sent to the printer and send the gentleman from Gallipolis in, please?"

"Yes, sir," the voice on the other end of the intercom said.

A few moments later, Jerry Temples barged in.

"Mr. Green, your letter of resignation has been accepted. Mr. Temples, here, has just been appointed into your old job as regional manager of Big Thicket Broadcasting. Congratulations, Mr. Temples."

"It's too fucking bad that Randy here has decided to leave the organization." Temples was mocking, adding to Randy's humiliation. "So, do we hold him a going away party or do we just let him go home and start looking for other 'suitable employment'?"

"We need to keep him with us for the next, say, eighteen hours or so… at least while we wrap up some unfinished business. We wouldn't want to have any interference going on with what we're about to do, would we?"

Randy felt that he was about to become part of a really bad "B" movie.

Francine Meyers made copies of Randy Green's letter of resignation without thinking until after she had finished her task. She didn't particularly like it when Joe Campbell came to town. This time he was being particularly irksome. Not only that, but Jerry Temples gave her the creeps every time he came up from Gallipolis. She got the distinct impression that Jerry was attempting to undress her with his eyes.

She re-read the letter again.

Something wasn't right.

She drummed her fingers for a solid minute before she took the master copy and fed it into the fax machine to send it to her grandmother. Granny Becky would know if there was something wrong. She would know what to do. After all, Granny Becky had worked and was still working at the very same job <u>she</u> was working at, except that Granny Becky was working for Zeke at the radio station in Magnolia.

Dodging the Goons

"You got what?" he asked. He motioned for Bill to come closer and listen in on the call.

"Glenn's cell phone rang as he; Bill, Tricia and Brenda were getting ready to leave the cemetery to go to dinner.

I got a fax, a resignation letter from a Randy Green from Big Thicket."

"Campbell might be on to him," Bill whispered, overhearing the news.

"Thanks for telling me, Becky, and no one else is to know what you just told me, especially not Jack. Okay?"

"Yes, Mr. Michaels."

Bill nudged Glenn as a reminder.

"That's right. Tell no one; not even Jack. By the way, just call me Glenn."

"Yes, Glenn."

He took a deep breath after hanging up the phone. "What do you think?"

"I think that Randy might be in trouble."

"Could they be watching us?"

"I wouldn't put it past Jerry," Tricia chimed in, "he seemed royally pissed about Saturday night."

"If we're being watched and if we act like we <u>know</u> we're being watched, Randy may be in even bigger trouble… assuming he's in trouble, now."

"Brenda's right. Let's think this one through before we do anything else, okay?"

Everyone agreed.

"Good. I'm probably the primary target here. Tricia, you may be in for a rough ride, too, presuming that Temples knows you're with me."

Tricia nodded. She understood.

"If we are being watched, I'm guessing that there'll be someone parked on Fifth Street waiting for us to head downtown. Bill, you and Brenda follow us after waiting one minute. Head up the hill, cross over on Grandview, then go down Carlisle. Pick us up in the alley which turns into Caldwell there on Fourth, by the green house. We'll make the rest up as we go along."

Tricia started her Mustang and headed out of the cemetery toward downtown.

Just as he thought, Glenn spotted what he presumed to be a Big Thicket issued Impala parked on Fifth Street which started to follow at a discreet distance once they passed it.

"We have company…" Tricia told him.

"Make a left at the light on Paint, then left on Fourth. Pull into the parking lot at the corner, find a spot then use it."

Tricia eased her Mustang through downtown exactly as Glenn had told her. Glenn looked as they pulled into the parking space to note that the Thicket car was headed west on Fourth Street. They secured the car, took out their purchases and walked across Paint to head east on Fourth. Bill was waiting for them half a block down as they had planned.

"I owe you one," Glenn remarked as they headed south down the alley to where it turned into Caldwell Street.

They zigged and zagged through the maze of streets Bill and Glenn knew so well, eventually winding up in a restaurant at the far east end of town.

They were able to eat their dinners in relative peace, tarrying there until seven-thirty.

At about ten till eight, they entered the Cross Keys Tavern after parking the hulk of the Matador in a nearby church parking lot.

"Corner table by the window," Bill told them. "Brenda and I can watch who comes in and make plans from there."

"If the Big Thicket crowd comes in, won't they be looking here, first?" Tricia questioned.

"Glenn and I have a habit of sitting near the band either at the family table or in one of the back booths. Randy knows this and that's where he'll get them looking if he has to. We can make our getaway quickly and cleanly out the front door when and if the time comes."

"What if they see us here?"

"I don't believe that they'll make a scene. Too crowded, but I wouldn't discount them coming up with some diversion or another."

They were able to sit down, order a round of drinks and listen to the band through their first set with no problems. Greg Fischer came and sat with them for a little bit. After reviewing the situation with Bill and Glenn, he went to station himself at one of the back booths as a decoy in case trouble came in the front door.

Half way through the third set, Brenda got up to go to the back to use the bathroom. Glenn watched her stop for a moment on her way back from the restroom to talk with Greg. At the same time, Bill hustled Glenn and Tricia off into the corner as Randy Green, Joe Campbell, Jerry Temples and two other men come in, their attention focused on the back of the building. Brenda came toward them discreetly. When she came up to Randy, it looked to Glenn as if they had deliberately bumped into each other. The men with him took no notice as she bent down, picked something up then continued back to the table, signaling Glenn and Tricia that they needed to get out of the building.

Moments after they exited, they heard a loud explosion from the direction of the parking lot on Fourth and Paint where Tricia had parked her car. They ran pell-mell back to the Matador, disappearing from the sidewalk just as the crowd from the Tavern started pouring out the front door to investigate the explosion.

Escape

RANDY SAT.

It was all Randy was allowed to do from the moment he was dismissed from his position of authority as Regional Manager for Big Thicket Broadcasting.

He had been relieved of everything he had which belonged to Big Thicket including his cell phone, his company credit card and his cache of business cards.

Joe Campbell was sitting at what was once <u>his</u> desk perusing <u>his</u> personal files on <u>his</u> company provided laptop copying files onto disc, asking about those files then erasing the files from the computer.

Randy had spent fifteen, no, eighteen years of his life dedicated to the radio station and to Big Thicket Broadcasting. He never protested about anything that the company did which might be seen as being slightly dishonest. He had job security, he was building a pension and he was able to afford an indoor swimming pool at this house tucked away just outside of town.

Joe Campbell and Jerry Temples were stripping him of his rights and privileges right in front of him in the most humiliating manner they thought possible.

"You're a traitor, Green. Traitors deserve to be shot, but we can't do that these days, can we?"

Randy stayed silent through Joe's constant taunting. His silence only heightened Joe's temper.

The hubbub of the building went silent after five when everyone else left, unaware that their boss was now a virtual prisoner in his own office.

Joe finally shut down the laptop at seven-thirty and declared that he was hungry. After a short discussion, Joe sent Jerry for some Chinese take-out which was eaten back in the office. Randy picked at an egg roll, not knowing what his fate would be.

He started to think about escape.

Perhaps Francine at the front desk would have thought it unusual for him to be cooped up in his office after hours and would have mentioned it to someone. On the other hand, he had a habit of sneaking out the back door to head to the Cross Keys to relax for a while - especially on those days, like today, when his wife was working an evening shift.

The kids running the programming were usually too damn busy with smuggled girlfriends or trying to sneak cigarettes out the back door while letting the automation run the place for a while. Once in a while, one of the evening operators would try to sneak into his office to try and take advantage of the couch where Jerry was now lounging. Jerry was talking about getting laid there someday or at the very least, convincing Francine to give him a blow job.

Randy stayed quiet. There would be an opportunity, he knew it.

Shortly after eight, Joe and Jerry shuttled between the office and the front lobby. There was one, possibly two men there who were planning on something. Thirty minutes of waiting followed thirty minutes of frantic activity. Finally, at nine-fifteen, Joe announced that they were taking a walk to the Cross Keys Tavern.

"I understand that Glenn Michaels is a creature of habit… and one of those habits has been to drop in at the Cross Keys on Thursday nights when he's in the area."

Randy squirmed. He had once told Joe Campbell that very same thing.

"Listen carefully if you want to enjoy your retirement in good health, Green…" Joe Campbell was not in a good mood. "There are going to be five of us going into the Cross Keys to meet up with Michaels and the girl.

"We're going to offer him a place to cool down for the night… you know, a place where you all can stay, safe and sound until, say, noon tomorrow. If he agrees, you go with him. He doesn't agree… well, let's just say I have some insurance that he won't leave town quite yet."

Randy wasn't sure what Joe's definition of "insurance" might be.

"So let's take a walk… any funny business and you might end up missing, Mr. Green."

Randy, Joe, Jerry and another man who was waiting in the lobby walked from the radio stations to the Cross Keys Tavern, being joined by a second man Randy didn't recognize just before they entered.

Randy's senses sought out an opportunity.

As they entered, he thought he noticed Glenn and Bill at the table nearest the front door. He managed to place himself between his captors and their quarry while pointing to the back of the room.

"They're usually back there…" he managed to yell at Joe above the music.

The men passed by the front table without noticing that their quarry was almost next to them.

Halfway down the bar, Randy spotted Brenda Preston coming toward the front of the Tavern after talking with Greg Fischer at one of the back tables.

Brenda looked as if she didn't want to recognize him. "Help," he mouthed as he got closer. She deliberately bumped into him to raise a bit of a stir while the band kept playing.

Randy deliberately dropped his wallet. Brenda deftly picked it up and kept going.

When he arrived at Greg's table, Greg stood up to let Randy sit down. Before anyone could protest, the muffled sound of an explosion outside grabbed everyone's attention… except Randy's.

Quickly, he rolled to his right and punched through the crowd, whose attention was focused on the front of the building, to head to the back exit.

He sprinted through the alley to the parking lot next door where he expected to find a car belonging to either Glenn or Bill. The sounds of Bill's Matador starting and pulling away from its parking place never sounded so sweet.

The car paused momentarily before pulling into the alley… just long enough for a back door to open to so that he could fling himself in before the car roared through the alley to get the hell out of Dodge.

Randy had barely gotten seated properly when a familiar voice piped up: "Hey, Randy. I understand you might need a job…"

Earl Strikes Out

Earl told his buddies at the bowling alley that he had an unexpected call from work and had to catch up on a few things. They managed to persuade him to come in for at least drink one beer before his ride was scheduled to arrive.

One beer ended up being three and a couple of fistfuls of sourdough pretzels before Earl walked out to the parking lot at the designated time to meet with Jack Jankowski. Earl popped an Altoid just as Jack drove up. He didn't want Jack to know that he had been drinking.

Jack was a congenial host on the way down to Magnolia, asking Earl about his family, his home and his job. Earl became slightly disturbed when Jack touched on a couple of subjects he thought were confidential… just between him and Zeke. Zeke kept records. Jack probably read the records.

The amicable conversation continued as Jack and Earl loaded the radio station's equipment into the back of Jack's Buick station wagon.

Jack and the night manager of Father Linguini's flirted for a few minutes, yielding a carry-out of a large pizza and draught beer which Earl consumed with gusto before they left.

"Earl…"

Jack's voice cut through the hint of fuzziness growing in Earl's mind as a result of three Millers at the bowling alley and whatever it was on tap at Father Linguini's.

"Your continued employment with WZEK will depend largely on your cooperation here in the next eighteen hours. I am in charge now. If you say anything to anybody about this escapade, you're gone. It's as simple as that."

"What do you mean, Jack? What's going on?"

"Glenn Michaels won't be doing his show in the morning. He will be unavoidably detained. Since he won't be on the air, he can't be Zeke's heir. I'll be in charge of WZEK after a hearing tomorrow afternoon."

The beers caused Jack's words to float in his head for a few moments before he understood the basic gist of what was being said to him.

"By the way, if somehow our activities are construed as criminal in nature, you are now considered an accessory."

Lawyer talk.

Earl never understood lawyer talk, even when he wasn't a sheet and a half to the wind.

They drove north, past the bowling alley and through Prentiss. Earl sat in silence until they started up the road toward Omega.

"I gotta pee."

"Wait… it won't be long, now."

"I really gotta go."

"Less than five minutes."

Earl spent the next five minutes trying to think of not peeing.

Jack finally pulled off the road into a long driveway of the lone house where Tricia Knox lived. The moment the car stopped, Earl poured out of the passenger seat and relieved himself on the front lawn.

"What now?" Earl asked while he was adjusting his zipper.

"We go inside and we wait."

Jack popped a couple of pills and took a pull from a whiskey bottle he had hidden under the front seat before leading Earl to the back door of the house.

They went in through the kitchen into the front room. Earl took a side trip into the bathroom to have another go at relieving his bladder before coming back out into the living room to stretch out on the couch.

Earl saw Jack sit down on the lounge chair before he finally dropped off for a fitful night's sleep.

Cutting It Close

"It looks like we've picked the right place to park tonight," Bill remarked as they ran alongside the church to get to the car in the church parking lot.

The four of them quickly got in while Bill started the car and put it in gear.

"That would be Randy," Bill stated as a dark figure came racing out of the back door of the tavern. "Let him in, Tricia…"

She opened her back door and the figure lunged in. Bill turned into the alley and squirted in the opposite direction of the entire hubbub.

"Hey Randy, I understand you may need a job," Glenn quipped when Randy got in and situated.

"You got my message, I take it."

"Yep…"

"They're after you, Michaels, you too… um…"

"Tricia. Tricia Knox."

"One of the guys seemed to know you."

"That would be Jerry Temples. I dumped him on a date the other night. So far he's taken rejection to a whole new level."

"So it would appear," Randy told her. "So… I take it we're on the way to Magnolia?"

"We need to," Bill told him. "Glenn needs to be on the air in eight hours or so. The boys from Big Thicket, Joe Campbell and Jerry Temples, are doing their best to stop it from happening."

"You probably want to call Margie," Brenda piped up. "She'll want to know that you won't be in tonight. Use my phone. Oh, and here's your wallet. Great move on your part back there in the Cross Keys, by the way."

Randy called his wife at work and explained the situation. Bill drove south to Magnolia. When Randy was finished with his call, Brenda called the Highway Patrol and Roy Ball at the Fuller County Sheriff's office to alert them to the possible trouble.

Within thirty minutes, they were in the parking lot at Zeke's Café talking with Magnolia Police Chief Richmond.

"Maybe the best thing to do is to lay low and see if any of the goons show up later tonight," Harold suggested.

After some discussion, it was decided that Bill and Randy would camp out at the transmitter to keep away intruders. They took Glenn's car, leaving the Matador parked as inconspicuously as it could be up at the library. Jessica Collins volunteered to take Brenda and Tricia in for the night. Brenda accepted the hospitality; Tricia opted to spend the night with Glenn on the third floor in the apartment. A rotating shift of police officers would stand guard outside of the building. Harold, Glenn and Tricia combed the building from top to bottom before securing it and calling it a night.

"There's only the one bed, you know," Glenn apologized when he and Tricia were alone. "I'll go ahead and sleep on the couch. Just give me a few minutes to use the bathroom to get ready, okay?"

"I have no problem sharing the bed with you," she smiled.

"I didn't think you would, but, I'm…"

"You're not ready to have sex with me yet. I'm not ready, myself, but I can trust you," she told him while she pulled the dress she was wearing over her head to reveal herself. She was as naked as the day she was born, yet she had all of the curves of a woman.

"We'll consummate our union another night," she continued. "Not tonight. I'm tired. I need to get some rest. You go ahead and sleep on the couch."

She took her dress to the bedroom, taking care to hang it in the closet. Glenn followed her lead. He undressed and went into the bathroom to perform his nightly rituals without saying a word. When he finished, he took a blanket, went into the living room and almost immediately fell into a deep sleep.

He became aware of a peculiar silence propelling him into the conscious world. The usual sounds of cooling fans and clicking thermostats were conspicuously missing. He rolled off the couch in a state of alertness. He quickly went into the bedroom to check on Tricia. He covered her and gave her a quick kiss on the forehead. She stirred slightly while he stole back into the living room.

There was a click and the sound of an opening door.

Glenn froze.

A flashlight shone directly into his eyes.

"Good Morning Mr. Michaels."

The voice sounded familiar.

"Earl is… ill this morning. I'm here to take his place."

"Why the hell are you up in my apartment, then?"

"Because you're going to be ill this morning, too. WZEK will be taking a short vacation from the airwaves.

Steve Carver. In an instant, Glenn knew that Steve Carver was the mole inside the radio station, passing information along to the operatives at Big Thicket.

"I presume that you'll still want a paycheck this morning, Steve…"

"I'm getting more than what I would be getting from you. Move, so I can keep an eye on you."

Glenn moved slowly toward the couch. The light remained on his face until he was able to sit down. He calculated what his next move might be.

"Jesus! You're naked!" Steve exclaimed once he moved the light off of Glenn's face.

"So is everyone else at some point of the day or another," Glenn explained. "I happen to sleep this way."

He sat down on the couch, but only for a moment.

"Would it be all right with you if I went and got a drink from the refrigerator?" he asked, getting up almost as soon as he sat down.

"Go ahead, I suppose," Steve sighed. "Just make it snappy."

Glenn's heart was pounding. He had to buy time for Tricia to call for help, presuming that she was aware of his predicament.

He opened the refrigerator door. No light. The power had been cut.

"I suppose you have a gun…"

"What do you think?"

"I think that if you have one, you'll be facing more jail time when this is all over than if you didn't."

"Don't be a smart ass, Michaels."

"Just saying…"

"Fuck you and shut up!"

"My, what a witty comeback!"

"Shut the fuck up and get the hell back in here!" Steve Carver was becoming increasingly frustrated with his captive.

Glenn took a small sip of his tea before setting it on his kitchen counter. Just as he got back into the living room, Tricia spoke from the bedroom doorway:

"Glenn, it's five twen-"

Before she could finish uttering the time, Steve swung around in response to Tricia's presence.

"FREEZE, SCUMBAG!!!" Glenn lowered his voice and yelled, disorienting his would-be captor while he rushed to put a full nelson on him. The gun and the flashlight went flying as Steve Carver was pinned to the floor.

Tricia came in, revealing that she had wrapped herself in a bed sheet. She kicked the gun away from the man on the floor and calmly proceeded to the front door to let Harold Richmond in.

"From the looks of it, you don't need my help Miss Knox. It looks like you and Glenn – Jesus, Glenn, you're naked!"

"You noticed," Glenn said, half mocking the officer as he got up off of his former assailant. "I didn't have the time to put on a tux and a tie when this joker came in. Where were you anyway?"

"He showed me his key card and told me that he had to get in to get the station started, so I just assumed that he was okay. Where are the lights?"

"There's a cut-off at the top of the stairs. I'll go turn them back on," Glenn volunteered.

Glenn was out the door before Harold realized that Glenn hadn't excused himself to throw something on. He returned calmly, going into the bedroom without comment while Harold was reading Steve Carver his Miranda Rights. After throwing on a pair of slacks, Glenn came out of the bedroom to confront his assailant before he and the officer headed downstairs.

"You said that Earl was ill. Where is he?"

"I have no idea."

"You're sure about that?"

"He was someone else's detail, that's all I know."

"If he doesn't show up, you're the only person who might know what happened to him."

"Let me talk to my lawyer, first."

Harold escorted the miscreant downstairs and into his squad car for the trip to the County jail. Glenn and Tricia took stock as to where they were.

It was five forty five. Fifteen minutes to air. They were expected… he was expected to be at his table doing the morning show no later than five after six.

"Do we need to go to Father Linguini's?"

"I'll call Jack to see if we're all set up. If we are, I'll do a quick shower and hustle over there."

Tricia shed her toga and got dressed while Glenn tried to call Jack.

There was no answer. The call went immediately to voice mail.

He called Father Linguini's.

Still no answer.

Tricia adjusted the dress she had worn the previous day. "Well?" she inquired.

"Jack's cell phone seems to be off and there's no one at Linguini's."

He called another number.

"Bill… are you and Randy still at the transmitter?"

"Yeah… we're getting ready to give you a carrier as promised at 5:59:45."

"Are you getting a feed from Father Linguini's?"

"Not a thing. We're assuming that you're ready to go from the café."

"We've just had an incident here. Earl's missing and so is Jack Jankowski. We may be royally screwed."

"Just a minute…" Bill was heard talking to Randy in the background. He was soon back on the phone. "Randy just said that the original plan was to keep you off the air today, but to leave everything in the station alone. The equipment on the second floor is way too valuable to ruin."

"What's the percentage of getting either you or Randy down here to run the board while the other stays with the transmitter?"

"That percentage would be a hundred."

"Can you link this phone into the transmitter for station ID?"

"I can do that. No problem. I can pull the news network through here, too."

"Then here's the plan…"

Glenn outlined a plan to get them through the next half hour. Tricia would go downstairs to see that Zeke's Café would be open while Glenn showered, gave the ID, dressed and assumed his place in the window. Bill in the meantime would turn on the transmitter and then come into Magnolia to be the board operator for the morning show while Randy stayed to mind the transmitter.

The plan was quickly agreed to. Glenn looked at the time when he hung up the phone to take his shower. Five-fifty-four. He had five minutes to be back on the line to give the station identification. He knew that there were people listening, hoping that he'd fail.

On the Razor's Edge

Tricia Knox hurried downstairs while Glenn was taking his shower. She was met at the back door by Jessica Collins and Brenda Preston. Quickly they went into Zeke's to get the grills started and to let the staff and customers in.

Tricia's mouth hung open when she got to the front door. It seemed as if everyone in Magnolia was outside, waiting to be let in. The staff was first followed by a literal throng, every one of them wondering what was going on that morning. She looked desperately to see if Jack was in the crowd, or Earl, or someone who might be able to help.

The loudspeaker of the radio came to life just as the clock on the wall read 6am: "Good morning Magnolia, Ohio. This is WZEK and WZEK-FM, Magnolia. We're on the air. The final Zeke Collins radio show is coming up, right after the national news."

Tricia heaved a sigh of relief. They were in. Glenn would be in his place inside of five minutes. She kept looking through the crowd, finally spotting Steve and Millie Mulligan. She tried to get their attention.

Minutes ticked by.

Glenn finally arrived through the back door, wading through the crowd, holding his cell phone. The crowd parted as he came through. Perhaps the day would turn out alright after all.

The sirens started, first at a distance, then coming closer. Glenn started the morning show from his cell phone right on cue as the sirens came closer. Tricia looked over at Sonia, the dining room manager. She was on the telephone, her face became pale. She screamed loudly and dropped the phone.

"BOMB!" she screamed. "THERE'S A BOMB IN THE BUILDING!!"

Before panic set in, Tricia gave a loud whistle. "DON'T PANIC… DON'T RUN! GO TO THE NEAREST EXIT AND GET AWAY FROM THE BUILDING. **NOW!!!**"

The assembled patrons did not panic. The building was emptied inside of a minute while the Sheriff arrived and roped off the area. Glenn kept on the air on his cell phone, the last person to leave the building aside from Tricia.

Minutes seemed to take hours as the Sheriff made a thorough sweep of the building. It would take at least an hour, maybe more, they were told.

Bill Preston arrived on foot, having had to park Glenn's car next to his at the library parking lot. After a quick conference with the Mulligans, it was decided that the show needed to be moved to Father Linguini's for the rest of the morning.

Glenn had no choice but to continue doing the show without script and on the run on his cell phone. The only respite he had came when the network news went on at seven.

They arrived at Father Linguini's at a minute past seven.

There was nothing there.

Laptops, mixing boards, scripts. All gone.

The crowd had followed.

"Save your battery," Tricia advised, "get on the land line and we'll wing it from there."

"Hey… Mulligan! You have a laptop we can use?"

"Sure, it's at the house, though…"

"Get it and bring it over here. I need to get Glenn some support."

Glenn had taken up position behind the order counter and was getting ready to start the second hour of the show.

"You can do it, babe… I love you," she told him from across the room.

"I know," he mouthed back, just an instant before he was back on the air.

The second hour went rather smoothly. The crowd shuffled in and out of the pizzeria to watch Glenn pull together a show without a script or any support. Just before eight, the Sheriff gave the all-clear to Zeke's. Bill switched over during the eight o'clock news, extending the break after the network news long enough for Glenn to travel between the restaurants.

Tricia was still on pins and needles.

The last couple of hours of the show went as smoothly as it could have with no more glitches. Tricia's enthusiasm grew as the audience in the street in front of Zeke's grew. For some reason, the hardships endured in the past eighteen hours had seemed to pay off. What was happening was something she hadn't thought would happen… Glenn seemed to be increasingly energized by what he was doing. He had bonded with the people of Magnolia and everyone beyond. He had become the new Zeke Collins.

"We need to finish up some business up in Chillicothe."

He was matter of fact. He wasn't short, just matter of fact.

"I need to stop by the house and get something else to wear," Tricia pointed out.

"That's good, yeah. We'll do that."

Glenn made arrangements for Bill to take Randy home and to see about the damages to Tricia's car. Just before they were about to leave, Greg Fischer showed up.

"You go ahead and take my car and go home to take a shower," Glenn instructed Tricia. "I'll have Greg drive me up when we're finished, okay?"

"Sure. See you in a bit." Tricia gave him a kiss before she left.

She went to the library, got in Glenn's car and drove back up to her house.

Something didn't feel right when she got there. She had lived in the place long enough to know the feeling of her house. Parking the car, she walked up to her front porch, cautiously looking around for the source of her uneasiness.

There was the sound of a gunshot.

She turned around.

John Jankowski was walking around the back of the car.

Before Tricia could react, Jack aimed a pistol at the rear tire of Glenn's Fusion and pulled the trigger again.

He then pointed the gun in her direction.

She dove as he pulled the trigger again, putting a bullet in one of the second floor windows.

"THAT WAS JUST A WARNING, LITTLE LADY," he shouted. "IF I WANTED TO KILL YA, YOU'D A BEEN DEAD ON THE FIRST SHOT."

He was right.

She got up to see him ambling in her direction.

"You can put your cell phone down here so both of us can see it. When I'm finished with you, you can have it back."

He had gotten up to her. She placed the cell phone down in front of him. He picked it up and threw it as hard as he could toward the highway.

"You've been pretty lucky up to this point, young lady. As of now, your luck has run out."

Missing Puzzle Piece

"Between the police and the Ross County Sheriff's department, Joe Campbell, Jerry Temples and the two thugs who held Randy last night have been rounded up and put in jail."

Greg Fischer caught Glenn up on what had happened while Glenn was on-the-air.

"What's the word on the car?"

"It's under investigation. Most likely a time bomb set by Frank Danson. He was one of the thugs involved in the kidnapping. The car's toast, though."

"No shit."

"You and Tricia don't seem to be much the worse for the wear."

"Well, between being chased, losing a car to a car bomb and almost being held hostage at gunpoint this morning, I guess you're right. We have done well for ourselves so far today. The only loose ends are Earl and Jack."

"Really… what's the deal?"

"Earl was a no-show this morning. Harold came up and extracted our afternoon guy who was trying to make me a no-show, too. He told me that Earl was ill."

"And Jack?"

"Jack was supposed to be at the pizza place this morning with an alternative set-up in case Big Thicket's goons tried something. He's gone;

along with a good deal of equipment and at least two lap-tops filled with information."

"Do you think that maybe Earl and Jack are in trouble with Big Thicket?"

"I'm not sure. I'm starting to be puzzled by this whole deal. I can't quite figure out exactly what Jack had in mind."

There was a soft knock on the door to Glenn's office. Harold Richmond peered around the doorframe.

"Hey, Harold, what's the deal?"

"I've been trying to find out what happened to Earl. His wife said he didn't come home last night after bowling up at Prentiss. Funny thing is his car's still up there in the parking lot. I've talked to a couple of people from Magnolia who were there last night and they don't even remember him coming in. His team ended up being short a man and had to forfeit."

"Mr. Fischer and I were just talking about that, Harold. You have met, haven't you? Greg is my attorney."

"Yeah, we met. I've seen him a time or two in town or at the County Courthouse."

"We have another party missing, Harold. John Jankowski otherwise known as Jack Jay. He's gone and so is a good deal of our equipment. Any ideas?"

"Where was he staying?"

"I think at the Magnolia Inn."

"I'll call the Wilsons here in a minute and see if they know anything. What's missing?"

"Radio equipment and a couple of laptops, that's all, I think."

"This almost sounds serious."

"I would hope it isn't, but we need to check into this. If operatives from Big Thicket are willing to resort to kidnapping and car bombing, there's no telling where they'll stop."

"I'll alert Sheriff Ball, too."

"Thanks, Harold."

Harold left Glenn's office and hurried down the hall.

Greg was looking through the collection of items still left behind by Zeke when he passed away. Glenn looked idly down at what was now his desk.

"There's something missing, here," Glenn mused, "something important… it was right here on top of the desk."

Glenn looked around on the desk, carefully pulling things out and putting them back. Zeke had a system of organized confusion which would have tried the patience of a saint. After several minutes of fruitless searching, Glenn stopped.

"Two files. Mine and Jack's. They were right here on top of the desk. They're gone… as is the file on The Incident."

"Who could have taken them?"

"Any number of people, Jack among them. This office seems to have had a revolving door these past few days."

"Are any other documents missing that you know of?"

"I'm not sure…" Glenn got on the intercom. "Becky, could you check the public access files and tell me if they're still there, please?"

"They should be, they're under lock and key,"

"Just check to make sure, would you? And call me back as soon as you have them."

"So I wonder what's going on here." Glenn was puzzled.

"Way too much, it seems."

The intercom crackled into life.

"I have the files, Mr. Michaels. They're right where I left them. Do you want me to bring them in?"

"That's okay, Becky. Just put them back, okay?"

"Okay. And oh, Harold's on line four."

"Thanks."

Glenn punched up line four and put it on speaker.

"Find out anything Harold?"

"I was just talking with Bill Wilson at the Magnolia Inn. Apparently Jack Jay left at some point last night. The bed hasn't been slept in and he hasn't noted any unusual activity."

"Thanks for the update, Harold."

"By the way, there is one more thing. It may be nothing, but it seems that Jack paid for his stay using a corporate credit card issued to an outfit from Texas called Big Thicket Broadcasting. Ever hear of it?"

Captive Audience

Jack Jankowski took up the overstuffed chair in Tricia's living room while she sat next to Earl on the couch. Earl's arms were bound in duct tape in such a way that he could, if needed, tend to personal business. He had on a bowling shirt which was, by now, getting slightly rank with sweat.

"I hear you've been asking about The Incident," Jack said as he tried to get comfortable. "There's a little bit more to it than you know about, Miss Knox. Let me be honest. You may not like what I'm about to tell you."

"If it's about Hannah Smith's unborn child belonging to Glenn Michaels, I already know. He told me about it the other day."

"So he finally confessed to it, did he? I've known it for years." Jack settled back. An air of smugness surrounded him.

"You're talking about the murder/suicide involving the preacher and his wife?" Earl asked. He had no clue. "Damn! Zeke would have really loved that story…"

"Zeke kept it to himself as long as he lived. He knew, Earl; he knew." Jack told him.

Tricia looked back over to Jack. "What's going on here? Why are you keeping us here? Why is Earl here and why are you pointing a gun at us, Jack? This makes no sense."

"I want what's mine," Jack told her. I want my child, I want my grandchildren and I want Zeke's radio stations so I can afford my retirement. Glenn took them all, and now he gets to go back to Texas scot-free with the bonus which should have been mine!"

Jack got up out of the chair and started pacing the room, occasionally reaching over and massaging his left arm.

"Brian Thompson would have paid me a quarter of a million dollars to hand over control of the radio stations to him. Now Thompson will be paying Michaels instead."

He turned and looked directly at Tricia.

"If you think your precious Glenn Michaels is going to stay here and share the wealth with you, missy – you've got another think coming. I'm keeping you with me until the storm's over for your own good."

Jack reached for his left arm again and winced in pain.

"He's having a heart attack," Tricia thought.

"The man uses women, Miss Knox. He used my Hannah; he used a string of women. I have the folder on your kitchen table, the folder from Zeke's files which I think will paint an uncomplimentary picture of your knight in shining armor. Get up. I'll take you back and show you."

He waved the gun, indicating to Tricia that she was to get up and lead him into her kitchen. As she went down the hallway, Jack continued his diatribe:

"Hannah would have been nearly fifty, her kids would be grown and that goddamn preacher your Glenn Michaels left her with would have been dead by now. Her mother would have been, too. She said I was trash. She said that I was no good; that I had no business being in contact with my child. Bitch even claimed that Hannah <u>wasn't</u> mine! Hannah's mother never acknowledged me as her father; but I looked after her the best I could all the same. I never told my first wife that Hannah was my child until after Harlan Murphy's suicide. You see, Harlan Murphy was my first wife's brother. It killed her to know that. After I told her, she fell apart and so did our marriage. She blamed me for her brother's death – but it was really Glenn Michaels' fault."

Tricia tried to keep up with Jack's rant, but he appeared to be increasingly incoherent as time went on. Jack went to lean on the kitchen table. It was obvious to her that he was in pain and that he would collapse at any moment. Jack's grip loosened on his gun and it fell to the floor. Tricia took advantage and kicked it out of reach while Jack slowly slumped to the ground.

"EARL! GET IN HERE! NOW," she yelled.

"Yes, ma'am." Earl didn't waste any time. He was there in mere seconds. Tricia directed him to her utility drawer to get a knife so that he could cut his bonds and completely free his arms. She then sent Earl out to look for her cell phone while she tried to assess Jack's condition.

"Jack, are you on any medication?"

Tricia heard the sounds of sirens heading up the road toward her house.

"I was going to humor him. I knew Glenn would probably reject the gift, go back to Dallas and leave me with the chance to propose something almost as good. Me."

The sirens were getting closer.

"Damn it, Jack, answer the fucking question. Are you on any medication?"

"I didn't count on Zeke passing so quick. I didn't count on Glenn actually stepping in like he did. I didn't count on him being liked so well and so quickly by the people here. I didn't count on the two of you…"

She heard the sound of car tires crunching up the gravel of her driveway. Jack's face seemed to freeze, his eyes were screaming for help.

"Shit…"

She rolled him over. His face was starting to turn blue.

"EARL!! SOMEONE!!! ANYONE!!! GET IN HERE **_NOW_**!!!"

"Sorry..." Jack barely managed to say as Tricia desperately ripped open his shirt to try to start CPR. "All I wanted was to be near her..."

Earl and Sheriff Roy came barging into the kitchen. Roy called for a paramedic before relieving Tricia in her attempt to resuscitate Jack's lifeless form. When the EMS arrived fifteen minutes later, all they could do was declare John Jankowski dead at the scene of an apparent heart attack.

Racing to the Rescue

"Tricia's in trouble."

"What are you saying?"

"I'm saying Tricia's in trouble, Greg. Harold just told me that Jack had been using a corporate credit card from Big Thicket." Glenn was already frantically searching his pockets and the desk to make sure he had everything he needed for a quick getaway. "My guess is that Jack may have holed up somewhere, but somewhere close. Tricia lives out far enough that her house could be a handy place to lay low. Besides, Zeke owned the place. If Tricia's out there, she might have found Jack and maybe Earl, too."

"What are you babbling about, Michaels?" Harold was still on the phone. "What's an outfit like Big Thicket got to do with Jack Jay?"

"Harold, you need to get a hold of Sheriff Ball and tell him to get out to where Tricia lives as fast as he can."

"Where's that?"

"I'm hoping he knows the street address… all I know is that it's on the state highway on the way to Omega."

Glenn turned off the speaker phone before Harold could say goodbye. He dialed Tricia's cell phone from his cell phone.

"*We're sorry, the number you are trying to call is unavailable. Please try---*"

Desperately he tried again with the same result.

"What are you driving?"

"The Prius. It's out front."

"We need to skedaddle. I'm worried. Her phone's off."

Glenn wasted no time getting out the door of his office and down the back stairway.

Greg was right behind him.

Glenn did a quick turn through the back door of Zeke's, wading through the remaining crowd of customers gathered in an impromptu vigil. He burst out the front door as if he were on fire, desperately looking for Greg's car. He raced across the street, finding the car in front of the memorial bench. He grabbed the rose in its holder on the bench before getting in the car, slamming the door and putting on his seatbelt.

"GO – GO – GO – GO!!"

Greg made a U-Turn, almost hitting Harold's police cruiser coming down the street in the opposite direction. Harold turned on his light bar, passed Greg and led them out of town, sirens blaring.

Glenn tried to call Tricia a third time, again with no response. They were practically flying down the left lane of the causeway between Magnolia and Prentiss.

As they were headed through town, Glenn tried one more time to see if he could raise Tricia. This time the phone rang… twice.

"Hey…" It was Earl's voice on the phone. He sounded out of breath. "This is Earl. That you, Glenn?"

"Earl. Where's Tricia?"

"In the kitchen with the Sheriff and Jack Jay. Paramedics are on the way."

"Is she okay?"

"Seems to be… Jack don't look too good, though…"

"What the hell's going on?"

"Not sure… he collapsed just before Roy got here."

"Can you get Tricia on the phone?"

"Sure, just a minute…"

It was no more than half a minute, but to Glenn it seemed like an hour. Greg was concentrating on the road ahead, trying to keep from getting too far behind Harold's cruiser. Before Tricia came on the line, he saw the small collection of Sheriff's patrol cars and the EMS vehicle in Tricia's front yard.

"Knox's mad-house. Tricia speaking. How may I direct your call?"

"What gives?"

"I've been shot at, kidnapped, rescued myself and have been watching the EMS try to revive a corpse. How's your morning been?"

"Dull and boring, as usual. I'm here."

Greg had just barely stopped the car when Glenn leaped out, still clutching the rose. He went into a dead run through the front yard to be met by Tricia just as he was about to come up the steps to the porch. It took Glenn at least three minutes before he could be convinced to let go of Tricia so that she could tell him what had gone on in the past hour.

An hour and a half after they were reunited, Glenn and Tricia headed back toward Prentiss in Jack's Roadmaster station wagon to get Glenn's car which had been towed to the dealership for a new set of tires.

"Jack made some interesting statements about Hannah Smith in the last few minutes of his life. He told me that he was Hannah's father and that he blamed you for her death."

"He said something to me about it, too. Honestly, I'd like to know. I've kept a lock of her hair. We'll see if we can get a good DNA sample from Jack and run some tests."

"What if he is?"

"I'm not sure. I do know that if he was her father, he might rest better knowing that she was loved for once in her life."

"He at least knew that you loved her. What more can any father want for his daughter?"

"Would it change what we have?"

"No… that's in the past. I want to look forward to what's to come. I'm looking forward to being loved again."

"Me, too," he told her.

In the Best Interest of Magnolia

GLENN NOTICED THAT TRAFFIC WAS heavy as he approached the dealership in Prentiss. It was way too heavy even for a Friday. There seemed to be a throng of people on the sidewalks, too, headed in the direction of the Fuller County Courthouse.

"What do you know about Alvin Bates?"

Greg Fischer's almost whispered voice came through on Glenn's cell phone.

"All I know is that he was once Zeke's attorney."

"Well, he's here at the Probate Court at this very moment on behalf of Jack Jankowski attempting to get the will I made out for Zeke a week and a half ago declared null and void. I need you at the Courthouse as quickly as you can get here."

"I just pulled into the dealer's lot to get my car. I might be able to wade my way through the crowd and be there in five to ten minutes… what's with all the people, anyway?"

"You'll find out… just get here."

Glenn parked the wagon and headed to the service desk to pay for his tires. The man at the service desk paid little attention to him as Glenn approached.

"Sir…"

The service manager looked up.

"Mr. Michaels!" he exclaimed. "You're on your way to the courthouse, right?"

"I came to pick up my car-"

"No time for that. Come with me." The manager literally jumped around the corner of his counter to lead Glenn and Tricia out the back door of the dealership. He called for one of the mechanics to take over for him while he ran his errand.

The block and a half between the back of the dealership and the courthouse was jammed with people.

Glenn's phone rang.

"Glenn… are you and Tricia still at her house?"

Becky sounded anxious.

"No, we're trying to pick our way toward the county courthouse."

In waves, it seemed, the people in the crowd looked back toward Glenn and Tricia and parted to allow them a path to the courthouse door. As they passed, the crowd closed in again behind them… calls of "We're behind you, Glenn!" or "You tell 'em, Glenn" echoed in his ears.

"Brian Thompson is here to see you."

"Becky, I don't want to see him for all the trouble he's caused for me in the past day and a half."

"He knows about it and he says that he's here to make amends."

"It may take a while for me to see him. If he's still there after I get out of court, maybe I'll talk with him."

Glenn finally mounted the steps leading to the Probate Court. Greg was there to meet him when he arrived.

"You couldn't have timed it better. The judge is just about to come back from recess."

"What's the deal, here?"

"Alvin filed a motion yesterday contesting the will. We only found out about forty-five minutes ago that the hearing is going on despite Jack's not being here."

"What's with all the people?"

"They're _your_ people, Glenn. Jessica put out a plea on the air to get anyone and everyone here to the courthouse to come and support you."

Glenn looked around before being ushered into a seat near the bench. Otherwise it was standing room only.

"All rise!"

The bailiff introduced the judge as she walked into the room and sat down at the bench.

"We seem to have picked up a few visitors," she remarked, "and I presume counsel for the estate of Ezekiel Collins?"

"Yes, your honor," Greg replied.

The judge looked at Glenn and Tricia. "I presume that you are Mr. Michaels?"

"Yes, Your Honor."

"Could you…" She motioned him to come to the bench. "Have a seat." She indicated a seat near the bench, close to the court reporter. Before he could sit down, the bailiff came over and swore him in.

"It is my understanding that you have been named the sole heir of the estate of Zeke Collins. Is that true, sir?"

"I understand it to be true, yes, ma'am."

"Zeke's Last Will and Testament was dated and notarized by the estate's attorney on July the fifth of this year. Where were you on the fifth of July, Mr. Michaels?"

"I was at home in Dallas, Texas, Your Honor."

"Did you know or have any foreknowledge of your inclusion into Zeke's will?"

"I only found out that I was Zeke's heir on the day Zeke died."

"Was there any indication that he might leave you with such a generous gift, Mr. Michaels?"

"He did make an offer to give me the radio stations when I met him on Sunday night…"

"Did you accept his offer?"

"No I didn't, Your Honor. I just wanted to do what I had to do and head back to Dallas."

"I take it, then, that you came to Magnolia just for a visit."

"Yes, Your Honor."

"How long have you known Mr. Collins?"

"I met him back in… I guess it was nineteen-seventy-five. He hired me to work for him in January, nineteen-seventy-six. We've been in contact ever since."

"You've held other jobs in radio, then."

"Yes, ma'am. I was on the air until about fifteen years ago. Since then I've sold appliances."

"Have you ever had the desire to get back into the business?"

"Not really, Your Honor."

"I take it that's why you rejected Mr. Collins' gift."

"At first, yes, Your Honor."

"And then you stepped in to do his show when he died on Tuesday morning."

"Yes, Your Honor."

"I was listening, Mr. Michaels. You handled the show extremely well, sir."

"Thank you."

"I was listening this morning as well. I must say that you seem to have grace under pressure. Tell me. Did Earl ever show up?"

"I'm here, ma'am," Earl jumped up and shouted out from the back of the room.

The judge chuckled. "Earl, normally we don't speak up like that in open court, but under the circumstances, you're excused."

"Thank you, ma'am." Earl sat back down.

The judge looked over toward Tricia. "You're Patricia Knox. You did a profile on me a couple of years ago. Would you come over here for a moment?"

Tricia got up and approached the judge.

"Ms. Knox, I read the story you wrote concerning Zeke Collins that appeared in this morning's Columbus paper. When was the last time you spoke with Zeke?"

"That would have been Monday, ma'am."

"How was he? Did he show any signs of dementia or loss of memory?"

"I'm not a doctor, ma'am, so I couldn't really give a diagnosis. As a journalist and an observer, though, Zeke seemed to be in control of his faculties and his destiny until the very end. He knew what he wanted and knew what to do to get what he wanted."

"When or did Zeke tell you that he wanted Glenn Michaels as heir to his business interests?"

"He never said anything to me directly, ma'am. I picked up on his intentions on Monday morning."

"Was that during or after Zeke's last on-air appearance?"

"It was during. Zeke backed off in the last hour and a half of Monday's show and let Mr. Michaels take over. If anyone in that room didn't know Zeke's intentions by ten on Monday morning, they surely knew it by seven-thirty on Tuesday."

There was a murmur of agreement in the Courtroom.

The judge turned her attention back to Glenn. "Mr. Michaels, if the Court decided that Zeke was not in his right mind when he decided to allow you to run his various enterprises in and around Magnolia, what would your plans be?"

"Your Honor, I would accept your decision with humility and grace. All I ever wanted when I came to Magnolia was to get my life back under control and say goodbye so that I could go back to Texas and make a living doing what I've been doing for the past fifteen years."

"If we weren't in this courtroom… if Alvin, I'm sorry, if Mr. Bates here, had not raised an objection to Zeke's gift to you, would you still walk away from the radio stations, or from Magnolia?"

Glenn took a look around the courtroom. He had been in Magnolia for less than a week, yet he felt as if he had known everyone in there for most of his life. There were the farmers who came into Zeke's every morning, it seemed, to have a cup of coffee and swap stories with each other. The Mulligans were there, as well as the members of the Town Council and the Mayor. There were other familiar faces, too. He didn't know the names, but they were familiar, just the same.

He felt Tricia's hand take hold of his.

"Wherever you go, I am going, too."

He didn't hear her say that, or did he? He felt a sense of belonging he had not felt before.

"Your Honor… Magnolia Town Council voted that I was the new Zeke Collins the other day. Yesterday I proposed to a woman I only met on Monday. My boss back in Texas would probably think that I am crazier than a pack of wild coyotes, but yep… I intend to stay in Magnolia!"

The audience in the courtroom erupted in applause and cheers. The news spilled outside of the chambers, through the courthouse and out to the street. Tricia held on to him tightly as Glenn was rushed by nearly everyone in the room.

The judge allowed the pandemonium to continue for the better part of five minutes before she banged her gavel to restore order.

"Mr. Michaels, you seem to have the support of a good sized portion of Fuller County. Zeke chose his successor well, it appears."

She looked over to Alvin Bates.

"Alvin, you and I both knew Zeke. Yes, there were times when what he did didn't make sense, but in the grand scheme of things, Zeke always had the best interests of Magnolia in mind. As much as I have to agree that switching family lawyers within two weeks of passing on would be ill-considered in most instances, in this instance, Zeke again had Magnolia's best interests in mind. Nothing personal, Alvin, but I have to rule that Zeke's will dated on July 6th as being as genuine. Mr. Michaels, here, is heir to all of Zeke's business interests, including and especially the license to his radio stations."

Alvin nodded his head. "I… have to agree, Your Honor. Since my client hasn't appeared, I'll withdraw his petition."

"Thank you Mister Bates. Court dismissed."

The Odds and Ends

It took about six weeks for Glenn to fully settle into his new responsibilities. He was, as he put it, busier than a mouse in a barrel full of hungry cats. Various pieces of business had to be taken care of relating to Zeke's legacy. For the most part, the transition went smoothly. Glenn made Zeke's show his own; gently, seamlessly, building on to the reputation.

Zeke was laid to rest in a corner of a cemetery outside of Lucasville. It was a private burial with only two dozen close friends, workers and family members in attendance. The memorial service itself had to be held at the high school football field in Magnolia in order to accommodate the rush of mourners.

Brian Thompson of Big Thicket Broadcasting waited in Magnolia until Glenn and Tricia came back after the court hearing. It was a tense meeting. Brian personally apologized for the actions of his employees, giving his personal assurance that the actions of his employees were theirs alone. He paid restitutions (Tricia was thrilled with getting a new Mustang) to all affected and promised to change company policy to allow more competition in markets where they had gained a virtual monopoly. He explained that he had once worked for Zeke before moving out west to start his career as a station owner. Brian and Glenn started talking with each other on a regular basis and buried the hatchet inside of a month.

Bob Beasley found out that he lost "the best employee I've ever had" when Glenn called him on Friday afternoon after most of the excitement had died down. It wasn't until Glenn and Tricia came down to Dallas to organize his move up north that the reality of Glenn's new life hit home for Bob.

"We'll see you at our place in a month or so," Glenn assured his old boss when they parted. "In the meantime, y'all be careful."

On the first of October, Glenn signed off the broadcast with an apology to his regular listeners. He asked to be excused for the next couple of weeks so that he could take care of some personal business. Magnolia's Town Council looked up from their meeting to give their approval.

"And it's about time, too!" Steve Mulligan shouted out loudly enough to be heard on-the-air.

Everyone knew what would happen the next day. They were all invited.

Glenn Michaels got up early on Saturday morning after spending the night in the guest bedroom at the house north of Prentiss. He was showered and out the door by seven to head into Magnolia to have breakfast with the Beasleys at Zeke's Café.

"I thought you'd bring her with you," Bob remarked when Glenn arrived alone.

"I hear it's bad luck for the bride and the groom to see each other before the ceremony."

"You know it's bad luck to be superstitious…"

Glenn went into fits of laughter.

After breakfast, Glenn got in his car and drove up to the cemetery to visit with Hannah Smith.

"You know I loved you… and I will always love you."

Glenn laid a bouquet of yellow roses on Hannah's headstone.

"Patricia loves you, too. She told me to tell you."

He felt a warmth inside which belied the crisp, autumn day. He stood there contemplating his situation, thankful for being as lucky as he was.

"There were times when I hated myself," he continued, "times when I didn't respect myself, wanting to have what we had, thinking that having sex was the same as making love. It took me twenty-five years to figure things out."

He backed up, took a deep breath then slowly exhaled.

"You taught me love when we first met at the radio station. I was too dumb to learn. There was more, you know. It was a lesson we needed to learn together, but never learned at all. Tricia's been teaching me, though. It's work. Love is nothing if we don't work together, and keep working for the rest of our lives just as hard as we did when we first met.

"You'd be proud of me, Hannah."

He kissed the tips of his fingers then laid them on her headstone. He glanced over to the newer grave next to hers and smiled. There was a simple metal marker, soon to be replaced by a granite marker with the inscription: **John Jankowski – Loving Father**.

The plan was set.

He entered Community Baptist Church through the side door, dressed in a conservative business suit. The guests were already in place, the last of the Saturday sun streaming in the windows, painting vivid colors from the stained glass windows on those assembled.

Glenn and Greg waited at the front of the church as the organist played and the bride came down the aisle.

Patricia Lynn Knox was radiant.

He had not seen the dress she was wearing… at least in the living world.

When she arrived to meet him, the Reverend Ezra Kellough handed each of them a candle, lit from an altar candle. The bride and the groom in turn started a chain, so everyone present was holding a candle, illuminating the church.

They repeated their vows. When they were finished, they melted into each other as they had so many times before in his dreams. This time he knew that he had finally found the 'Woman in White' who had been part of his dreams for as long as he could remember. They belonged to each other, inseparable.

As the people of Magnolia applauded their union, she looked at him and smiled.

"C'mon, Mr. Michaels, we have work to do."

You're Welcome to Come Back to Magnolia!

THE FOLKS AT ZEKE'S CAFÉ have a place for you at a table, in a booth, or at the counter so you can sample a helping of Miss Annie's Biscuits and Gravy, a cup of Mr. Zeke's Special Blend Coffee, or how about some fresh eggs served the way you like them, provided by one of several local farmers?

We're mighty proud to share some of the stories about the goings on here in Magnolia.

For instance, there's a tale about Miss Lizzie, and how she and her nephew opened up a new Bed and Breakfast down at the corner of Main and South Streets, despite some powerful opposition by Coach Chuck and his loyal cadre of former Magnolia Marauders. *The Magnolia Chronicles* tells about the run-up to the big announcement on Heritage Day. You'll meet Pastor Dan and his family as they try to make peace during his first month as the new pastor of the Community Baptist Church.

There's also been talk about the former child television star who came to Magnolia to get away from it all, only to find that her biggest fan lives in an apartment over on Walnut Street. Will Chaney finds that true love was just around the corner in *Goodbye to All That*.

Glenn Michaels' son, Christopher eventually makes it to Magnolia as well in *The Magnolia Connection*. Yes, he's kicking and screaming – an unwilling partner to a most surprising and unlikely young woman – in a trip from his efficiency apartment in Houston, to Jumpstart in western Fuller County.

So, kick back and relax. Come and visit us here in Magnolia! We'd be tickled to have you!